Akram's War

Akram's War

NADIM SAFDAR

ATLANTIC BOOKS
LONDON

First published in trade paperback in Great Britain in 2016 by Atlantic Books, an imprint of Atlantic Books Ltd.

This edition published in 2017 by Atlantic Books.

1 2 3 4 5 6 7 8 9

A CIP catalogue record for this book is available from the British Library.

Paperback ISBN: 9781782397328
EBook ISBN: 9781782397311

Printed and bound in Great Britain by Clays Ltd, St Ives plc

Atlantic Books
An Imprint of Atlantic Books Ltd
Ormond House
26–27 Boswell Street
London
WC1N 3JZ

www.atlantic-books.co.uk

For Sahar, Zain, Iman and Zakariya

II

Prologue

Grace stood directly before the memorial steps. A slow wind buffeted her bare legs and the cold of the tarmac had seeped through the thin soles of her shoes, spreading upwards until her legs felt like stone. The memorial had three steps on each of its four sides, leading to a square plinth several feet high, and above that, as though reaching for the heavens, stood a tall grey cross. One simple wreath decorated the base of the plinth, surrounded by red paper poppies stirring gently in the breeze. Her gaze shifted down a granite face carved in relief; towards the bottom of a long list it stopped at PRIVATE A. HARTLEY, THE QUEEN'S OWN YEOMANRY, 2003. She clenched her teeth and closed her eyes, feeling a renewed blast of damp air against her cheeks.

At precisely nine that morning, Grace had telephoned the social worker who was to bring her daughter Britney and supervise their contact. Nervously, Grace had suggested a change of venue, hoping the voice at the other end of the telephone wouldn't object. For two hours on the second Sunday of each month Britney was brought to her at McDonald's, the only place the social worker could think of that was reliably public and warm. The woman had been brusque, complaining that she would have to find a winter overcoat and provide breakfast for the child before they left the home. Before Grace could go into a long, rehearsed soliloquy of her reasons for the alteration, there was a deep sigh at the other end and the call was terminated.

Grace had arrived early, the chill slowly freezing her face into an expressionless mask with a brim of stinging ice settling on her lower eyelids. She had witnessed a white coach pull up. From it the members of a military band had alighted. After putting out a trestle table, bread rolls and a large urn from which steam rose, they had quietly breakfasted standing. Then from cellophane wrapping they had pulled out splendidly bemedalled tunics in hues of brown and green and black, pulled them on snugly over their fleshy girths, and it seemed to Grace that with each brass button fastened the men and women stood further towards full extension. Finally, as though to affirm a sort of confident power, peaked caps with polished badges were squeezed onto heads.

The band had tuned their instruments, the sharp notes mixing with the voices and footsteps of the gathering crowd. Afterwards the band members had filtered through the growing assembly, trading jokes and laughter and pressing hymn sheets into waiting hands.

Stepping away from the memorial, Grace looked around, her spine as erect as anyone's there present, and searched expectantly among the crowd. She observed the purposeful stride of young men in uniform, some with their girlfriends or wives and children. She saw elderly men propped on walking sticks or sitting in wheelchairs, behind them stoical women, their heads wrapped in silk scarves. Brass instruments and buttons glittered in the cold sunshine, and shiny medals and colourful ribbons dangled off chests; the emblems these people carried, she thought, to them they represent life.

However, among a shifting focus of stiffened backs in ceremonial dress and peaked caps gazing poignantly upwards, Grace did not see the particular peaked cap she was looking for. She was troubled. Here, a solitary brown face should be easy to spot – so where was he? He had said he would be at the ceremony. She hardly knew him, had only met him in the early hours of the morning, and had slept for some of their time together. But still, the thought of introducing him to Britney, as she knew she would, filled her with tense anticipation. Fleetingly she pictured the three of them standing before the cross like witnesses bound by some solemn oath.

The band sergeant issued a sharp order, followed by a crack of boots as some stood to attention. Immediately, the assembly, both civilian and military, removed their hats, tucking them under an arm or holding them solemnly at the waist.

The call of a bugle started up. Its lingering, spaced notes left goosebumps on the nape of Grace's neck and somehow made her feel important. She realized that if the notes were for Adrian Hartley then they also belonged to her.

With the last note of the bugle still ringing in her ears, there followed a silence broken only by the occasional muffled cough and, once only, the cry of a baby. The silence amplified the sound of the wind and she thought about Adrian Hartley, suddenly grateful that in a profound way, one she had discovered only hours earlier, he had left her with something that she might use: *hope*.

She had hardly slept and had woken with a fog of fatigue circling her head, and that morning she had forgotten to take her pills. While she wasn't entirely convinced that everything had changed overnight, for once – if only for today – she felt part of something, although she couldn't articulate what it was. She listened intently as a prayer was read.

Ever-living God, we remember. . .

The words seemed to pass through her like an instruction written in electrical current, and she vowed that now she had missed her dose she'd give it a week and see how she felt.

. . . from the storm of war into the peace of your presence. . .

Grace felt a small squeeze of her hand and turned away from the cross. 'Hey,' she whispered. Her heart leapt like cold steel in her chest and a grin spread across her face. Taking half a step backwards to accommodate the short space between herself and the girl, she stared lovingly into her daughter's eyes.

Britney's hair had grown, the wind picking at fine blond filaments across her brow. Her cheeks, suffused with cold pink, momentarily trembled and then, screwing up her face as though deep in thought, she said, 'I'm cold.

Why are we here, Grace?' Her voice too seemed to have changed, her words articulate with a confident glottal stop.

The social worker held the girl with an arm around her shoulders. Britney shook free of her chaperone. She retrieved a poppy from her coat pocket and held it out towards her mother.

The prayer concluded: *Through Jesus Christ our Lord.*

Grace swallowed hard and checked her tears. 'Amen.' She took the poppy and reached for her daughter's hand, feeling the small fist curl into her own.

Britney seemed to be searching for words. Anxiously the child tucked the loose hair on her forehead into a woolly hat and cocked her head up at the social worker as though seeking permission. Then, addressing Grace, she said slowly, 'Mum.'

Grace felt a surge of pride. *Mum.* There it was. She was Mum. Again. For two brief hours: Mum. She tasted the word in her mouth.

As conductor, the sergeant major threw his hands into the air, summoning a short triumphant chord from the horn section that punctured the cold atmosphere. The remainder of the band raised their instruments to their lips and the crowd seemed to brace itself.

'What now, Mum?'

Grace bent down and whispered, 'Do you still like to sing?' She enjoyed saying that. It seemed like a connection between the two of them, however small.

Britney nodded, a bashful smile quivering on her lips.

Grace looked down at the hymn sheet clutched in her fingers. The paper flapped in the breeze. Summoning what seemed to Grace the sort of mother's voice the social worker might approve of, she said, 'Now, my love, now we sing a hymn.'

1

I am Akram Khan, formerly Sergeant Khan of the Queen's Own Yeomanry, and in a short number of hours, at a place not far from here, loaded and enabled, I will submit.

My wife Azra sleeps in our bed, a white linen sheet pulled tightly around the bony geometry of her figure. Her thin hand, curled into a fist, is wrapped in the sheet, her wrist weighted with gold bangles. In profile, her nose is studded with a pinprick of gold. I lie next to her, every muscle contracted towards a knot in my gut, and although our bodies at their nearest point are merely an inch apart, I am careful not to touch her. I lie as though trapped, perfectly still under a shared sheet. When Allah wills it, and soon He will, it will be my time for eternal sleep, my conclusion. As I pass into the hereafter the brothers will wrap me in a shroud of linen, and they will chant the names of Allah as they lower my remains into the earth. And over my body they will heave a single slab of stone.

For Azra the membranous sheet is protection against my efforts to consummate our marriage. I have tried. For a time my hands were hopeful: brushing against her shoulders, playing with a loose strand of her hair, twisting it around a digit as tightly as I dared; when feeling bold my fingers would trace the bony contours of her spine. In the cold house, listening to the rain lash against the bedroom window and feeling lonelier than I imagined possible, again and again I would try.

The strength of my want surprised me. Even as I trembled, perspired, clutched myself to still my jerking muscles, the sensation felt decent. Later, shamed by her and branded a failure, a humiliation tempered only by the cumulative incantation of a thousand *Bismillah*s, I abandoned my earthly desires and accepted the inch or so between us. She snores lightly, contentedly, still a virgin.

She is not for me. Not in this life. I tell myself: I am saving my pleasures for when I am dead.

It is time to make ready, and carefully I swing my feet to the floor. A bullet fired from close range has left me with titanium and gristle for a knee joint. Below it I have no feeling, and I move awkwardly, trying not to wake her. I make it to the door and take one last look at Azra. She has turned away, her long black hair falling across the pillow, one knee bent up to her chest, stretching the sheet taut. By day my bedfellow covers herself in a black burqa that, save for a rectangular screen through which she sees, completely enfolds her body. She says the burqa is to conceal her from the lustful eyes of men. I say that her virtue is a strange game.

The narrow hallway is dark, and with the help of a walking stick that I leave by the door, I carefully place each step, keeping to the edges to avoid creaky floorboards. My fingertips brush against the wall for orientation and balance. I hear a faint rumble as the last train from Birmingham slows, ready for a last draw of breath as it pulls into Rowley Regis station, its great energy transmitting through the house.

The railway came first, then factories and workers' houses, small damp houses like the one I have lived in my entire civilian life. In the early days the voice of our street was the echo of great steam-powered hammers and bubbling fires of molten steel, and to us this was regular and bucolic, as birdsong might have been for others. It was a disembodied noise, one I heard but could not see, shielded as it was by high perimeter walls. Children would assemble as the factory gates drew open at the changing of shifts, hoping that their fatigued and oil-stained fathers would buy them a pop on the short walk home. But more than that, we gathered for an opportunistic glimpse through a gap in the gates, of giant hammers and spitting fire.

The carpet is threadbare underfoot and the wall rough and crackly beneath my fingertips, and it startles me that there is knowledge here I have yet to acquire, and that the house has silently aged, sagged and worn. I hear a gentle sound of stretching bedsprings as my mother or father turns in their sleep. Reaching blindly into the room I pull at a light cord, then take a sideways stride into the loo and ease the door closed. A small extractor fan cut into the window picks up speed and settles into a constant rhythm. The overhead light blinks, casting the movement of my limbs in slow motion.

I look into the mirror on the small cabinet above the sink and clutch my beard. Abruptly the flicker flatlines to a thin fluorescent beam. My beard is thick and densely black. It has grown to just beyond the length of one fist and is immediately recognizable from a distance. It marks me as one who has rejected the vanity of the infidel. One who has chosen. I release the hot tap. Pipes rumble as though summoning strength from distant corners of the house. A jet of water issues, becoming scalding; as it meets the cold parabola of the sink it generates steam. I turn it off and watch it glut.

From the cabinet I select a small pair of scissors, a disposable razor and a can of shaving foam, placing each item on the porcelain ledge between the taps. I pinch at a tuft of beard and take a swipe at it with scissors – a sinful thing. Out in the street I hear a cat cry and then all is silent save for the mash of the scissor blades. Short clumps of hair collect on my palm stretched below. I whisper a short prayer, '*Bismillah ir-Rahman ir-Rahim*', a consolation for my loss.

About prayer I am superstitious, and superstition is a magic not permitted to the believer. Although we are born perfect, few of us remain in that state, and it is enough to reach out, to strive, to hope for forgiveness. At night I leave a gap in the curtains, and the very moment I awaken, raising my head from the pillow, I catch a piece of morning sky and whisper, '*Bismillah ir-Rahman ir-Rahim*.' It is like saying hello to Allah, and every new scene seems to warrant it. A thousand times a day, maybe more – tucking into breakfast, pulling my trousers over my bad knee, leaving the house, sidestepping a crack in the pavement, seeing someone I know or don't know, putting a fruit to my nose, watching a bent old lady crossing the street, washing my hands or rubbing my sore knee. Remembering Allah lends a kindness to each scene, slows down our fast lives, so that even the little things are lived in a state of suspended grace. And the more I say the *Bismillah*, the more it seems necessary. It is instinctive, important. It reminds me of the vastness of I, a mobile dot under the spread diaphragm of a ceaseless heaven.

I snip carefully around the vermilion border of my lips where brown skin meets pink flesh. Between my fingertips the hair feels thick and wiry. It is densely black, glossy from the application of palm oil scented with sandalwood and something else, something eastern and exotic, an *oud*, a pleasant odour, something like night-blooming jasmine, a scent that keenly fills the air wherever a group of brothers assembles.

Brothers: drawn from distant corners of the world and merged in Cradley Heath. United beyond blood and flesh, the strongest of brotherhoods falling under the cast of Allah's love. Brothers at the mosque, and afterwards brothers walking hand in hand and arm in arm, brothers brimming with excited thoughts as we repair to the Kashmiri Karahi House and Sweet Shop. Brothers who, before a word is said, upon the instructions of Brother Mustafa (our first-in-command) scan the sparsely furnished kebab shop, sweep memory for the slightest change in the walls, look underneath green plastic tables and chairs, patrol behind a counter at the far end, and unscrew, inspect and replace a solitary pendant light bulb.

Under a dim fluorescent light at the Karahi House the brothers and I (although I no longer wear three stripes, clearly I am second-in-command) feel safe. We talk about martyrdom and search each other's eyes for the difference between doubt and sincerity.

'What would it be like?' Second-in-command.

'Who will go first?' First-in-command.

'Will Allah greet us personally?' That could be any one of the brothers, lightly swaying to a scene secured under clamped eyelids.

And, although no one will say it out loud, we are each picturing voluptuous houris, their bodies stretching against the slippery silk of the most exotic garments – and we each struggle to hide that thought from our brothers.

'Boom. Boom.' That's Ali, the Karahi House proprietor. He is a joker and speaks carelessly as though to shame us. 'I can see ladies dancing in your eyes.' A spatula in one hand gesticulates lewdly while with the other he flips lamb chops on a sizzling grill. 'Their feet, garlanded in silver anklets, dancing on your filthy souls.' Oily spice fills the room.

Carefully I drop the hair into a plastic Ziploc bag retrieved from my pyjama pocket. The uneven crop of close-cut bristle now reveals something of my former face. I have a square jaw, full lips, and eyes a girl once described as gentle. When it mattered to me, I considered myself handsome. It flashes across my mind that before I shave it all off I could groom myself something fashionable. A goatee, perhaps? Just for a minute, to see what it would look like. But those thoughts are the diversions of Beelzebub, a temptation to infidelity, and to compensate I whisper a quick *Bismillah*. Staring into the mirror, I allow myself a small smile. A smile in recognition of the unfortunate fact that we can never be truly faithful to Allah, that within my weak mind there is still resistance, rebellion.

I shake my head vigorously as though it will scatter those thoughts, and with the razor I cut neat tracks into what remains of my beard, dispersing shaving foam thick with black hair under the running tap. The skin underneath is smooth and stretched taut like a canvas over my chin. Already I feel colder without the beard. My face itches and burns and I rub and press at it as though kneading dough, leaving behind short-lived, thumb-shaped welts. The image staring back at me is boyish: it is the vanity of the infidel and reminds me of my earlier self, of a time before belief in the one and true God. That there was a time before belief seems hardly possible, and I turn my eyes away.

I rub in a splash of Cologne, gritting my teeth as it stings. It has been a long time since I felt that particular pleasurable pain.

My gaze tilts upwards, squinting through a small rectangular window to the marbled black sky, imagining the hazy horizon, the join between sky and land that determines the end of the visible world. A scene that Allah will illuminate at dawn. '*Bismillah ir-Rahman ir-Rahim*.'

I concentrate my eyes into the distance, connecting with what I cannot see, the great invisible being just beyond. I am barely conscious that I am standing before Allah. I see through the clouds to a crescent moon. As I concentrate harder, I view a colourful scene of an orchard with round bushy trees of a wonderful brightness, the likes of which I have never before seen. Bulbous red pomegranates grow on the trees, and in the air is the scent of sandalwood and jasmine and roses. A stream flows across the foreground. On its golden waters glides a wooden barge propelled by a fisherman punting with a long pole. In the background, as though painted in, are the snow-capped peaks of the Himalayas, places colder and more isolated than man could ever stand. As I now look down, out from this dizzying height, a wind spurs like sharp knives at my face, and as my arms waver for balance I open my mouth for one final breath of thin, giddy air.

I feel a knot in my throat; my heart races and a surge of adrenaline makes my whole body shiver. Despite the coldness of the bathroom, strangely I feel warm. It takes all my control not to cry out loud.

And suddenly an ugly pain works my knee. A familiar antagonist that is worse between the hours of sunset and sunrise. The doctor assured me that all pain increases at night-time, but its eagerness surprises me. Sweating, I rest on the edge of the toilet seat and clutch at my artificial knee and hope that might banish the sensation that grips, like the branches of an electrical tree, the nerves above and below the wound.

When finally it eases, I pull down my pyjamas, letting them drop to my ankles. My cock I shield with one hand and, with the other, first trim the hair, snip and deposit. I adjust my position, but very carefully in case I reignite the pain, bending low to my task. I rub in a very thin layer of shaving foam and carefully guide the razor around the curves, pulling and tweaking at my anatomy, stretching the skin flat.

The razor, sealed into the Ziploc bag, I dispose of in a pedal bin under the sink. The shaving foam and scissors are replaced in the cupboard. It is better to return things to where they came from, always better.

Quietly I unlock the bathroom door, turn off the light and step into the hallway. It wasn't as satisfying as I would have had it. I had imagined an overwhelming serenity, but it was more practical than that, and at times, shivering in the cold bathroom, I had wanted it to be over as quickly as possible. I have to admit, the martyr's penultimate scene would, to an infidel, seem a strange one. But that is the point, the very point that only true believers in the one true God understand. It is the very thing that separates the martyr from the infidel. It is about faith – a compulsion elevated above all others. About doing what Allah wills. And belief, belief is faith, believing in His justice. Like any soldier in war, orders must be followed. Not satisfying nor serene, but successful. No razor cuts. Not a drop of blood.

I turn one last time and see a patch of sky through the window. *Bismillah*. I smile. Not a drop, not yet.

2

Briefly I look in on my parents sleeping. I am not yet dead and cold and devoid of feeling, and I regard them with pity. Pity for their worn ageing bodies and pity that there will be no one to care for them. Azra I do not wish ever again to gaze upon. Instead, as I pick up my number two dress uniform from a wardrobe on the landing and descend the stairs, I imagine her body twisted into the sheets and feel a bitter resentment in the knowledge that she will stop only long enough to collect her inheritance, my army compensation money. Again I am leaving my parents, and this time forever, or at least forever in this world. If they are heaven-worthy then I will see them, and if they are not, I as a heaven dweller may have it in my power to summon them. Or I may not. There are many contradictions. Many unknowns.

Downstairs, before a tinsel-garlanded picture of Mecca above the mantel, I dress quickly. My father's snores reverberate through the ceiling above, and in the loneliness of the night every sound grows, its significance amplified.

I leave the house, creeping out like a soldier on manoeuvre. The clouds are dense and the air dewy grey; absent is the crescent moon of my imagination. Part way down the street a fox slinks nervously across the tarmac, its beady eyes caught by the light of a street lamp, momentarily glowing a bold yellow. It stops briefly to consider me leaning on my stick and then skulks on. My best army boots clink on the pavement, their polished toecaps twinkling beneath the same street lamp under which the fox paused moments earlier.

On my head I wear a peaked sergeant's cap. It is black and across it runs a red sash. In its centre, like a third eye, is a brass cap badge bearing the emblem I once earned, a double-headed eagle. My tunic is olive green, with many utilitarian pockets, all of them empty save for a little money and another cap badge that I have, since my return, kept in an inside pocket next to my heart. The tunic is tight over my bulging waist, yet still I feel strong in it, as though the chest is padded with plates of steel. It was hand cut precisely to fit my body, my body in its prime, and wearing it for the first time on parade was my proudest moment. I stood a good inch taller than I actually was. Squinting into the sun, I saluted Her Majesty, our Colonel-in-Chief, and swore I would defend Great Britain, her territories and dominions, with my life.

I don't look back, picturing instead how the house diminishes from view. It grows not only smaller, but somehow also less significant. As I cross the road and take a left turn, already it feels as though the house, to which I will not return, is a place I never inhabited. The streets are deserted, yellow where illuminated, and seem to pulse quietly as though resting for the night. On the distant peak of Turner's Hill flashes an orange beacon mounted on an aerial, a tiny, almost imperceptible dot of light, one I watched as a child looking out of my bedroom window, mesmerized.

The soles of my boots are plated with steel and my footsteps clatter in the night air. I wore them often on a parade ground where noise mattered, my buddies and I falling into step, rehearsing complex manoeuvres until our legs, arms and eyes were in perfect sync. The boots are solid and hard, and when they were first issued (to one Recruit Akram Khan), several of my toenails bruised so badly during route marches that they fell off. Each night I polished the boots to a mirror shine then stuffed them with newspaper soaked in leather-softening tea and urine, and like a trophy I put them in a closet bearing my rank, name and number. Working them to a shine was competitive, an act akin to pleasing God, and deprived a recruit of sleep. A mixture of spit and boot polish dried to a crust and then, with a clean cloth, rubbed in small circles until the new layer reflected resplendent. To a soldier, looking after kit is a precious and satisfying act akin to worship, and these particular boots that I first trained in I later kept aside for special occasions. They shine again as they catch thin yellow windows of light.

I turn into Coopers Street. Ahead, perhaps fifty yards, is the figure of a female. Narrowing my eyes, I make out a shortish woman in a red miniskirt and a cropped denim jacket. The volume of her wispy hair catches the light. She walks slowly, her legs balancing on what look like pins, her arms swimming for balance. I slow, adjusting my pace to hers. It would be indecent to catch her up, and I might frighten her. But at the same time I know immediately and without question that, like a chaperone and from a safe distance, I will follow her.

It is three in the morning and at eleven I must be at the war memorial two point five miles from the house I left minutes earlier. Two and a half miles, even with my bad leg, even with a small detour to pick up ordnance, will take no more than an hour.

The woman stops below a pub sign. Crouching down, she rubs the back of her ankles, muttering something I cannot make out. I catch up a little and get a clearer view. The miniskirt exposes thick white thigh flesh and her low-cut top squeezes folds of skin at her waist. On her feet are stiletto heels. She stands, struggling in her seemingly drunken state to stay upright, and carries on up the street.

I can smell her perfume as I reach the pub sign. It is a pub I know. I know everything here. Every bend, every shopfront, every wall and the quality of the brickwork, and I have seen it age, but that is not a comfort. Maley's dad would drink in this pub, drinking being a preoccupation of all grown white men akin to reading the daily paper. They were men who measured time by when and with whom they last drank, and distances by how far someplace was from the nearest pub. Now the pub is derelict, shuttered with a zigzagging pattern of plywood planks, although its sign is still intact: *The Gate Hangs Well*. Azra does not wear western perfume; she wears an *oud* purchased in tiny vials, purportedly from the city of Mecca. This female wears an English perfume blended with alcohol, rose-tinted and volatile, an alluring, ruinous scent.

She stops again and I do too. Flattening myself against a wall, I watch her intently. I feel my heart thump inside the confines of my chest, a strange thing, as though once again I am watching the enemy. This time she slips off her stilettos and places them to one side. Squatting, she squeezes each ankle in turn. She is caught under the yellow orb of a street lamp, her only concern the discomfort of her feet. She seems cast free but dangerously alone and trusting, and unlike the fox she appears to be blind to risk. *Only English women go out at night* – it is a common refrain among us brothers. I first heard it as a child, a saying that is passed down the generations.

The female stands up, lifts her chin and carries on along the pavement, forgetting the shoes. After fifty short strides I halt and stare at them, abandoned as though something sinister has befallen their owner. Ahead and unburdened, she is walking faster and gaining distance. I wait for her to disappear around a bend in the road. Then I pick up a shoe and stare at it, turning it over in my hand. Tentatively I raise it to my nostrils, smelling her sweat and traces of iron where her ankles had bled. I have a nose for blood. And then, as though I crave ruin, I inhale deeply. The action seems involuntary and surprises me. I thrust my nose into the triangular enclosed part where her toes were. The inner sole feels warm, the satin finish of the shoe gratifying to the touch. Its heel ends with a sharp point. The toe is blunt but perfectly smooth as it sweeps a pleasing curve.

'You a perv or something?' The female puts a hand on her hip and leans back a little to look up at me. She is even smaller close up, her eyes just level with the sergeant's emblem on my arm. I haven't known many girls, and I search her up and down, looking for some flaw that will diminish her to a level I feel more comfortable with. Her hair parts in curled waves from a perfectly straight midline. Her face, not beautiful, is more naive than pleasant, with blunted smooth contours, blue paint smudged under her eyes and red gloss on her lips. She has a brief nose and small circular eyes.

'Could I have my shoes back, please?' Her thin lower lip, held tight, still trembles. I look down at her feet where two cracks in the pavement run parallel.

'You shouldn't be out this late on your own. It's not safe.'

'Fucking minicab driver tried it on. Had to get out.' She takes in my attire, her face expressing surprise. 'Grandma always said I'd find my knight in shining armour.'

Self-consciously, I shrug my shoulders. 'Paki driver tried it on?'

'Shhh,' she says, putting a finger to her lips and looking around as though someone might be listening. 'You can't say things like that!'

I say in a mock Pakistani accent, 'Most trustable minicab, madam.'

That makes her laugh. She laughs uninhibited like a drunk, the still night extending the sound. When she stops she gathers me in her eyes and with a sharp intake of breath says, 'What's your story?'

I shake my head.

'A good story is as good as it gets, and I know you've got one.'

'Got to crack on.' I extend the shoes towards her but she doesn't take them.

'Went out with a Pakistani once. Bloody secretive bastard.' She pauses to think, a thin parting in her smile. 'Had a nice car.'

'Must have been a Muslim,' I say.

'He was a lot of things but not much of that.'

I tut. 'What type of car?'

'Went back to his wife.' She laughs again, her mouth wider and more expansive, as though I have gained her trust. Curiously, she has what appears to be a silver tooth in the front of her mouth.

'Was that not expected?'

She shrugs her shoulders, says 'It's just life,' and turns to go.

I call after her, 'You shouldn't be out alone like this.'

'What you waiting for then? You walking us home or what?'

For a while we walk in silence save for the clang of my parade boots and the soft yet audible pad of her feet on the tarmac. We are no longer walking in step and I feel an urgent desire to hear the press of her feet in between that of mine, as though that almost imperceptible sound is confirmation that alongside me walks a woman. Not Azra, a figure in a burqa, but a woman with flesh and arms and legs, smeared high-gloss red lips and sweat on her brow.

As she walks she veers briefly from side to side. I feel an instinctive urge to reach over and steady her but keep my hands to myself. I compare our shadows: hers short and squat, mine upright with a peaked cap.

She pauses for a moment. 'I'm Grace.'

'That's the best name a girl could ever have.' I shake her hand; soft and small and curiously warm.

'You got cold hands. Warm them in your pockets.'

'Army don't do that.'

We walk the length of Forge Row and then cross into Albert Road. During the day, we wouldn't be doing this. Not Grace and I, not together.

Even in daylight little can be seen through the windows of any of these houses, dirty lace curtains slung across each one. The doors are locked, and five times daily they open as the men escape for prayers at Best Street mosque or any of the five other mosques within a mile (some converted from previous incarnations and others cavernous, purpose-built institutions) that now compete with the original. Behind the lace curtains could be a birth, a wedding, a hundred women mourning a death, but you wouldn't know it as you pass by outside. It occurs to me that Grace is right: we Pakis are secretive. Brightly coloured cars fitted with extra-wide plastic wheel arches sit quiet and innocuous as their owners sleep, yet during the day these lads are always coming up fast, nodding to a beat, engines revving out of flared exhaust pipes and loud Indian music playing on custom sound systems. They wear a permanent scowl and have hungry, suspicious eyes. Their thin territorial ambitions and short-cropped hair remind me of the skinheads that moved on after the developers levelled the Mash Tun.

Seeing Grace and me together, the locals would jeer and laugh, shout insults, take off their shoes and show us their soles, lob stones from across the street, chase us out of their territory – and before I got home the scandal would have reached my parents and Azra.

Grace stops outside a narrow Victorian house part way along the third terrace we come to. She must be one of the few *gora* inhabitants still here. A poster has been placed in next door's window – the familiar white face of our first-in-command fills the frame, airbrushed to thin down his rotund cheeks and disguise the easy-blue blemish of the albino. His eyes, normally milky, have been painted the faintest brown – brown for the people – and somehow they appear sincere and kind. Above his bearded, benevolent face are the words 'Bismillah Events Presents – Live in Conversation with Dr Mustafa Al-Angrezi (the English)'. The event is to be held at a community centre this evening; brothers are instructed to pass through security at the front entrance and sisters at the rear. So my brother Mustafa who mourns his brother Faisal the martyr will at six o'clock mourn another, and he will have a twinkle in his eye and spout propaganda and they will listen; yes, after my *shahid* at eleven, they will prick up their ears and listen.

Mustafa is barely recognizable in the altered image. It is also vanity that compels him to take the appellation Al-Angrezi. Of course, he would justify himself in his usual wily way, perhaps squeezing my bicep while whispering, *Brother Akram, we each tweak our assets.* He is correct, of course. In war each side takes what advantage it can.

I turn towards Grace. She stands perfectly still outside her house staring back at me, perhaps wondering what I make of the poster. The light from an upstairs window bisects her face, dark and light. She fumbles in her pockets for keys then inserts one into the lock.

She turns the key and stops. 'What is your story?'

I shake my head.

'You can't be right, walking around at this time of night dressed like you've got an appointment with the Queen. I'll do you a tea.'

'Got to crack on.'

She adds quickly, 'There's toast, if you want it?'

'We Pakis only accept at the third time of asking.'

'Suit yourself.' The door opens and without another word she enters and closes it behind her. I stare at the green paintwork, wet with dew.

Moments later the door reopens. 'Shoes?' she requests.

I hand them over and smile.

'No story, and by the looks of it, no car,' she continues in a sterner tone. 'You had better come in out of the cold.'

I hesitate. Suddenly I am aware of a hot prickly sensation where I earlier shaved off the beard. I imagine welts spreading across it and self-consciously knead it with my fingertips.

'Come in or we'll have the Pakistanis talking.' She stands to one side to let me in.

To slow the action down I whisper a *Bismillah*.

The front door opens directly into a living room. She fumbles for a light switch, races to a corner to turn on a table lamp and turns off the main light. Then she looks at me, clearly pleased with her efforts. There is a small sofa in a blue fabric with an ample scattering of cushions, a wooden coffee table, and a sideboard on which is placed a small television set. Two shelves above the television contain a collection of porcelain dogs. The walls are painted pink. I stand, waiting to be asked to sit.

'You want a story and the only story I can think of is this, but don't take offence.' My gaze moves across the dogs. They come in various colours and sizes and some are arranged around a ceramic feeding bowl. 'A prostitute happens to pass by a dog, its tongue lolling out with thirst. Taking off a shoe, she fills it with water from a nearby well and offers it to the animal. For her act of kindness, Allah forgave her for being a prostitute.'

Grace notices me eyeing the arrangement. 'Collect them, when I'm good. Not always good, though – I can go for months under my duvet.' She laughs. 'You're lucky, you've caught me good.'

It's a long time since I have been this close to a white person, and I shiver. Now that I can see her in the light, she is fatter than I thought. Her face, although young, appears marked as though underneath the thick layer of make-up she has bad skin. She smiles, exposing the silver front tooth. It seems to move, and then, with a practised motion, flips onto the tip of her tongue. She retrieves it and rolls it between her fingers into a ball.

'Kit Kat foil,' she says, exposing a gap in her mouth. There it is – the flaw I wanted – and feeling immediately more relaxed I offer her a broad smile.

'Milk and sugar, or do you want something stronger?' Her shoes drop to the floor and she kicks them underneath the sofa. With one hand smoothing the cloth around her rump, Grace swivels on her toes and goes into the kitchen, leaving the door between the rooms ajar.

The ceramic dogs feel smooth and cold to the touch. I hear the kettle boil in the next room, the hot liquid pour, and the rattle of teaspoons against porcelain. Grace returns with two steaming mugs and places them on the coffee table. She lands heavily on the sofa. 'So the prostitute thing – would I be forgiven?'

'If you believe in that sort of thing.'

'What you doing dressed like that? You been to a party or something?'

'It's the armistice remembrance event at eleven,' I say.

'Yeah, what for?'

'It signifies the cessation of hostilities. In World War One.'

Grace gazes at her watch. 'Good eight hours until eleven.' She sighs and continues in a louder voice, 'Take your hat off, and drink up, it's better while it's hot.'

The tea has been mixed with whisky and burns my throat.

'How come you don't have a car? Pakis always have cars.' As she lifts the mug to her face a shadow falls across her pale chin, and where her fingers wrap around the mug there are thin, stained creases between the joints, blue and brown, as though coloured in with pencil. Her hands grow visibly redder as they grasp the warm mug. It startles me that *gora* skin is so permeable, soaking up like a sponge, and as though to confirm my sudden theory, when she puts down her mug and smiles, the lower part of her face is flushed from the conducted heat.

I notice a photo in a frame next to the TV. It is of Grace, younger and slimmer. She is holding a small child, a girl of about two.

'That your kid?' I ask.

'Man in your condition, thought you'd need a car.'

Grace's reference to my leg reminds me that it is hurting. I knead at the knee joint, more out of habit than in expectation of alleviating the pain. Sometimes I am hopeful when it hurts, as though pain signifies that there is still life left in that part of my body. In the bedroom Azra and I share is a full-length mirror. When I look into it, it is perfectly possible to squint out my bad leg. Tricking myself, I feel pride in the condition of my body, not quite as muscular as it was and sporting a decadent paunch, but otherwise buff.

'I did a course once,' Grace says, dropping to her knees.

I watch as her fingers work around my knee joint, the unexpectedness of her touch making me lean back against the sofa and close my eyes. Gradually the pain subsides, and as it does so, as if something else is switched immediately on, I feel a sliver of wet and a hardening between my legs.

'Thanks,' I say, opening my eyes and trying to wriggle free. 'It's better now.'

She ignores my statement and slowly rolls up my trousers to a point above the knee. I expect her to be horrified – the leg is a mass of dark keloid scarring, and the titanium articulation bulges from the skin at an unsettling angle – but she simply resumes massaging the affected area, the pain now replaced by pleasure. She wears no rings and the sight of her colour pressing into mine, alternately turning white and returning to pink, seems somehow wrong; I almost expect a dark brown to rub off me and creep up her fingertips. Her touch is soft and warm. My heart races and I clench my entire body as though my hands might jerk out to where they have not been invited.

'Armistice Day.' She sighs. 'Your leg's fucked and still you glorify the maiming and the killing.'

Through a gap in the curtains I can see still an unchanged black sky, ominous, a sky to die under. I recite, '*Bismillah ir-Rahman ir-Rahim.*'

'You what?' Her hands release my knee and she returns to the sofa. We sit pressed against each other and drain our mugs in one large gulp.

'You've got to have respect for the dead.' I feel light-headed from the alcohol.

Grace puts her knee to her chest and rubs her ankle. 'Been working since lunchtime,' she complains. 'Respect for what?'

I reach for her foot; turning sideways, she allows me to place it on my lap. Her eyes register surprise but not fear. Gently I press around a callus at the back of her ankle, careful not to touch a rolled horizontal tear in the skin where her shoes have rubbed. It feels alien, Grace's legs resting across mine, as though they're not part of her at all but objects of flesh wrapped in a thin membrane, specimens for inspection. Blue veins blanching to my touch zigzag downwards across the slope of the dorsum of her foot, joining and branching again at the toes. A soft bulbous sweep of flesh marks the limit at which the tissue squeezed into the shoes. Hers are working feet, not slender and pointed like Azra's. They're like the feet of a child, a triangular wedge of tissue with short toes rendered softly swollen at the nail. As I pull back on the toes she sighs, extending her foot gracefully like a ballerina's, and at the same time the malleoli at the ankle slide into prominent view. I recall an image of a girl standing on tiptoes reaching for fruit on a tree, her malleoli jutting out like something that might catch the sun and sparkle, bony and delicate like an Adam's apple – a picture I can't place, as though invented. I want to stroke the arch of her foot and milk each digit. A tense heat rises in me.

'Ooh, that's better. Murder out on those streets.'

I shake my head to free myself of illicit thoughts. 'Respect for the dead. For the uniform.'

'Looks good on you.' She takes off my cap and considers the badge at the front.

'Double-headed eagle, that,' I say.

'Two-faced, I'd call it.' She throws the cap onto the low coffee table before us.

'We're all two-faced. Didn't you say I caught you at a good time, not bad?'

'I didn't say bad.' Angrily she pulls her foot away. 'I have good times and other times when without the pills I'd draw the curtains and take to my duvet. They take the edge off it, like drawing back the curtain a bit, but that's all you need, isn't it, an edge?' She pauses as though waiting for an answer. 'They sort of slice off the worst bit at the top.'

'Give me back that foot,' I demand. 'I'm not done yet.'

'Have you ever killed anyone?' she asks.

'We had strict rules of engagement.'

'Sounds clever.' She looks over at the picture next to the TV. 'Pakis got morals, haven't they; they don't let shit happen for no reason. They got an edge.'

I stop rubbing the foot. 'Most of them have cars too.'

'A gentleman would have taken his hat off before he came into the house.' 'Bad luck, is it?'

She looks at me and for a while says nothing. She has the trick of a mother, the prolonged silence adding weight to her words when she finally speaks. 'Soldiers are stupid, they do what they're told.'

'They do what's right by their country.'

'That's worse.'

'There is a right.'

'All that soldier talk. Heard it before.' She swaps feet and I begin to rub her left ankle.

'Worse, this one,' I say, boldly touching the deep laceration behind her ankle. Around it the skin is yellow and raised. It amazes me that she could walk at all. The soles of her feet are black. She flinches but allows me to continue.

'I could fall asleep,' says Grace, clenching her teeth as though that might keep her awake. She lies flat on the sofa, leaning her head against the armrest and closing her eyes.

'I don't want to go,' I say.

'Don't then.' She keeps her eyes closed and smiles as I continue to rub.

As my other hand casually brushes against my chin I am suddenly re-awakened to the absence of my beard, and the very thought seems to make the skin sore and itchy. I pinch my chin, thinking back to the house I left earlier, my parents and Azra sound asleep and, before that, the ritual in the bathroom. I was then certain of something, and although that belief hasn't waned, I have put myself to a test. I still feel in control but I have been distracted. The martyr is permitted to act out any depraved fantasy – his sins are forgiven and that is a truth. Truths can't be overruled: they are written, and faith requires that however contradictory it may seem, you can't pick and choose from what is written. Still, really, this. . . Placing her feet gently on the sofa, I stand up. 'Thanks for everything.'

'You going?'

I nod.

'Free country.'

I feel tall and powerful standing over her supine form and she in turn seems smaller than before, as though she has shrunk into the upholstery. I glance at the photo and then at her. 'The kid in the picture, she's yours, isn't she?'

She nods. As my shadow looms over her I examine her face, but it betrays no emotion. Even with her eyelids screwed tightly shut she knows I am staring. Under exertion, her eyelids quiver, and a muscle twitches in the corners of her lips.

'What happened?'

'You have to earn that story,' she says.

'You got another drink?' I ask, giving in as I knew I would.

'Bottle's in the kitchen.'

I take the mugs from the table and go into the kitchen. After swilling them under a tap I quarter-fill each with Scotch.

Grace is asleep when I return. One cheek lolls against the sofa, her arms bent casually to each side as though in contentment or perhaps even defeat. Unlike my wife, Grace sleeps easy. I put down the mugs and pick up the photo. The toddler is cute. She stares out of the picture with sad eyes, a strange thing for a child. '*Bismillah ir-Rahman ir-Rahim.*'

'What you saying that shit for?' Suddenly Grace is awake and she leans forward, her eyes examining mine. 'Don't give me no Pakistani walla-walla. It can't help.'

'It can help.' I whisper another *Bismillah* and kiss the photo, and gently, as though it is a sacred object, return the frame to where I found it.

'If you had a car you'd get into it and piss off now.' A single black tear drops from her left eye. It stops momentarily at her cheekbone. She swipes it away, leaving an angular smudge from eye to cheek, and as she does so her upper lip pulls up, exposing the dark gap in her mouth.

'You should get that tooth seen to,' I say, regretting the words as soon as they are uttered.

'Can't,' she says matter-of-factly.

'Why not?'

She looks away. 'I'm in need of it.'

We each pick up our mugs and slowly we drain them, mostly in silence. From time to time her eyes lock onto mine and her lips purse as though she is considering me kindly. At those moments I clench against the adrenaline, my heart racing and stomach muscles contracting. A clock on the wall – the big hand has the head of Mickey Mouse at its tip – chimes weakly as it records four o'clock.

'Really, I should turn in. Big day tomorrow,' says Grace wearily.

'Big day?'

She glances at the photograph, closes her eyes and smiles.

Emboldened by the drink, I reach for her foot, suddenly desperate to make some sort of last connection. She claws it away under the sofa.

'It's been lovely, but I'm so sleepy.' She yawns, putting a fist to her mouth.

'Thanks,' I say. 'I mean it. Thanks.'

Grace stretches out a hand and pulls my wrist towards her. 'You're all right.'

'You're too trusting,' I say irritably.

'If you want to fuck me you can.'

I pull my arm away and shrink back. I feel tears welling up and struggle to hold them at bay. Finally I stutter, 'I'm a m-married man.'

'Men get sore when they think they can't fuck you.' Her voice is dreamy and warm.

'It's okay, I don't mind.' I pick up my cap and put it on my head. Finding my stick, I aim for the door. Then I backtrack and, stooping over the sofa, negotiate the thin brittle fibres of her wavy hair. They scratch my face and I kiss her lightly on the cheek. I recall the rose scent she left behind in the street and how it filled me with pangs of both desire and panic. Now I'm closer still but I don't feel it as keenly. It puzzles me, as though with proximity something has waned. 'I'm not angry,' I say. 'You're a nice girl.'

Grace turns her head quickly and plants a kiss on my lips. Hers feel dry and rubbery and nothing like the electrical charge of my imagination. Then she opens her eyes and, staring at the ceiling, smiles. 'Come on, soldier boy, let's go to bed.' Emboldened by the drink, I feel happy and careless.

Tidiness ends as we climb the stairs. Before the bedroom window sits a dressing table in laminated oak, an oval mirror attached above it. Its surface is covered with variously shaped bottles of scent and cosmetics, washes and creams, brushes for hair and for eyes, thick-handled safety razors and small, colourful vials containing lip gloss. Azra doesn't have much of that stuff, and what she does possess she keeps locked in the vanity case she was clutching when I first spotted her at Arrivals. I saw her open it only once. There were small mirrors inside the lid and numerous plastic compartments attached to pivots to pull out. Inside them were secret potions the purpose of which she never revealed. It smelt of woman, the vanity case, more woman than I ever got to see. In Grace's bedroom, shoes are discarded on the carpeted floor and books and magazines stacked a foot high in discrete piles along the walls. On one side of the bed is a small cabinet with a groaning ashtray and a small framed photograph of a baby, its round head filling the frame.

I take off my number two dress uniform, draping each item carefully over a chair, and naked, I slide into bed next to Grace. She feels warm and soft, and as I nuzzle her neck I feel a comfort beyond that of flesh and the aroma of her perfume, the soporific comfort of an intimate bed. My cock, ramrod straight, throbs against her skin.

'I'm sorry I'm a—'

She puts a finger to her lips. 'Shh.' She kisses me. Her lips are now soft and moist and with my tongue I probe the gap in her teeth. Then I stop.

'I need to tell you.' I pull away. 'I've never done it.'

She shrinks back and looks at me, her chin resting on her hands. 'I thought you were married.'

'Yes.'

'You lied?'

'No.' I search her eyes but she expresses no surprise.

'Pakistanis around here, they're all married. Not that that stops them.' She laughs. 'I should know. They cruise by and. . . Well, let's put it this way, for them all white flesh is game, and, if I might say so, the younger the better.'

'We have a thing about white. I used to think it was something to do with school, how we Pakis got singled out, but it goes back further than that. We are subjugated, a slave race. The white man is still our master and the only way to get at him—'

'Well,' she reaches over and puts my hand on her breast, 'you've conquered.'

I don't know what I'm supposed to feel. The breast is just tissue moulded to a shape, but strangely something that demands a response. I try to think of something to distract her. 'Why do you collect those dogs?'

She quickly replies, 'So I'll be forgiven.'

We burst out laughing and I take the opportunity to withdraw my hand. She reaches forward and presses her lips hard on mine.

'That tooth of yours, what's the secret?' I say when she releases me.

'You shouldn't speak to a woman like that. You really are a virgin.'

'Then that is proof?'

She nods, pressing her body against mine. 'Long time ago I went up to Newcastle to see my mum. Got drunk and in the middle of the night we had this terrible argument. Stormed off barefoot down the motorway. So you see from experience, I must know – are you on the run from Newcastle?'

'I'm on manoeuvre.'

'Lies. Tell you what, if the truth is a good truth, I mean one worth knowing, I might tell you about this.' She fingers the gap in her mouth. 'I'll trade you.'

'It's something to do with the little girl in the picture, isn't it?'

'It's personal, but I'll trade,' she says again.

'I'm sorry. About your daughter. I am sorry.'

'I thought you were mad and we would fuck wildly, but you're not mad, are you?'

'Never known a white girl who's invited me into her house.'

Grace corrects me. 'A prostitute.'

'Still a girl.' My head throbs from the whisky but I try to put on a serious face. 'As you say, I've conquered.'

She pulls the duvet up to her chin and considers me for what feels like ages.

'Sex,' I say dreamily, turning to look out of the window, 'is problematic.'

The view from the bedroom window is familiar. I can see the terraced houses opposite, separated from us by a narrow strip of road. A street lamp burns but overall the feeling is of quiet, a sense of lifetimes spun so fast, as though through a vortex, that they are over as soon as they have begun. A sense of death, as though our presence is proof of a long line of people passing through these identical houses.

I pull away from her, rest my head on the pillow. 'Any more grog?'

She wraps a sheet around her body, runs downstairs and fetches a fresh bottle and, shivering, returns quickly to bed. She pours us each an inch and inspects me with a kind gaze as though waiting for me to say something. Still holding her mug, slowly she closes her eyes.

Like a bird flapping lightly to ascend without moving in any other direction, my gaze carries out of the window and above the rooftops. I rise higher, wings catching air currents, suspended over a grid of terraces. Below me, the streets run in neat parallel lines broken only by large walled yards where the factories once stood. Like a bird of prey I zero in to street level and suddenly stop, surprised by the gentle sound of Grace snoring. She can no longer hear me but I describe to her a boy I can see in the street. Burnished by the sun, he is warm and happy. He wears blue shorts and his favourite Captain Astounding T-shirt. I was seven, I tell Grace.

3

I had wandered out of the house and down to the end of our street where stood a tall factory wall, taller than a man but not as high as a house. I was deep in thought staring at the wall and with one hand I was pinching at my hair. As I stood back to take in its full height, so impressive it blocked out the sun, my feet tottered dangerously on the edge of the kerb. Coming from behind the wall was a noise that could only be made by a hammer equal to the size of a car, and every ten seconds I could feel the crash of its great weight reverberate through my toes. I could smell it too. Halfway down the street the smell changed from cooked chapattis and damp clothes drying on lines to the cold scent of worked metal and oil and fire. It was well known by everybody that if you leant up against the wall when the hammer struck, your bones would splinter inside your body. I touched the brickwork with a fingertip and counted to ten. The hammer fell. Then I bent my finger. It still worked okay. I tested my palm flat against the wall. After three bongs I examined it, holding it up to my eyes and squeezing it with my other hand. Nothing bad had happened.

Suddenly a sensation like hot breath crept down the back of my neck, as though someone was watching me. Startled, I spun around.

'Hey, little bro, what you playing?'

The speaker, a man, took a step back and, turning his head sideways, spat into the road. He was old enough to be a man, yet he didn't match up to my ideas of what a man should be. Although he was tall, he was too thin, and he wore his hair long and had no moustache. He wore tight jeans that flared at the ends and a cropped leather jacket exposing a large belt buckle. He stood with his feet splayed and his thumbs dug into his leather belt. Behind him was the corner where the end of our street met the main road. I sweated, knowing I was already beyond the limits of where I was allowed to go.

'Are you a good-for-nothing?' I said, feeling my lips tremble at the conversation I was having with a strange, almost grown-up man. I was both confused and excited by his belt buckle, resplendent in the sunlight. It was square, and embossed on the silver were the numbers 786. 'Mum says street's full of good-for-nothings this time of day.'

He thought for a moment, his head cocked, examining me; his gaze lingered on my bald knees. I felt self-conscious, him looking at me like that, so I spoke up again. 'I bet you can't go tight up against that wall?'

Without a word, he stepped past me, pressed his back flat against it and spread out his arms like Jesus on the cross. A light breeze swept his hair across his face. He closed his eyes and with his mouth half open he took a long deep breath.

I counted to ten loudly, the hammer sounding.

'Does it hurt?' I asked.

He shook his head.

I counted to twenty.

He rolled his eyes and exhaled for a long time. 'Can I get off now?'

'You're definitely not a good-for-nothing,' I said, impressed.

'What's your name, little bro?' His eyes darted left and right, scanning each end of the empty street, before returning to me.

I wasn't sure whether to tell him. 'Akram. Akram Khan.'

'Pleased to meet you, Mr Akram Khan, I'm Bobby.'

He took my hand and shook it and I thought, Bobby is a strange name for a Pakistani man. His hand felt warm and smooth, like my mother's when she rubbed me clean in the bath. At the thought of Mum I stepped into the middle of the road, from where I could just about make out our red front door at the far end of the street.

'What you looking at?' Bobby asked.

I shrugged my shoulders.

'I got a pound here, little bro.' From a pocket he slowly pulled out a thin bar of Highland Toffee. He tossed it into the air. I leapt for it. 'Good catch.'

'Thanks,' I said, 'but that's not a pound.' My teeth tore at the plastic wrapper.

'No, but this is.' He dangled a blue-green note between his fingers. I leant forward and pounced for it, and at the last moment he pulled his hand away and jerked back his head and laughed, exposing chipped brown teeth. 'You can have it, but you'll have to keep a big secret. Can you do that?'

'Yeah,' I said, biting into the hard toffee.

He retrieved a cigarette from behind his ear and tapped the filter end against a spoon-like thumbnail. 'I don't think so,' he sneered, putting the cigarette between his lips and pocketing the pound. He turned away, about to cross the road.

'I can,' I insisted. Chewing the toffee was hard going at first and hurt as it pulled on a rotten milk tooth.

Slowly Bobby turned back to face me and lit the cigarette with a match. Shading his eyes with a hand, he looked at me for a long time. The smoke half covered his face in white clouds.

'Honestly I can,' I said. The previous evening I had sat on my knees on the floor by the fire, next to Mum, who was hunched over an exercise book at the table. Like a child, she was practising writing her name in discrete shaky English letters. Arriving home from the shop, my father had pulled a wad of notes out of his inside jacket pocket and placed them on the page of her exercise book. Mum had stopped what she was doing, folded the money into the leaves of the book, and stood on a chair to stow it away on top of a tall dresser.

'I can keep a massive secret for a pound – no, a gigantic one,' I pleaded. With every crash of the hammer his offer seemed to be slipping further away.

From the direction of our house a blue car hurtled past, and for no apparent reason it beeped its horn. My companion's eyes followed the car until it disappeared from view. He sucked on his teeth and a bead of sweat dripped off his brow. 'You don't look brave enough to keep a secret as big as that.'

He turned and crossed the road. His oily hair was plastered to his skull and straggled down his neck. Bobby walked slowly for a man and I was able to keep up.

After a minute he stopped and spun around. 'If you can follow me to the park and keep those cute little bro feet of yours exactly five steps behind all the way, then I'll know I can trust you.'

'No problem.'

I trailed him, struggling to keep the distance between us exactly five steps. As we walked, Bobby spat on his hand and put it inside the front of his trousers. He took it out, spat on it and put it back in. I followed him past the health centre where my mother took me for check-ups. Standing outside waiting for his mum was my friend Mustafa. He had been born different, it was said, with a special disease that made him the whitest Pakistani I knew. His eyes, pink-rimmed, were almost transparent in the centre, and he had been warned that if he looked into the sun for even a short time his eyes would hollow out.

'Captain Astounding!' Mustafa stared jealously at my T-shirt.

'See you later?' I suggested.

Bobby stopped and turned back to watch our conversation. He took out another cigarette, rapped it on his thumbnail and lit it, then blew the smoke out of his nose.

'Where you going?' Mustafa looked at my companion suspiciously.

'Far,' I said in an important voice. He put on a worried face. With the toffee binding my teeth I could not add to my report.

Resuming our walk, I followed Bobby past my old nursery and the infant school I'd joined the previous year. Each time we had to cross a road, Bobby would go first and wait impatiently on the other side, signalling with a jerk of his head when it was safe for me to cross. I could hear other hammers at work behind high walls, and sometimes I peeped through gaps in enormous iron gates. I still didn't spot a hammer but I did see dark-looking men lowering, on a chain, a gigantic ship's anchor. One man worked the chain and several others guided the anchor onto the tray of a truck. If it fell it would have crushed them. I felt a knot in my stomach, knowing I was far from home. I wouldn't know how to find my own way back. My aching jaw from the hard-going toffee was making me feel sick.

As we approached the Mash Tun public house, Bobby and I crossed to the other side of the road. The pub was a square building with wooden picnic benches commanding a thin strip of yard next to the pavement. Skinheads in boots, tight jeans and bomber jackets stood outside drinking out of tall glasses. Each wore a long chain folded over at the hip. Spotting us, they stopped and stared. One scratched under an armpit in imitation of a monkey. They mouthed words at us – *Wog, Paki* – exaggerating the lip movements so their meaning was impossible to miss. Bobby shrank back against a wall as though it would afford him protection. One of the skinheads, swinging his chain frighteningly fast at his hips, mouthed the word *Later*, and they all laughed. Among them, sitting on a low stool, was a boy, Adrian Hartley, a bully I recognized from school. He nodded to me and ran across the road towards us. I stopped warily as he approached.

'You wagged school then?' Adrian's hands were deep in his pockets. With his feet planted firmly on the ground his body swayed from side to side while his head nodded as though he could hear a song playing in his ears. I was worried that he might punch me, but his hands remained in his pockets.

'I'm not wagging. Mum says I've got a tummy ache.'

Adrian looked at Bobby and smiled, his white teeth dazzling in his pale round face blotched with blue and black stains, maybe dirt. 'I'm not wagging either.' He jerked his head towards the Mash Tun. 'My dad said I could skip today on account of my black eye.' His stubby finger traced the blue circle around his bloodshot left eye.

The skinheads shook their heads, and digging their thumbs into tight denim pockets they slunk off into the pub, through a swinging door like in a cowboy film. Bobby stood perfectly still exactly five steps in front of Adrian and me. He dug one thumb into his belt and twisted his long hair around a finger of his other hand. His feet were spread wide. He turned his head to the side and a bolus of spit shot out of his mouth to land fizzing on the hot tarmac.

Adrian gazed hungrily at the stub of Highland Toffee in my hand. 'Have it,' I said, offering him the gooey mess. 'You can buy twenty Highland Toffees with a pound, and I know how you can earn a whole pound.'

'Really?' said Adrian, his eyes wide. 'In the Mash Tun with a pound I could drink Tizer all day.'

Bobby squinted as though examining some detail on Adrian's skin. 'The white boy your friend?' he called.

A white friend, I thought, and nodded proudly.

He whistled, sucking the air through his teeth. 'You have good friends.'

It grew warmer as we walked on, and each successive street was quieter with fewer houses. Adrian kept turning to me, squeezing out a nervous smile, and I reciprocated with a reassuring nod. At what was to be our final turn, the view before us was like that of a country village. The road sloped lazily downwards, lined on each side by trees. A sign on one side read *Lye Park*, and a set of low gates led onto grassland. In the distance the grass sloped gently upwards, and on the crest of the hill was a playground, incongruous in its orange tubular metal construction. Emanating from it were the excited shrieks of preschool children and the guarded, muffled voices of their mothers.

Lye Park was huge, and after walking some way in the opposite direction to the playground, Bobby stopped and scanned the view. We stopped too, waiting. He dropped to the ground, and we followed, the three of us crawling on our knees and elbows over the warm earth like soldiers, towards a small dense orchard of crab apple trees. The fruit was tiny and wouldn't ripen until the autumn. Pointing to the base of one tree, Bobby instructed me in a harsh whisper to stay there as a lookout. I sank to my haunches, my legs quivering.

Bobby led Adrian by the hand to a nearby tree, one with a low canopy of dense green leaves. 'It looks like a camp in here,' I heard Adrian say excitedly as he disappeared underneath the thick mass of overhanging green. Bobby wriggled in after him. His big feet stuck out, their red rubber soles lolling out like tongues.

There was some sort of argument. Adrian's boots were ankle high and green with red laces and took him ages to get off. They were thrown, as though discarded, to the edge of the foliage, a Union Jack stitched on each side.

The sunlight was strong and it shimmered through the few spaces between the leaves. Bobby spat a lot and cursed and the wind shook the leaves on the tree. Then Bobby squashed Adrian underneath him and then he seemed to be propped up on his knees. He spat some more, rubbed himself and made gentle murmuring sounds as though he was coaxing a baby to sleep. Finally he let out a subdued grunt, and Adrian, pulling up his trousers, wriggled out feet first from underneath the bush. He leapt for his boots, looked inside them and then at Bobby, on his face an expression of confusion and betrayal.

*

Smarting again at the memory, I reach across and untangle a stray hair on Grace's brow. At the parting her hair is darker, almost black, like a water stain that re-emerges however many times it is scrubbed clean. Even in sleep her face looks thoughtful and disappointed as though she is about to cry. I wonder what she dreams about.

'That's not the whole story,' I tell her. 'Adrian looking so hard done by: that was because of me. I took the pound that Bobby had paid him. I slipped it out of his boot when he was inside the bush, and as soon as I stole it I felt a dullness, a despair I hadn't felt before. I knew that if I replaced the money the hopelessness would go away, but I didn't. For a reason unknown to me, at the time and even now, half a lifetime later, I feel I am in need of that despair.'

I expect Grace at least to stir, but there is only the shallow rise and fall of her chest and a gentle vibration as the breath passes across the Cupid's bow of her upper lip. All of me wants to touch her body, softly at first until she wakes up, and then I want her to say again that I can fuck her.

4

Bobby walked briskly away, and Adrian and I were stranded, wandering aimlessly until Adrian recognized a pub from which he was able to navigate, pub to pub, back to the Mash Tun. I tried not to look at him, out of fear of what he might report, and he carried a limp. A few times, suddenly remembering, he cursed the pound he had been cheated out of. I was glad when he went into the pub.

I got back to find Mustafa in the middle of the road, exactly halfway between his house and mine, which stood facing each other. Mustafa trembled and covered his eyes with his hands, muttering, 'Allah, oh Allah!' As though oblivious to the boy's panicked presence, a dog chased a cat in circles around him. The cat, I thought, would lose the dog. It would leap through a small opening in a fence or do an about-turn far too quickly for the lumbering dog, and scarper. The animals changed direction and disappeared, and Mustafa, slowly uncovering his eyes, looked cautiously around. His chest swayed rapidly and seeing me, a thin spray of tears ran down his cheeks.

I took him by the arm and led him off the tarmac, onto the pavement. We sat on the kerb, kicking our feet into the road.

'Did you go really far?' he said between shuddering breaths. His eyes were still narrowed suspiciously.

'You don't trust no one.' I pulled the pound note a little way out of my pocket for him to see.

'Did Bobby give you that?' His eyes widened.

'Didn't have to do anything,' I bragged, though I was secretly surprised that he knew the man's name. 'Anyway, how come you're wagging school?' I asked, changing the subject.

'Opticians.'

Just then, in a blur, the cat and dog went past us. 'Come on,' I cried, tugging at Mustafa's arm, 'we've got to save the cat!'

We followed the animals back and forth through slim alleys that ran between houses. When we reached an allotment where a neighbour grew radishes, I stopped abruptly, Mustafa colliding with my heels. I gazed intently at the cultivated earth that ran in neat lines across the small plot. Inside the troughs, small leafy shoots marked the position of each radish. It took a lot of rubbing to clean off the dried soil, but the taste of the radish would fizz on my tongue as though stolen food ought to taste bitter. Seeing them reminded me that I was hungry and that my mother would be wondering where I was.

We trailed the animals across a mountain of brick and timber where number eleven had collapsed one night earlier that year. No one had been in it, and the following morning our entire street had come out and watched in awe as a digger with a huge iron ball on a chain rolled in and flattened what remained; somehow, numbers nine and thirteen were still completely intact. Long nails studded the timber planks and Mustafa and I picked our way carefully across the debris. Where the garden had once been, the cat screamed like a baby but the dog made no sound, just the whoosh of air around it and the thud of its paws as they met the ground.

Nobody I knew had a dog, and if one came along the footpath towards us my mother would take my hand and we'd cross the road. Dogs were unclean and if you got too close to one Allah would be angry. But now, as though we were each proving something to the other, Mustafa and I were chasing the animals.

Mustafa was an albino. At first, his mum and dad were convinced it was an English conspiracy, or at the very least a mix-up at the hospital. But then an albino was born into his family in Pakistan, and after that they put it down to something they called Allah's will. Mustafa lagged behind me and clutched his chest as though he was in pain. He couldn't run properly, partly on account of his eyes and partly because of his fat little legs. He was prone to stumbling, and when he did he bled and it wouldn't stop until he got stitches. His eyelids trembled in the breeze, fragile like a butterfly's wings. His skin was paper white, and all summer long he'd squint, or like a soldier's salute he would shield his eyes with his hand, and when he looked at you he'd stand real close as though examining a fly on your nose.

Mustafa and I paused to catch our breath.

'The Prophet Muhammad kept cats,' I said.

Exhausted, Mustafa sank to his knees, fine wisps of hair trembling on his pink scalp.

'Get up,' I urged. 'We'll go to heaven if we rescue it.'

We found the cat in an alley. It lay, perfectly still, on the cobbles and tufts of moss. There was a tear in its belly and its guts spilled out. Rivulets of blood trickled in all directions, sinking into the gaps between the cobbles. The animal's eyes were wide open as though taking one last look at the sky.

'Have we failed? Will we go to hell?' asked Mustafa.

'Probably,' I replied.

'What we going to do?' His voice was agitated and sharp. He put an arm around me and I him.

'We can make up for it if we do good for the rest of our lives,' I offered.

'My mum says all children go to heaven,' he said.

'Cats too. If we keep an eye on it we might see its soul as it slips away.'

'I've never seen that before.' Mustafa shook his head, wiping away a tear.

'I have, lots of times – chickens,' I lied.

'What's it look like?'

A light breeze carried the scent of oil and smoke from the nearby works, and bending a little way towards the cat I could smell something sweet and warm. Drying quickly in the overhead sun, its blood carried the smell of the soil, the mineral-metallic odour that would remain on my fingers for days after rubbing the radishes.

'First we have to say a prayer,' I said.

'Our Father. . .' started Mustafa, remembering a prayer we recited at school assembly every morning.

'No, not that. The foreign prayer my dad says when the chickens are about to die.' I put my hands together and looked up at the sky. '*Bismillah ir-Rahman ir-Rahim*.'

'Still can't see the soul,' said Mustafa mournfully. He stared intently at the cat and nervously shuffled his feet.

'You have to look up to see it fly away,' I said.

He scanned the sky, keeping the cat within the lower border of his vision as if he was afraid it might jump up and dart at his legs. 'Maybe it's already gone?' A fresh bout of tears welled up in his eyes.

'You don't understand. I've released its soul with my power. It only goes once I've said the *Bismillah*.'

Mustafa kicked at a cobblestone, mindful not to stray into an imaginary perimeter about two feet deep around the body of the cat. Finally he spoke. 'I saw something worse last night.'

'In chickens they're called giblets,' I said. 'The bits coming out of its body, and they're dirty. My dad pulls them out of their bellies and wraps them in a plastic bag and when no one's looking he throws it into the canal. He says that *gora* put them in sausages to eat. Do you eat giblets?'

At school Mustafa was often mistaken for a *gora*, and even when he told the white kids that both of his parents were Pakis they couldn't quite accept it; as a sort of compromise they called him a Paki lover, not a Paki. He was whiter than the *gora*, so their eyes retreated into their sockets and heads shook in disbelief when he spoke Paki with a proper Paki.

Mustafa shook his head. 'Yesterday my aunty came to visit and the day before my dad kicked my mum. Aunty is my dad's sister and she said I was cursed like a *gora* but our kid Faisal he was all right because he was brown.' Tears rolled down his cheeks and he held out a hand and stared at it, one side and then the other. His face grew pink. 'After that, my aunty looked at me and wailed like I had just suddenly died.'

'They do that a lot, our mums,' I offered as consolation, giving his waist a squeeze.

Mustafa shook me off, irritated. He ran his fingers through his hair and raised up on his toes as though he was about to run away. 'In the night when my aunty had gone, from my bed I could hear my mum crying in the toilet. Afterwards when I went to go to the toilet I saw giblets in the base of the pan. Only then I didn't know they were called giblets.'

'I heard your mum crying this morning,' I said. 'She came over to visit mine and they both cried. After that they were talking about a baby and didn't even notice when I slipped out of the back.'

As though my confirmation had doubled his mother's pain, Mustafa turned from pink to white.

'Your mum having a baby?'

He stuttered, but no discernible words came out.

It started to rain in large warm droplets. The rain diluted the cat's blood to pinks and light reds. The damp air amplified the crisp, pungent scent of radish, the iron in the blood and the iron in the soil from the nearby allotment.

'Come on, mate, you hungry?'

Back at the allotment, our feet sinking into the earth, I picked and cleaned each radish before handing it to Mustafa. He ate slowly; watching in contempt as the rain mixed with his tears, suddenly I was impatient to be free of him. I felt agitated and fearful, not of being caught stealing but of something else, of being tainted in some way by Mustafa: by his fear of animals, his knowledge of Bobby, his skin that dirtied so easily, and by giblets in the toilet.

*

I pause and look over at Grace. She murmurs and her hands lash about as though seeking something. For a moment, her chest forms a convex arc, the small of her back lifted off the mattress; she breathes heavily until her thrashing hands meet the hard surface of her bedside cabinet, when suddenly her eyelids open and she looks around. She seems momentarily surprised to see me and then smiles. 'Told you there was a story in you.'

I reply gently, 'You didn't hear a word.'

The sight of Grace awakening has stirred memories of the house I have deserted. Is Azra still sound asleep, pulling the white sheet ever tighter around her bony limbs? Would she care that soon she'd be widowed? Or are they awake, Azra and my parents, looking out of windows, standing by the front door peering into the dark street, watching for me? Would they believe – this last thought gives me a curious satisfaction – that I lie not far away, in a stranger's bed? Would the knowledge of that evoke in Azra some kind of passion or only anger, anger and a disdainful curl of her lower lip?

'What are you thinking about?' I ask.

'Don't mind if I doze off now and then, I'm still listening.'

I laugh. 'But you're not.'

'I like the sound of your voice.'

'It's a soldier's voice. To my troops it was the booming voice of a sergeant.'

'It's familiar.'

'Strange thing to say.'

'It pleases me.'

Through the window I glimpse the sky, which has lightened from purple to grey, and even without consulting my watch I know less time will have passed than I think. Ahead of me are still many hours of walking the streets, and here it is warm and comfortable. This here is sin but I will be forgiven. That I will be forgiven is a truth beyond doubt, but still out of superstition I quickly whisper a *Bismillah*.

5

After that it rained heavily, the sky darkening suddenly, and the wind blew up. I went home, to be scolded, fed, bathed, and spent the afternoon sitting by the fire. As it spat I dared myself to rub the glowing embers into the carpet, leaving tiny black dots in its fibres.

The door opened and I smiled at my father as he came in, wet from his walk home from the shop. He draped his huge overcoat over the fireguard, sucking all the heat out of the room. A brewing steam gathered along its woollen surface and started to rise. The flames crackled as though straining underneath it.

'Miss that old thing,' he said ruefully, referring to the old sofa we had put out that morning for the rag and bone man.

I nodded. Misty-eyed, my mother had described it as a good sofa, and it was the only one I had ever known. Over time its spindly legs had broken one by one and been replaced by two stacked bricks. The seat was marked with inkblots and long scrawly lines ran along the armrests – my handiwork as a toddler, my father said. The seat part lifted up and inside Mum had stored old clothes and shoes. Behind the cushions we found various things – a penny that Dad let me keep, broken crayons, an old set of keys Dad had given up hope of finding – and just before we put it out, leaning it against the front of the house for the rag and bone man to take away, he took a Stanley knife to it, slashing the upholstery from end to end. My mother had not approved of this last act. She said it was vandalism and that he should have let it go as it was, with dignity. He should have thought about all the now dead people who had once sat on it. Embarrassed, my father had reached into it, working loose several pieces of wood for the fire.

Now he stood warming himself by the grate, staring at a framed picture of Mecca above the mantel. It was the only picture in our house. In the absence of the sofa, Mum had made me a daybed out of pillows covered by a duvet brought down from my bed. The old brown armchair rested in a corner next to a TV on a stand, and one tall thin dresser stood like a sentry by the door. A low table usually placed before the sofa had been pushed against a far wall. I stretched, enjoying the luxury of a relatively empty room.

'Where's your mum?'

'Out.'

Dad considered me as though I was lying.

'She's at Mustafa's,' I added.

'Mustafa?'

'Across the street, the house with the blue door,' I said.

'Stay here,' he instructed sternly. 'I'll be back in a minute.'

As he picked up his coat, the fire seemed to leap after it, its warmth instantly enveloping my face. I braced myself for a cold gust of wind as he opened the door to the street. From outside came an acrid smell of burning, as though someone had lit a bonfire.

They were arguing as the door opened and they came back in. Once again, the breeze through the open door brought in the smell of fire.

'You shouldn't be out tonight,' Dad said to Mum.

'She's all alone with two boys.'

'You have to think about your own family,' said Dad.

Mum opened her mouth to say something

'Shh, not now,' Dad said through clenched teeth.

He double-locked the front door and draped his coat over the armchair. Lifting the living room curtain at one corner, he looked out into the dark street. He lowered it carefully and wrung his hands, a scowl on his face. Mum went into the kitchen and then joined us in the living room. Sinking to her knees with a sigh, she settled herself onto the duvet next to me. On the carpet in front of her she had placed a bowl of potatoes. She began to peel them. I looked at them and then at her, trying to work out what day of the week it was.

She smiled, patting me on the head. 'Yes, it's chips tonight.'

There were noises from the street, at first distant and muffled; yet somehow I knew they were linked to the smell of fire. My heart was pounding, all of my attention suddenly focused on the sounds in the street. My parents were listening too, their faces frozen and eyes wide. They glanced at each other and my mother gave a tiny shake of the head. The footsteps outside – boot soles studded with clattering metal – grew louder and then stopped abruptly like a loud slap. They had stopped outside our front door. Bravely, my father returned to the window and put out a hand to draw back the curtain. Mum shrieked and Dad pulled away. Outside someone shouted, 'Pakis, come out, you Pakis!'

The warmth of the burning planks in the grate was in direct opposition to the scene I tried to imagine outside and I shuddered, fearful for my parents more than myself. A loud beat started up, something being struck repeatedly against a bin lid. At intervals the crashing stopped, replaced by jeering and monkey noises.

'Put the TV on loud,' Mum said to Dad.

'We will go one day,' said Dad, moving to stand by the fire and adjusting a stray corner of glittery tinsel that had been sticky-taped around the edges of the Mecca picture.

My mother looked up at him and forced out a smile. She patted the space on the carpet next to her. Dad shrugged his shoulders and remained standing.

Outside I heard the screeching brakes of a car and someone cried out – a noise not dissimilar to the scream of the cat earlier, only louder.

'I have to go,' said my father.

Her eyes showing fear, my mother shook her head. 'Sit down, come on, next to us,' she said softly.

'If I could only get to the end of the street to a phone box I could call the police.'

I could smell the oil on the stove in the kitchen heating up. Although no potatoes had yet been put into it, the fat gave off the aroma of frying chips.

'Police!' Mum cackled. 'Don't worry,' she added unconvincingly, 'they'll be gone in a minute or two.'

'We can't show them we are weak.' Dad's voice trailed off as he went into the kitchen.

The door to the backyard opened and then slammed shut. I heard the latch being bolted. My father reappeared in the kitchen doorway, holding a long broom handle. Mum put down the potato she was peeling and sprang to her feet. She grabbed the broom and stared at my father. 'No, not in front of the boy,' she said.

'You're wrong, missus: especially in front of the boy.'

Mum shot me a panicked glance. 'Go upstairs!' she cried.

I didn't move.

'There's no hiding it from him,' said Dad.

'You can't fight them all.'

My father let go of the broom, leaving it dangling loosely in Mum's hand. He stooped slightly so that his face was level with hers and did something I had never before seen him do, nor have I seen him do it since: he kissed her. Then he turned to me, his face suffused with a violent, incomprehensible anger. 'Get your coat!' he shouted.

Before I could obey, Mum moved to block the front door, the broom handle across her body. She looked back and forth between us, her expression gradually charging to one of fixed determination. 'I won't tell you again,' she said fiercely to me.

I got quickly to my feet. Putting one hand on the banister, as though to climb the stairs, I lingered on the bottom step.

She turned to my father. 'Do you see anyone else going out there? Think for a minute. What would we do if we lost you? What would happen to me as a widow? And the boy, what would become of him? You want him to grow up into some sort of hoodlum without a father?'

'You don't understand,' said Dad softly.

'Upstairs!' she screamed, without glancing in my direction.

I scrambled up to my room and peered out the window. Across the road, four men stood before Mustafa's front door. Even in the poorly lit street, I could tell they wore bomber jackets, tight jeans and long boots. One had a spiky Mohican and another swung a thick chain at his hips. The headlights of a car passing slowly at the other end of the street caught the men, frozen for a split second, like startled burglars. In that moment, I recognized the man with the chain as Adrian's father. He shook the chain, opening it out to double its length, and swung it. I watched it spin, glinting as it caught the grim overhead streetlight at its maximum height, and winced each time it cracked against the pavement.

The end of the chain met the windowpane. The glass fractured but held together for a moment; just as the men ran away, the entire pane collapsed into the front room.

Inside the house a light was switched on, the brightness of the interior contrasting sharply with the dark night. Mustafa's mother came up to the window, clutching his little brother Faisal. Faisal was swaddled in a white blanket. She bent to the floor and picked up a shard of glass. She looked at it, shaking her head in resignation. Faisal, too young to know better, cocked his head up towards the broken window and smiled. His mother shivered and pulled her headscarf over her brow. Mustafa came into the room, rubbing the smoke from his eyes. He wore proper pyjamas like English people. Mustafa pulled his mother away from the window and the light went out.

Our windows were closed but I could taste black smoke. I coughed, and rubbed my stinging eyes. There were no lights on in any of the houses, and the widely spaced street lamps glowed discreetly in yellow orbs high above the deserted road. The factory hammer broke the silence every ten seconds:

bong. I listened intently, expecting to hear glass breaking further along the street.

I could make out my father's angry voice. 'We must defend ourselves.'

'*Inshallah* we will, but not like this,' screamed Mum. It was as though by shouting louder she would get her own way. She muttered a *Bismillah*; I heard her footsteps going into the kitchen and then a hot bubbly sizzle as she cast the freshly cut potato sticks into the oil.

Noticing a glow from the street below, I pressed my nose to my bedroom window and looked down. Flames leapt off the sofa. I heard my mother scream, 'Allah!' The front door was flung open, letting in thick black smoke that curled up the stairs and into my room.

From the window I saw my father kick at the fire. He ran indoors, picked up his coat and returned to the sofa, draping the garment over it. It was a stupid thing to do, I thought. The fire licked around the edges of the coat and quickly through it. From my elevation it felt like I was watching television. Then I saw my dad drag the sofa into the middle of the road, away from the house.

I heard jubilant jeering from the other end of the street. My father cried out, '*Allahu Akbar!*' Raising the broom in his hand, he marched down the road. Fearing for him, I said a *Bismillah*. Then I saw my mother staggering after him down the street, pulling her headscarf tightly down on her head. I hurried downstairs and stood, with one foot outside, at the open front door. The wind had turned, blowing the rain and thick black smoke high above my head, and the warmth of the burning sofa cast me in a pleasing orange glow. Halfway down the street, Mum and Dad stood guard like ancient sentries.

Suddenly, I loathed the idea of being brown, a Paki, with Paki-bashers out on the streets and Adrian's dad ready to pounce. I hated too the weakness of my parents. Of what my parents had become.

Digging one hand into my pocket, I felt guiltily for the crisp edges of the pound note. The pound note was bad luck and right then I should have got rid of it, thrown it on the fire, but I didn't. I kept it.

*

I watch Grace as she gently stirs. She cracks a benevolent smile. It takes ages for her eyes to fully open.

'Kids think daft things,' she says. 'It's not like that anymore, is it?'

'There's a flaw. Somewhere inside of me is a deep flaw.'

'It's just life. Not all white people – what is it you call them?'

'*Gora*.'

'Not all *gora* are the same, just like not all Pakistanis are like the lying bastards I meet.'

'The *gora* is a simple humble being, but you were right – almost the first thing you said was that we Pakis, we're liars.'

'We all have things we'd rather not. . .' Grace's gaze strays towards the baby picture on her bedside cabinet. 'I didn't use that word.'

'We don't fit in,' I say emphatically. 'Never will.'

'You,' she draws back a little and observes how I am comfortably reclined next to her, 'seem to be making a good fist of it.'

'You don't get it. We don't want to fit in.'

'Not even soldier boy?'

'You miss the point. It's how we think.'

'You're better than us?'

I hesitate. 'Yes.'

'As a kid you were a thieving little bastard, and for what it's worth I don't mind that. Admitting to your dishonesty in some way makes you honest.'

'You want me to be really honest?'

She nods.

'Earlier, I wanted to. . .' I glance across at her belly and up towards her breasts. 'When you were asleep. . . I mean—'

'That would spoil it. Don't stop. It's like. . . As I said, your voice is familiar. It's good to fall asleep to.' Her head sinks into the pillow and she closes her eyes. I watch her breathe, waiting until the rise and fall of her chest is regular and shallow before I resume.

6

Being Craig Male was worse than being a Paki. As always, he was dressed in an oversized moss-green vinyl parka. At school I had observed from a safe distance how a gang of boys would wait at the top of the stairs and spit balls of chewed-up paper that slid down his parka as he crossed the foyer several floors below. Between classes they'd run up silently and kick him from behind. Then they'd form a circle and laugh as he tried to keep an eye on all of them at the same time.

I was eleven and took myself to and back from school. That morning, I tiptoed past, hoping he wouldn't see me. But he turned abruptly and offered a friendly smile. 'My mum died last night,' he said.

Maley had bad genes and close up he didn't look the same age as me. He was a younger version of an old man. He was thin, really thin, and short. He had a comb-over, because the hair on his head was too sparse to cover his scalp. The skin on his face hung off his bones, and for a thin person that was unusual. He had spots too – bright pink against his paper-white skin.

'Is it all right if I walk to class with you?' he asked.

I shivered at the thought that he might tell other kids about his dead mum. 'Mate, you really shouldn't go to school on a day like today.'

'It's Tuesday.' His pace quickened. 'Pasta.'

'It's not a good idea. Wag it. Go tomorrow.'

The 247 eased to a stop just ahead of us. In the absence of Maley, I would have caught it; from the upper deck of the bus most days I would see Maley as he walked to school.

'Why?'

'If they find out they'll kill you.' I stared at his plimsolls. His big toe was just visible through one.

'I never miss Tuesdays.' Maley gazed up at me. His matted hair sat flat against his scalp, revealing a flaky patch of skin.

'I can't wag school, Dad will kill me, but I'll say I have to go home for lunch. Wait for me somewhere. You can come to my house.'

'Your mum won't mind?'

'No, why should she? Anyway, she'll be at the shop.'

He looked unconvinced. 'The thing about pasta is that it really fills you up.' He said it slowly, like a challenge.

I made up my mind. 'Look,' I said, 'I've never wagged before and if I get caught it's not worth thinking about, but I'll join you. We'll hang out. I hope you like curry?'

'Never tried it.'

'It's much better than pasta.'

'You sure?'

'It's the best food in the world,' I added in a serious tone.

His eyes brightened. 'Really?'

After checking behind me in case Mum was watching from the window, I turned into a street in the opposite direction from school, and Maley followed.

'Pasta is special. It's what is called a slow-release carbohydrate. It keeps me full for four hours. Six if it's Mrs Cole – she puts extra on my plate.'

'Why? Do you know her?'

'I think she used to work with my mum.'

'Your mum had a job?'

'Yeah, 'course she did. She worked at Danks's. Clerical, like. They made boilers for ships. My dad says it's the boilers what made him go deaf.'

'Clerical?' I didn't know what that meant.

'She got sick and my dad finished up too.' Maley rubbed his hands together for warmth. 'So he could look after her.'

'Sounds horrible, your dad's job.'

'It's all right.' He shook his head. 'It was before I remember.' He stretched out a hand. 'I've seen you around but we've never spoke. You're Akram Khan, aren't you?'

I smiled and shook his hand. It was cold and bony with tiny wrinkles criss-crossing the pale skin. 'And you're Craig Male.'

'How come you know that?'

'You're famous.'

This seemed to please him, and he smiled. The small park nearby was deserted and we took a swing each, even though they were for younger kids. As we swung I noticed he wasn't wearing socks.

'My dad doesn't believe in a God,' he said thoughtfully. 'Mum didn't either.'

'What will happen to your mum?'

'Nothing.'

'Nothing?'

'They're going to cremate her.' He pulled a marble out of his pocket and held it up to an eye like a pirate looking through a lens. 'We're going to keep her ashes.'

'We believe in Allah. When we die we go to heaven.'

'There's no p-proof of heaven,' he stammered angrily.

'What will you do with the ashes?'

'Put them in a pot in the cupboard.' Maley looked down at his feet.

'Why?'

'What they good for?' He shook his head and stamped his feet to the ground; his swing abruptly stopped. He got off. 'You coming?'

'Where?'

He glanced up at the sky as though reading the time. 'We got three hours forty-five minutes until dinner.' He thought for a moment. 'Could go up Turner's Hill?'

I jumped off my swing and began to walk beside him. 'Never been.' I looked at the hill looming about two miles into the distance. It was the tallest point around. On its peak was a huge steel aerial, and at night a beacon flashed from its tip, warning low-flying aircraft. Viewed from my bedroom window and at a certain angle the aerial stood precisely on the rim of the horizon. Once, when I was little, I had been reading a story about giants and just as I looked out of my window I saw the silhouette of an enormous man stride across the top of the hill. Terrified, I dived under my bed, and only emerged when my mother called me down for dinner. And although, at eleven, I no longer believed in giants, the hill still seemed like an alarming, almost mythical place.

A truck hurtled closely past, scattering tiny stones at our feet.

'It's best when there's lightning,' said Maley. We looked up at the clouds, greying.

'Doesn't it scare you?' I said.

'The lightning conducts through the aerial so you won't get hit, but you can get real close.'

We took a path that skirted the Old Hill tower blocks where the poor *gora* lived. It led to a stretch of canal with pretty ironwork bridges. Further ahead, as the canal curved, was the sharp outline of an abandoned mill.

'That there' – Maley pointed to a bird idling in the canal – 'is a Canada goose, and that one, the smaller one with the white bill, that's a coot.'

They were names I had not heard before.

'Once I saw a kingfisher diving from that willow up there by the mill,' he added proudly.

'A kingfisher?'

'Yeah, I saw a flash of blue and I knew in a split second what it was, even before it flew off with a fish in its beak.'

'Must have had a nest somewhere. Maybe along the bank?'

Maley stepped off the path and scanned the ground along the canal edge. 'Rains were heavy, probably flooded.'

'Kingfisher dead then?' I raised my eyebrows.

'It's just nature.' He smiled cheerfully before leaping back onto the path.

'How come you know stuff like that?' I said, catching up.

'Don't you ever come here?' Maley wore a face of disbelief.

'Go to mosque after school. Then homework, and when that's finished it's telly and bed. Weekends have to help out in the shop.'

'You own a shop?' His eyes bulged like the marble he still held in his hand.

'Yeah.'

'You must be rich.'

I laughed.

'You sell pasta?'

'We only have Pakistani customers.'

'You should ask your dad to stock it. Spaghetti's my favourite.'

The mill had thick walls like a castle and one small doorway. Although the lack of roof tiles rendered it open to the elements, from inside the darkening sky had cut off a clear view of its height. Maley paced its four sides, measuring them out with his feet, before declaring it a perfect square – like a prison cell, he added. Craning his neck, he peered up. 'Strange. No bats today.'

'My dad keeps live chickens and if a customer orders one he kills it in the sink at the back.'

'We are the strongest species on the planet,' Maley replied.

'He makes me hold the bird while he slits its neck. They're strong, chickens. It's not a job for a kid.'

'But not the wisest,' Maley added ruefully.

We left the mill and continued upwards along a rough path.

'He says a *Bismillah* as he presses down the knife. That way it's halal. Then he tips it upside down so that the blood washes down the sink.'

'Slitting its neck would really hurt a chicken.' Maley's face seemed to contort into a frozen mask. 'I'm glad I wasn't born you.'

I stared at him. It was a shock hearing that. I was about to say the same thing to him, but something stopped me. I closed my mouth and considered the view.

'Look,' I said, pointing, 'I can't see the top of Turner's Hill anymore. It's disappeared into the clouds.'

'If we hurry we might see the edge of the rain.' Maley's eyes bulged with excitement.

'The edge of the rain. How come I don't know that?' I struggled to keep up with Maley. Having little weight to carry he was sprightly.

After another hour of climbing circuitous, slippery paths, often having to fight our way through the undergrowth, we got to the top of Turner's Hill. The rain had stopped, and we didn't catch the edge of it. The low dark clouds limited our view to the large clumps of manure below our feet.

'It's fresh,' said Maley seriously. 'They have grazing up here, see.'

'What, cows?'

'Mostly horses,' he said. 'Scrap iron men. Gypos. Fairground when it comes. Must have gone into some barn on account of the weather. They're clever, see, horses, can sense a storm.'

'How do you know?'

'Rode one once. At Pontins. Used to go every year. Don't remember it though. Dad keeps a picture in a frame on the wall. Been on a beach as well and sat on a tractor.'

'Thought you said you were poor?' I looked him over, taking in his trousers that were a few inches too short, the vinyl parka falling like an apron to somewhere around his knees, his lively face painfully dotted with leaking acne.

'I've seen pictures of me as a kid when we were rich.'

'What happened?'

'This bottle of pills she got from the chemist's was wrongly labelled. She got irreversible liver disease.'

It made me suddenly angry that he was referring to his dead mother as *she*. 'Wrongly labelled?'

I said it reflexively, and regretted it faster than a kingfisher could catch a fish. Maley didn't reply. He took a few steps towards the base of the aerial and disappeared into the clouds. I kicked at the sodden earth, the air cold around me. Before I could start to worry about how I would make it back alone, a bush shook as though caught by the wind and Maley reappeared from behind it, his hand outstretched and covered in manure.

'Look, I found a slow-worm. It's a big one.' He seemed happier than he had been all morning. Cupping his hands together, he held them out to me. I looked inside them, not putting my head too close. I could see something brown wriggling between a crack in his fingers.

'They break easily.' He turned away, guarding his hands. Carefully he lowered the worm onto the grass, then collected some foliage to tuck around it. 'Mum said I should go watch them cremate her,' he added.

'I wouldn't go,' I said.

'People do weird things. It's just human nature. Animal kingdom, now that's much better.'

'I find animals boring.'

'You think kingfishers are boring?' Maley's neck began to flush red, just like it did after a spitball was dropped on him from the stairwell or he was kicked from behind. 'Well then, you're an idiot like the rest of them.'

'Well, I think kingfishers must be okay,' I allowed.

'They're one of the fastest species on the planet.'

We meandered back down the hill. Maley stopped frequently, crouching to examine a plant or a bug, and once a wasp, apparently with no fear. He used words I had never heard before – alder, alderfly, ecotone, cowslip, gastropod, mallard, vole, cow parsley – and each time I'd nod and murmur a non-committal *Yeah, sure*, which seemed to satisfy him, and he'd get up and we'd carry on. Before we got to the road he stopped once again, next to a hedgerow.

'Listen, can you hear it?' His face was frozen in concentration. I shook my head. He put a finger to his lips and then carefully teased apart the branches of the hedgerow. 'In here,' he whispered, beckoning with a slant of his head.

I was cautious at first, fearing another dirty slow-worm, but when I looked in I saw the most beautiful thing. Deep within the hedgerow was a nest containing four tiny brown birds. They craned their necks and chirped with beaks that seemed paper-thin but far too big for their small heads.

'Best not to disturb them,' Maley whispered. He carefully replaced the foliage and tiptoed backwards. I couldn't say anything, still enraptured by the image of those pink beaks, the tiny bodies chirping for all they were worth, short sharp tweets. 'Their mother must be watching us from somewhere around here.' Maley scanned the trees above us.

Once on the road we were both suddenly aware again of the fact that we had wagged school. As much as possible we kept to the side streets, and as the roads got busier we quickened our pace.

Maley led, lifting his chin and sniffing as though he was following his nose back to my house. 'I'm hungry,' he said, rubbing his stomach. 'I can feel it turning over.'

'Mum says that hunger is the very worst thing.'

'She's right,' said Maley. 'More than hungry, I'm starving.'

'Mum doesn't allow me to use the word *starving*. If I use it by accident she says a hundred *Bismillah*s.'

Already Turner's Hill seemed a distant memory as I led Maley into the house. He peered wide-eyed into a large pot on the cooker. The steel sides of the pot were still warm. Mum had cooked the curry before going out to help at the shop. She didn't serve customers, she worked out the back: plucking chickens, sealing them over a gas ring, gutting them and chopping the meat to order. She soaked chickpeas and lentils in brine so they could be sold soft, and she always had a large cauldron of oil on the go, deep-frying samosas and other battered savouries that were put on a large tray and sold up front. The back room was as much a part of the store as the shop itself. She also collected eggs from hens we kept in a yard to the rear of the shop, and boxed them ready for sale.

Maley pocketed the marble he had been turning over all day, smiled, and stirred the pot with a large wooden spoon.

'It's butter chicken, is that okay?' I said.

Maley thought for a moment. 'Well, if I ate a balanced diet I think I would be a vegetarian, but because of the way it is I allow myself some meat protein when I can get it.'

'There's bread in that cupboard.' I pointed at it. 'Can you get us some?'

I thought he would take two, perhaps three slices for each of us, but he placed the entire loaf on the table. I felt powerless to object and re-assured myself that he'd probably eat only a few slices. I put some curry into two bowls and placed them on the table. Maley sat motionless, elbows on the table, his eyes fixed on the steam emanating from his bowl. He sniffed, looked at me and then back at the bowl, a worried expression on his face. He picked up a slice of bread and stopped.

'You dip your bread in the curry,' I instructed.

'Dip it? What with?'

'With your fingers.' I broke a corner off a slice of bread, and pinching it into a scoop I gathered up some curry and put it into my mouth.

'Hot,' Maley observed after his first mouthful, blowing out repeatedly. Again the redness began to creep up his pale, acne-littered neck.

Despite the apparent hotness of the mild curry, Maley ate eleven slices of bread and two bowls of curry, containing what must have been half a chicken. By the time he had finished he was pinker than I had ever seen him. I managed only two and a half slices and half a bowl of curry. The *gora* way he ate – taking huge mouthfuls, one after the other in quick succession, the next one going in before he'd swallowed the first, licking his fingers, and also the way he slurped and dropped crumbs and curry drips with almost each bite – put me off my food. Halfway through, as I watched his unwashed fingers grasping the bread, I remembered the grubby slow-worm and turned away.

'You were right,' he said, 'it is better than pasta, although if you mixed spaghetti with curry I think that might be the perfect meal.'

'I'll tell my mum,' I said seriously, hoping that would please him.

'I always have tea to settle my food,' he said eventually. 'Don't you?'

'Tea has always confused me.'

Maley looked up, his mouth furiously working, but didn't reply. To me, tea was something Mum boiled in a pan with an equal volume of water and milk and heaps of sugar, but sometimes kids at school said *Going home for my tea*, and I hadn't fully worked that out. I imagined fish fingers, Yorkshire puddings, gravy, roast chicken, Vestas and boiled potatoes fluffy on the surface. Sometimes as I walked home from school I could smell tea coming from the English houses: pies, steaming carrots and Cadbury's Smash. I'd seen it too, at the supermarket: trolleys loaded with shiny colourful packets of ready-made food and bottles of condiments, green peas, sausages, crispy pancakes, ravioli, corned beef, tomato ketchup.

I found a pan for Maley, and when I told him how Mum would apportion the milk and water he didn't believe me. 'A drop of milk, that's all it takes,' he said proudly, 'a drop.'

He put two china teacups filled with pale brown liquid on the table. To his own he added six sugars.

'We have biscuits,' I offered.

His eyebrows arched high into his forehead. 'What sort?'

'All sorts.'

'Let's have a look then.'

The tin on the shelf was empty, so I reluctantly went and got the two unopened packets that were kept in the pantry. 'Only custard creams and chocolate bourbons today.' I slipped them onto the table.

'I like both,' he said, his eyes now loose in their sockets.

I shrugged my shoulders and he took that as a sign that he could have whatever he wanted. I was okay when he opened the first packet and crunched through four chocolate bourbons, but I felt a clench in my stomach as he tore open the second. I was thinking that perhaps if I went to my dad's shop at home time and while no one was looking put two identical packets of biscuits in my bag, then I could sneak them home and replace the ones we had opened. It was stealing, but only sort of. In a way all I would be doing was moving things that belonged to us from one place to another. And another thing, we would have to tidy up and leave things exactly as we had found them. Exactly. Mum wouldn't notice the eaten curry, would she? The pot seemed big enough to last for days.

Maley ate four Custard Creams – to even up the numbers, he said, crumbs dropping from his lips – and his happy face reminded me of my mother's refrain, *Hunger is the very worst thing*.

For a moment he looked up at me, deep in thought. He licked his fingers, although there was no need to when eating biscuits. He hadn't even dipped them in his tea; 'Soaks up too much,' he had said. He looked down again, his eyes lining up the remainder of the biscuits, giving them a quizzical smile. 'I was right, you're rich.'

I slid the open packets across the table. 'Take them home for your dad.'

Maley stared at me, a scowl gradually forming on his face, and his fingertips rapped nervously on the tabletop. 'We don't want no charity.'

*

Grace whistles at the beginning of each exhalation and at the same time her eyelids seem to contract ever so slightly. I smile to myself. I am conscious of the time; in my trouser pocket is a watch, but my trousers are out of reach, draped over a chair, and next to them sit my boots, solid and incongruous on the peach-coloured carpet. I dare not move, in case I wake her, but more importantly, as I gaze at the half-moons of her flickering eyelids, I sense a serenity I have never before known. She murmurs something, her lips barely moving; it sounds like *sleep*, perhaps an instruction to me, or to herself? Looking at the bedside table, I consider the round face of the baby, pale and bald with eyes cutting a horizontal exactly halfway down her face. Grace sleeps soundly, as though she is cheating on the child in the picture.

Resting my palms on the mattress, I ease myself up to a sitting position, my back against the headboard. From here it is as though I am watching over Grace, observing protectively as the fine tendrils of her brown hair fall across her forehead and the whistle emanates from her broken mouth. Suddenly incredulous that Grace would shape silver foil for a tooth, I am reminded of what she said, *I am in need of it*, as though the gap is a talisman she carries.

Without opening her eyes, Grace slowly composes her mouth. 'It's just life. When your mate went on about nature, what he means is it's just life.'

After that statement she raises the curtains of her eyelids and considers me with a kind frown. She catches her lower lip between her teeth and bites gently, the colour draining as the pink flesh stretches. I recall the moment she had pulled me into her and said I could fuck her. I had twitched all over like a greyhound primed with the scent of the rabbit.

My thoughts conduct a forceful arousal and I feel hot and sweaty with a rising panic and want her to ask me again. I look for her nearest hand, which is tucked into the small of her back. If I could only reach for it. I offer vacant eyes, hoping she will draw closer, but she doesn't sense my desire. Then, disappointingly, I watch as slowly her hand moves out from behind her back, but not towards me, instead pinching lightly at her own cheek. She has small fingers, the nails painted a golden colour, painted some time ago and now grown so that the paint starts halfway up each nail.

I turn away, speaking once more to the window. It seems safer somehow not to address her directly, as though, distracted, I might catch sight of her eyes or breasts, or painted fingernails or feet riding out from beneath the sheet, and I might urgently want something she does not want to give.

7

It was a Friday a few weeks after the death of Maley's mum. He had not attended the cremation – another Tuesday pasta day – but he and his father had collected the ashes, and Maley offered to show them to me, an invitation I had declined. At lunchtime, I retreated as usual to a stony step at the side of the school, shielded partly from Adrian and other bullies like him. I peered lazily into the playground. The bottoms of my trousers flapped lightly in the breeze, and out of boredom I scuffed my shoes on the wet tarmac.

Maley appeared, laughing. He swiped the air with an imaginary sword as he looked across the playground, empty except for a few scurrying late to lunch. 'Now taste ye my wrath and my warning!'

I followed his gaze. At the far end of the playground a boy I didn't know was knocked to the ground. I shivered and recited a quick *Bismillah*.

'Talk about wrath, he'll kill him if he carries on like that.' Maley narrowed his eyes as though concentrating on some scenic detail.

I stood up to get a better view.

'Natural selection. Survival of the fittest,' Maley continued complacently. Then, turning his attention to a small green plastic coin, a free-meal token, between his fingers, he patted his stomach. 'Have to stock up for the weekend.' Without waiting for my response, he raced nimbly off towards the canteen.

The fallen boy was crawling about on his hands and knees, and circling him was Adrian Hartley. Each time his victim tried to push himself up,

Adrian would kick his feet out from under him. The lad, his clothes wet from a puddle on the tarmac, sank back to the ground. There was something terribly wrong with that lad. There was something terribly wrong because there was nothing obviously wrong. He was a *gora* and stocky, and yet Adrian struck him hard and carelessly like he would a Paki.

I went over, negotiated a gate and stood on the far side of a tall wire fence separating Adrian and me. The wire was cold and rusty. Adrian and the boy were about six feet away.

'Hey,' I called out, 'leave him alone!'

Adrian ignored me.

'I'll tell your dad about Bobby.'

Adrian stopped and looked at me. A wave of panic flashed across his face, replaced by a grin spreading in slow motion as though the small movements of his face were catching up with his thoughts. In Adrian's language I had volunteered for a beating: his eyes grew wide and wild and the grin worked itself into a snarl. I ran first. Adrian would have to go the long way past the exit gate that led onto the street; by that time, I had disappeared into a side street.

I circled back and cautiously approached the school gates. The boy, alone now, was leaning against them, fingering a new hole in the knee of his trousers. His knee bled.

'All right?' I asked.

'I owe you,' he said, pulling a pound note from his pocket.

'Put it away.'

'Have it. I've got fifteen left.' He smiled. 'Coming to the chip shop?'

'Okay.' I could already smell the pungent aroma of chips and bits with extra vinegar at Ivan's.

'I'm Dax Cogger,' he said, limping beside me. 'Just here for the winter.'

'How come?'

'Fairground,' he said. 'What you call a gypo. I didn't steal the money, by the way, I run a stall.'

I examined him closely but could still find nothing obviously wrong.

He had a kind face, square with ruddy cheeks, and short brown hair. He had gentle eyes you immediately trusted and a snub nose. He wore trendy Dunlop trainers and his school uniform was bang-on regulation. His lower lip seemed to hang loose and every now and then he'd gather it between his teeth as though holding it in position.

'Coconut shy. Darts. That kind of thing,' he explained.

We cut down a slippery bank to a babbling stream dotted with mossy green stepping stones where my feet got wet, and then walked through a short section of woods.

'Odds stacked in our favour though.'

'What did you do to Adrian?'

'Nothing.' Dax shook his head. 'I just told him I don't cry. I can't make tears. I can't even make an ouch sound.'

'You've just made one,' I said, laughing. Dax laughed too. 'They're stupid around here, especially that Adrian. His dad's a skinhead and when he grows up that's what he wants to become. Just don't tell him anything else that marks you out.'

Dax nodded. I led him along a path that avoided the main roads and emerged by a graveyard. Beyond the damp tombstones was a chapel, grey and solid in the gloomy afternoon, and from the gates of the chapel you could just about see Ivan's chippy a bit further along the high street.

After we'd been to Ivan's we spread our coats on the tombstones and ate our chips. Dax had bought me a drink, and when he was paying for it I had seen him pull out all fifteen notes. Eating chips on a cold day was one of the best things you could do. Although the clouds threatened, it didn't rain.

'I've seen most of the country,' Dax said.

'What's the best part? I mean, if you were going to live in a house, where would it be?'

'You mean like to stay?' He thought for a while. 'There's plenty of nice places. London's nice – we get to camp in a park right in the middle where the millionaires live and you see ripe cars rolling by – and Yorkshire's nice too, you can go for hours in just fields.'

'What's your favourite?'

'I met a girl in Ripon once. I'd like to go back there.' His thick lower lip trembled.

I had never even spoken to a girl at school. 'A girl?'

'Her dad owned the land we camped on. She'd bring us eggs in the mornings. Yeah, if I were a settler I'd go to Ripon, but I'm not. I'm going to marry a fairground girl.'

'Marry?'

'It's important,' he said. 'Keeps the fairground ours.'

'Would you cry if the girl in Ripon died?' I said.

He shook his head.

'How about if your mum died and you had to watch her being cremated?'

'There's nothing wrong with me,' he said, stamping a foot angrily against the ground. 'I just can't cry, and what use is crying anyway?'

We ate for a while without speaking, the silence broken only by the rustle of chip paper and the sound of our cans clinking on the stone. The wind gathered leaves, blowing them across the path and piling them up against the church door. As it grew in strength it carried a wetness with it, as though it had already started to rain.

'What's wrong with you then?' Dax asked eventually. 'I'm never in one place long enough to make any proper mates, just the kids no one else wants to be mates with.'

'You can't see what's in front of you?' I replied harshly.

He stared at me and shook his head. 'You seem all right. You risked a kicking for me.'

'I'm different.'

'I didn't notice. It's what you're made of what counts.'

'You didn't?' Scrunching up the chip wrapper, I sprang to my feet and set off along the path. Dax caught up with me and put a hand on my shoulder. I stopped. The rain was real now and we were getting wet. He looked at me kindly.

'Don't worry about it,' he said. 'It's a big world.'

We walked side by side through the school gates. Thankfully Adrian and his mates weren't waiting. Dax was in the year above me. He slipped off to his class and I went to mine.

At home time there was a crowd at the gates. I caught a glimpse of Dax as they swept him, like a wave, across the street, his head bowed and arms hugging his sides. Kids conspired in excited whispers, *a scrap*, and I followed the tail end of the group as it sped across the road and down a side street towards a square of green turf with grassy mounds on two sides and tall council blocks on the other two. I scrambled up onto a bank where I had a panoramic view.

Two entire classes of year seven and eight, boys and girls, circled Dax. I looked for Adrian but didn't see him. Perhaps he had detention. Dax put up his fists, like an old-fashioned boxer. Kids shouted at him, urging him to cry. I heard one of the boys say they'd let him go only if he shed a tear. Dax grunted, an almost inhuman sound, as though he was a bull breathing through enormous nostrils.

One boy punched Dax square on the nose. Clutching his face, Dax cried out and reeled backwards into a girl with hooped earrings. She screeched like a cat and scratched at Dax's face with her fingernails. A second boy put his arm across the girl, pushing her back. 'You've hurt my girlfriend,' he declared, kicking Dax in the shins with a sickening crack. Dax fell onto his knees and the crowd jeered, urging him to get up. He staggered unsteadily to his feet but remained bent over.

There was blood running from his nose and it covered his hands where he had wiped his face. His trousers were caked in mud, and grass stains like claw marks ran down his shirt. Bent double, he stared at the ground and shivered, stumbling like a blind man inside the circle. They punched and kicked him and pushed him from one assailant to the next. Dax panted like a wounded animal. He put up no further defence, and the quality of the beating seemed to change. Now they hit him in places they wouldn't have before: a kick between the legs, fingers gouging at his eyes, fists striking the top and back of his head, and when he fell, boots too. He flinched at each blow, doubled up, fell over, but he never cried, and each time he got back up onto wobbly legs. He should have stayed down. 'I'll be the one to make him cry,' one boy loudly boasted. Having had a go, like a boxer venting all his fury on a punchbag, he slunk back into the circle, disappointed. In consolation his girlfriend kissed him on the mouth.

I jumped up and down, trying to keep my eyes on Dax. I thought about running for help but didn't want to leave him. I scanned the blocks of flats as though that would suffice as an appeal. Curtains twitched, windows closed, briefly a door opened and shut.

Eventually, after what seemed like hours, a pickup truck pulled up. Alighting from it, construction workers barged into the middle of the scrum. They picked up Dax, limp and bloodied, and carefully, as though handling a baby, put him into the cabin of their truck. Fearlessly, the kids banged the side of the truck as the builders drove off at speed.

My head low, I walked away slowly, so as not to attract attention to myself. I heard the odd shout – *Paki* – and dug the toes of my shoes into the tarmac, wanting to damage something, anything. I slowed down further, abruptly changing my mind and now willing them to come for me, but I knew they wouldn't. For that day, they had had enough.

Already I would be late home, and I could foretell the beating I would get at my father's hand. At that moment I resolved that I would defy him, that like Dax I would rise up from the floor and challenge him to *hit me again*. While my mother as usual tried to mediate between her husband and son, I would tell my father the truth: that I had gone to watch a fight. That would incite his anger: *Fight,* gora. *I'll give you a fight.*

I tried to rehearse the narrative I would recount later to Mum, after the beating. But a simple explanation would not come, my thoughts instead crowded with images of Dax. They seemed to zoom in on his face: the frightened eyes, the trembling lip, the tilt of his mud-caked chin as he again rose from the ground.

I walked, but not by any defined route, as though whatever turns I made, ultimately and disappointingly, they would lead me home. The sky was a thick purple: broiling, darkening, shifting and flattening. It was a cold evening and I clasped my arms around myself, shivering.

The streets were nearly empty. Through front windows I saw *gora* huddled around their television sets, cooking smells wafting out to the street. Normally I'd stop and sniff the air to determine what was for tea – potatoes, beef, carrots – but that day I strode mindlessly on, without purpose.

The Mash Tun was quiet, its curtains drawn, its patio benches desolate. About a mile on, a fish-shaped neon sign flashed orange in the window of Ivan's chippy. As always, the door stood ajar and pop music mingled with the reassuring sound of spitting oil. Like an actor spotlit on a stage, Ivan offered me his cheerful salesman's smile while ladling chips onto a waiting spread of newspaper. I had no mood nor money for chips.

After maybe another hour I was tired and nervous and no longer convinced I would welcome my father's cane. I paused at the end of our street, resting my back against the tall factory wall, no longer afraid of it; robbed of its mystery, it was now just a wall. The brickwork was warm, as though borrowing heat from the furnace within, and the rhythmic beat of the hammer reverberated through my body. I closed my eyes, a gentle wind stirring across my face.

'Carry on like that and your bones will shatter.'

I opened my eyes and Mustafa offered me a nervous half-smile. He clutched the handlebars of a bike, its weight balanced against his waist. Perched precariously on the seat was his brother Faisal, a child of about six.

'That's what they tell little kids, but it's not true,' I said.

'You look like you're in trouble,' said Mustafa.

I nodded.

Unlike his older brother's, Faisal's skin was a pleasant brown. He had a small cherubic face and big round eyes that stared intently at me.

'Cold?' Mustafa added.

Again I nodded.

'Come with us.' He patted his back pocket. 'I've got matches.'

'Number eleven?'

Faisal giggled and repeated, 'Number eleven.'

Mustafa and I each took one side of the bicycle with Faisal propped between us. We went a few yards down the street and turned abruptly to our right as though passing through what had once been the front door of number eleven. We found ourselves surrounded by the heaped remains of our neighbour's house: roof slate, bricks, plaster, shattered windowpanes, and timber studded dangerously with rusty nails. Here and there a scrap of wallpaper or a decorative kitchen tile served as reminders that this had indeed once been a house.

We built a small pyramid of timber and settled down on brick stools around it. There was plenty of paper and kindling left over from previous fires, and Mustafa tucked it expertly into the hollow at the base of the triangle. From his pocket he pulled out a handful of bent kitchen matches. 'Our lad stole them when Mum wasn't watching.' He tapped his brother on the head and the kid beamed. 'She doesn't suspect you, does she, lad?'

Faisal put a small pudgy finger to his lips. 'Shhh.'

Mustafa struck a match against a brick; it flared and he cupped it protectively in both hands, lowering it slowly into the hollow. The light flickered in the gaps between his fingers and the paper caught fire. He knelt low, his head perilously close as he blew air gently onto the tiny flicker of orange. The flames grew and licked at the kindling. Mustafa settled back on his stool, pleased with his work.

I stared as closely as I dared into the fire, the smoke catching my eyes. One by one the faces of each of Dax's assailants were consumed by the flames, first melting at the edges and then collapsing inwards and vanishing entirely. I rubbed my eyes with a knuckle, grinding in the stinging soot.

Finally, I said, 'In hell, you burn up only to be given life to burn up all over again.'

Faisal pulled a frightened face and went to sit in his brother's lap. Mustafa seemed at ease as his brother's guardian, cradling the small body in his arms.

I continued. 'You beg Allah for a drink of water and he just laughs in your face.'

Faisal's head nuzzled his brother's chest and after a long pause I could hear the faint rhythmic rustle of his sleep.

'And it's worse than that,' I added. 'Mum says imagine the most terrible thing you can and times it by a thousand.'

'It's my fire.' Mustafa sounded irritated. 'You're not welcome talking like that.'

'He brings you a cup of molten steel spiked with the hair of a pig and says, *Drink this.*'

'God don't talk.' Mustafa looked up at the sky, orange changing to grey as his head tilted further up. He sighed. 'Should get our kid to bed.'

'If you die and you're not a Muslim, do you burn forever?'

'Nothing is forever,' said Mustafa matter-of-factly.

'I know one thing that is.'

Still holding his brother, Mustafa got to his feet. 'What?'

'Infinity.'

'What's that?'

'It's like counting upwards from one and never stopping.'

'Until you die.' Mustafa propped his charge onto the saddle, balancing the weight with his own.

'You don't get it. The worst thing is .. you just never die. You just count and count and count.'

Mustafa wheeled the bike away, quickly diminishing from view in the semi-darkness. I kicked at the fire, now about two feet high, watching gleefully as sparks flew. I pulled out a thin stick of wood still burning at one end and held it up to my face until I felt it burn the hairs over my forehead. I got to my feet, my chest beating tight and fast in anticipation of my father's reaction when I got home.

Our house was only a few doors down and nearing, I looked around for somewhere to dispose of the lit torch. A letterbox? A petrol cap on a car? A post box? Somewhere it would cause the most damage. My face contorted into a snarl, and then again, as though no matter how much I tried I couldn't straighten it out.

The next school day was Monday. I watched the year eights line up in the playground before class, laughing and joking, ribbing each other as they always did.

'You seen Dax?' I asked Maley as we joined the line for year seven.

'Animals kill, but not in malice or wrath,' he said angrily.

'You shouldn't talk like that.' I felt sick in the stomach.

'Told you we were a cruel species.'

And then from the year eight line-up we overheard: 'Mum was on the night shift. She says they brought some gypo kid in.'

'Oh yeah.' The words were accompanied by a nervous laugh.

'Says doctors tried everything, says he was born with a weak heart.'

I clenched my teeth as hard as I could and looked up at the sky. '*Bismillah. Bismillah*.'

8

Grace's hands again make a clawing motion in her sleep, disturbing the duvet, and as I silently will it to do so it falls slowly like a furling banner to a point below her breasts.

Her hands find my arm, gripping it tightly, and she awakens and looks at me. 'There was a prostitute and a dog,' she murmurs in a soft sleepy voice.

I smile.

'And someone who was kind to them called Allah.' Her voice is broken and confused, and self-consciously she pulls the duvet up over her breasts.

'You invited me up,' I say.

She says slowly, as though recollecting our meeting, 'Soldier boy?'

I nod. 'Hush now, go back to sleep.' I chant to myself almost inaudibly '*La ilaha il Allahu. . .*' It is soothing for me, takes me to a place far back. I am just beginning to gather a coherent set of early childhood images and already she is fast asleep again. I would have liked to tell Grace about that distant place, lying in bed watching my mother's lips inches from mine as she hummed my infant self to sleep, and for a moment I resent Grace for her slumber.

I swing my feet onto the thick carpet. I look for my stick but cannot see it. How I got into bed I cannot remember, and I search for things to hold on to on my way to my clothes.

But it seems too permanent a thing to dress, I am not ready to leave, and instead I find a towel and wrap it around my waist. Another towel I lay on the floor at the foot of the bed as a make-do prayer mat. Owing to the limits of the titanium articulation I cannot bend and prostrate, so I decide to pray seated on the edge of the bed with only my feet placed on the towel. From there I can bow my head to signify a deeper movement. Although it is not yet dawn and time for the first daily prayer, *fajr*, a Muslim can instead pray at any time, a simple prayer composed of two repeating sections. I say it once and then again, and each time I raise my head I catch, through the window, a patch of sky. After the second recital I cup my hands before my chest, and gazing through the window, seeking Allah, I wonder what it is I should say to Him. Behind me sleeps Grace, making barely a sound. I should pray for her. I bend towards the towel until the knee hurts. The towel is scented with soap and shampoo and lotions that Grace would have applied to her water-dripping body, and trapped between its fibres is also a scent unique to her, that of her body masked by the things she applies. These are impure thoughts I quickly block out, and as I stare at the blackish nothingness, grateful that somewhere up there is Allah, what comes to me is landscape – streets I have known. Like smoke I drift through them, taking in the details. At the end of a typical road two lanes run off, left and right. Down one is a series of prefab houses hurriedly put up after the war. They are clad with concrete blocks about a metre square, and between each block the joints have slipped and grown with age, rendering slits and gashes along the entire terrace as I view it from the street. Further on, the road curves out of view. The other lane is terraced with red-brick houses, and before each front door is a neat path and a patch of green. Outside one such house the path is gone, replaced by a gently sloping concrete ramp with a metal handrail on each side. The council installed it after the elderly occupant, Maley's father, lost the use of his legs. There was no need for it. He had called time on his days at The Gate Hangs Well and, with his pride dented by incapacity, the old man no longer left the house. The handrail is cold and wet with dew. The green paintwork on the door is flaking, and a plastic sign reads *Beware of the Dog*. The windows are grimy, the curtains drawn. Mr Male has been moved into a home.

I speak quietly so as not to wake Grace. 'I stood here once, with Maley.

He opened that green door, newly painted then, a foul unhygienic smell emanating from within, and then he said a strange thing, brightly, with a smile on his lips. He said, "I don't feel pain like normal people.'"

I thought about his dead mother. 'I know that, pal.'

We were sixteen years old and it was the last day of school. While our classmates were signing each other's shirts with thick marker pen, we had slipped away.

'You're lucky you got one of these new places,' I said to Maley, wrinkling my nose at the smell.

'It's not that new,' replied Maley. 'We moved here when I was born.'

Inside, the smell of boiled cabbage and cigarette smoke clung to the air. We passed quickly into the living room, wallpapered in an orange and brown geometric design, the sort of thing you would usually only find once you had removed several layers of existing wallpaper. Placed against the walls were two heavy-set armchairs and a matching sofa with roughly textured brown cushions and thick sweeping arms. Between the chairs was a steel coffee table, one his father had welded out of steel plates, Maley told me, and tidily at its centre sat a thick glass ashtray, a packet of cigarettes and a lighter. The room was square and cold; it had a low ceiling and on the mantel was a line of empty brown beer bottles. A glass-fronted cabinet was crammed with miniature drink bottles and on top of it stood two framed pictures. One picture showed a chubby thin-haired infant maybe a year old; on each side of him, leaning into the shot, were a mum and dad who looked more like grandparents, dressed as though from an earlier generation. In the other picture the same boy, now about four, sat atop a horse, a cowboy hat on his head.

'That's me,' Maley said proudly.

I followed him up a steep carpeted staircase into his bedroom. The window was open and the smell was different there, of damp and perspiration. Save for a single bed and a small table there was nothing to see. I stuck my head out of the window, observing how the grassy bank at the rear swept in a graceful railway-like curve before disappearing behind the houses.

Back in the room, now that Maley had flung open the doors, I saw that two walls had concealed floor-to-ceiling cupboards. Inside them were shelves stacked to the top with boxes of toys and puzzle sets. In places the cardboard had coloured like rust but otherwise the boxes appeared pristine, as though unopened. One large box caught my eye. It bore a picture of a steam locomotive painted green. Other pictures in shadow showed what else was in the box: trees, a signal box, people, and a village railway station.

Maley, seeing my interest, offered to assemble it for me, but then seemed to abruptly change his mind and said there wasn't time. He said I could have it, and I declined. As a Pakistani I knew it was polite to decline twice but on the third offer I could accept. I waited but he didn't ask me again.

I didn't often get toys when I was a child, and to compensate I had learnt the toy section of the Littlewoods catalogue by heart. On Christmas Day, I would jealously observe from our window the *gora* kids wobbling on their new bikes and racing battery-operated vehicles, and I knew precisely the maximum adjustable seat height of a Raleigh Chopper and what batteries a Milton Bradley Big Trak required. Even then, aged sixteen, I would have liked a toy train set.

Maley slammed the cupboard doors shut. He pulled a green rucksack out from under the bed and beamed. 'Got it on sale from the army and navy shop.'

We went back down the stairs into the kitchen, where the mustiness, mixed with the smell of frying lard, was most intense. It was the coldest room in the house and the cabinets were made of plastic-coated metal. Against one wall stood an upright cooker, the sort I remembered my mother throwing out a long time ago. A latticed window was cut into the back door, and a thin black dog sat with its nose squashed up against it.

Maley saw me looking at the greyhound. 'Races it sometimes, my dad. She's called Betty.'

'Does she win?'

'Hate dogs, no substitute for nature.'

I couldn't imagine Maley hating anything, least of all something belonging to the animal kingdom.

Shaking his head, he peered into the fridge and pulled out a thick yellow slab wrapped in cellophane. I laughed. 'Bloody hell, look at the size of that!'

'Cheese, equal parts protein and fat, keeps me going.' He stuffed it into his pack. I watched as he tied a bow in the drawstring on the backpack. His fingers seemed to work opposite to how it was normally done, his left hand twisted into the string while his right trembled as it swept around to make the knot.

'One more thing before I go,' he said, carefully tearing open an empty cornflakes box. Crouching over the kitchen table, he took out a marker pen from his pocket. As he wrote on the cardboard, I looked down at my shirt and made out the name *Craig Male*. Only then did it really sink in that it was the last day of school. Earlier, in the classroom, Maley had signed my shirt, and somehow that now seemed a long time ago. I looked back up at Maley. Proudly he held up a square of cardboard on which he had written the word PLEASE. Through the window, Betty marked circles around a child's swing, her claws tearing up the lawn.

'You really don't know where you're going?' I enquired as Maley locked the front door behind us. Scanning the terrace, I saw that each house had a willow tree planted in the centre of a small front lawn, blocking the view into the bay windows. I always felt a compulsion to look into *gora* houses. I wanted to know what they had.

Maley with an idea always walked fast, and I struggled to keep up with him.

'There are lots of places I'd like to see,' he said.

'Like where?'

'The Australian outback. You can die of loneliness out there.'

'The outback? Can't think of anywhere further?'

'I've got this idea. I'm on this uninhabited island somewhere in the Pacific and one day this surfboard washes up.' The breeze teased at Maley's hair and rippled into the surface of his large parka, a fashion he still wore, whatever the weather. He didn't smile, but then he didn't appear his usual tense self either. His arms swung at his sides, the vinyl under his armpits squeaking.

'What about your dad?'

He ignored me. 'Depends on which stats you read, but Australians live longer than us.'

'Maybe they have different genes?' I said.

'Your environment can compensate for your genes.'

'Does he know you're going?' I persisted.

'He's an alc. Has been since Mum—'

'He's still your dad.'

'When he was last sober he wished me luck.'

'And your mum?'

'She's dead, remember.'

'Don't you say goodbye,' I was confusing myself now, 'to the ashes or something?'

'Are you stupid?'

'So that's it? Nice knowing you, Dad, see you, I'm off?'

Maley stopped walking and turned angrily towards me. 'You keep thinking there's got to be more.' A familiar pink blotch crept up his neck from the collar of his school shirt. 'I tell you about nature and you seem to say it's not good enough, like there's something higher – God – but there isn't any proof of that. I tell you about my dad and you want me to speak to a jarful of soot in the kitchen cupboard. Life is what it is. Can't you just see me off?'

'Sorry.'

'It's like you're holding me back.'

'You're holding yourself back.' I wanted to hurt him for leaving me.

'How?'

'Well, why do you need me to see you off?'

'I thought it might do you good.'

'Oh, that's all for me, is it? It isn't because you have no one else?'

'I wanted to do it properly. To say goodbye. You've been kind and fed me and that. But I also wanted you to see that it's perfectly possible to just leave.'

'Why would I want to leave?'

Maley slowly spun on his toes, taking in the full circumference of the view. On one side was a row of Victorian terraces, neat and homely from a distance but close up the paintwork was peeling and the brickwork chipped. There were piles of litter too, as though someone had taken a giant broom and swept up against the faces of the houses. On the other side of the narrow street was a high black oily wall that marked the rear of Blackheath Forgings. It was tall enough to block out the sunlight to a degree, and beyond it, save for the occasional crack of metal against metal, there was silence.

'You're not blind. When. . . well, you know. . . when people are at their worst, I think of my island, and the more they go on the clearer it seems to become. But you, I pity you, because I know you don't have an island.'

My heart sank at the thought of being left behind. 'I don't need some imaginary island.'

Maley stooped to pick up a small stone and held it close to his eyes, examining it. 'I tell you what I think. I think you're going to carry on taking it for the rest of your life.'

'I w-won't,' I stammered, looking away.

'You'll be living in one of these draughty terraced houses waiting for the next brick through the window, and every morning you'll be scrubbing off graffiti, and just because you've got a shop and maybe a car you'll think it's all okay, but it won't be. It never will be okay. You'll have lost your imagination and become one of them.'

'You quite finished?'

'No.' He squared up to me. 'What you going to do about it?' With two needle-like fingers he pushed me hard in the chest. The pink flush had spread rapidly up his face.

'Steady on, mate.' I pulled away from him, and to make light of it I forced myself to laugh.

Maley came closer, his face craning upwards on his thin neck. With my back to the road I could feel my heels balancing on the edge of the kerb. Again he pushed me in the chest. 'Paki. Wog. Blackie.' His spit splattered my chin.

'Blackie?' I retreated, putting one foot into the road and wiping my face with a sleeve. 'No one says blackie anymore!'

I saw a curtain twitch in one of the windows and suddenly the ridiculousness of the situation became clear. 'Someone's watching, cut it out.'

'I'm sorry. You just don't react, do you?' Maley took my arm, yanking me back onto the pavement.

'I've heard it before,' I said, as we continued on up the street.

'We were northerners, but my grandfather's grandfather came here because of the steel.' He shook his head. 'It's time to move on, that's all.'

'I get it, you're just trying to justify your new life as the only inhabitant of an Australian island.'

'The only *human* inhabitant,' he corrected and smiled, exposing a jagged row of large teeth crammed into a tiny pinched jaw. I had never seen him so happy. I pictured the bittersweet scene of a ghastly white Maley running along some beach in his tatty Y-fronts.

We crossed a dual carriageway and scrambled up a steep bank on the other side. Again Maley stopped, bending down to look at a plant. 'Have you noticed how those wasps, the yellow ones with the black stripes, you don't see them anymore?'

'When we were little we used to trap them in a milk bottle, wet them and make them fight each other,' I said.

'Know what this is?' He caressed a small yellow flower with the back of his hand.

'Never paid it much attention,' I said.

'It's a ragwort. Oxford ragwort. It's not indigenous. It was brought over by Indian railway workers.' He scanned the horizon. 'Railway used to join up here.'

'Won't you miss that? The knowledge? The stupid kingfisher and your dad going deaf from the boilers. It's special.'

'I'll put it to good use,' he replied cheerfully, springing to his feet and sliding down the other side of the bank. 'This is it,' he said.

Following him, I looked around. It was a familiar busy intersection with traffic lights posted on each of the four sides. The 247 hurtled past and stopped further ahead.

'Here?' I gazed at the bus, wondering if he was about to run for it.

Maley held the sign reading please across his chest. We stood for an hour, scanning each vehicle hopefully as though it would be the one, and we hardly said a word. Some drivers tooted their horns, some slowed to jeer at us, their voices lost to the rush of wind past the moving car.

'I got an idea,' I said eventually, 'but if I tell you, you mustn't object.'

'What is it?'

'I'm going to go over there.' I pointed to the top of the grassy bank. 'It's because of me. That's why the cars don't stop.'

Maley shook his head, but without waiting for him to answer I scrambled up the slope. It was calm sitting up there, and quiet, as though it was a long way from the road. I plucked an Oxford ragwort; it had a dark orange feathery button and I counted twelve thin petals coming off it like spokes in a wheel.

A few minutes later, a truck stopped next to Maley. I felt a sudden wave of panic. After signalling to the driver, Maley raced up the hill. Standing over me, panting, he said, 'Just so you know, kingfishers aren't stupid.' Then, without looking back, he raced to his waiting lift and climbed into the cabin. For a minute the truck remained eerily still. I felt a strange foreboding, but not for him. Maley would be okay. The fear was for me.

*

I search for words to explain why I am here. It is warm and there is Grace asleep. I feel passive and content and beyond that I cannot provide an answer. I should leave, but the view through the window, the luminous presence of Allah in the near dark, it keeps me glued.

The evening of the day Maley left, like most evenings, I went to Best Street mosque, but that day I went of my own volition, without my father having to nag. Best Street mosque is on the junction of Best Street and Garratt's Lane. A small green sign above the door announces the purpose of the building, and across the windows are steel bars. It is shabby and unkempt and it was once an ordinary house occupied by the foreman of Rowley Works. Ordinary, but with the bonus of being located on a corner and hence having a side yard and two street-facing walls. When the foreman died it was sold at auction, and the local Pakistanis, all of whom sent their children to school in tatty clothes and lived in dingy, cold houses, clubbed together thousands of pounds and bought it.

When we got the key, we entered en masse, about twenty men and boys, and without a word began to strip the walls and floors, piling everything unholy outside. We laid bricks, later rendered, to make stools and installed before them a long strip of cold water taps, and there the men and boys shivered as they conducted ablutions before prayer. Later, dividing walls were knocked through to make a prayer room, one that could hold – we counted – fifty-three seated worshippers. We fixed to the walls pictures of Mecca and Medina and one other of the oldest mosque in Jerusalem, cheaply framed and with Christmas tinsel around the edges. A carpet was purchased at great cost. On a Sunday morning exactly five years after it was installed, we took out the carpet, spread it across Best Street, closing off the public highway, beat the thick wool with sticks and soaped and rinsed it using buckets of water. Finally, when the imam was satisfied, we hung it to dry on the side wall on Garratt's Lane. Under its sodden weight the wall collapsed and blocked traffic to the lane. Quickly arriving were the newspapermen and council inspectors. While they reported and called their superiors, they over saw like colonial masters supervising the natives as we relaid the bricks – the first wall any of us – factory workers, bus drivers and children – had built.

Every day after school throughout my childhood and teenage years I went to Best Street. There we boys and girls sat in a line with our backs to the wall, a Koran spread open before each of us on a wooden, easel-like stand, rocking back and forth to the ebb and flow of the metre we could not hope to understand. Of the Arabic words we recited I knew only one, Allah. At first the routine seemed relentless and without joy, and I found it difficult to find the word Allah, appearing as it often did as a prefix or suffix in a long string of curling calligraphy, but even then I knew it was about faith, about carrying on. Like a parade sergeant the imam patrolled the line, lashing his stick painfully at anyone who displeased him, often apparently at random. Later I grew to understand that the word Allah was synonymous with justice; but at the time of the imam's thrashing stick, the Bible passages read out at school assembly, in direct contrast, were all about love. God was love. Jesus loved us and we loved him and he had come as a baby to save us all. We Muslims, we have missed a trick, I used to think, and it is a simple fix – just add love. After Koran lessons I'd go home for supper and then return to the mosque with my father for the last prayer of the day. *It is important to sleep on a prayer* was my dad's refrain, and the same day Maley left I sat on the mosque carpet, gone eleven at night, staring at the age-defying tinsel garlanding the picture of the Great Mosque in Mecca.

Loudspeakers transmitted the soft voice of the imam, muffled and sleepy, as he closed the night prayer. It was black and wet outside, and mid-prayer a brief storm passed overhead. We were seated facing the imam who was at the front, and on the wall behind him were six wooden clocks, like those used by children to learn time. Five were set, by the imam's finger, to the hours of the five daily prayers, and the sixth established the time of Friday prayer, usually around lunchtime. I closed my eyes, feeling a clock beat inside my head, in rhythm with the imam's final chant, and tried to imagine how Maley must be feeling. He was alone and surely he was scared. How far had he got? Where was he sleeping? I said a *Bismillah*, and as I prostrated myself for the last time, my forehead to the ground, the imam ahead of me and worshippers either side of me, silently I prayed in English. I prayed for Maley.

I straightened to a sitting position and turned to the brother on my right and whispered, 'Peace be upon you and the mercy of Allah,' and then recited the same words to the brother on my left, and the prayer was over. Easing the stiffness from my legs, I sat cross-legged on the soft prayer-room carpet, leaning back with a palm stretched flat behind me.

I looked around. A few of the brothers leant into each other, conversing in hushed tones. As though showing off his wealth, one thumbed a mobile phone, and several got out their prayer beads. A yawning child received a light slap across the head from his father. Readying for a reading, the imam sat down on the only chair in the room, a copy of the Holy Koran in his lap. Like a blind man he felt underneath the chair for his spectacles and, finding them, put them on. He leant back and then did a double take. Peering over our heads, he stammered loudly, 'H-hello!' The word hello was for the *gora* and the world outside and was never used inside Best Street mosque.

We all turned at once. In the corner by the door, a figure was curled asleep, and in the brief, tense silence that suddenly prevailed, I could hear him snore. I stared in disbelief. The boy had fine blond hair and a pink nose, and a layer of steam gathered on the surface of his wet T-shirt. I recognized him as Adrian Hartley and felt a strange shiver in my chest, as though that knowledge made me an accomplice.

We rose carefully to our feet and gathered to form a semicircle about three feet from him. He was lying on his side, his head buried in a bent arm. He had his back to the wall and his T-shirt was rucked up, his jeans sagging, exposing his underpants. My father stood directly in front of Adrian and I pressed up behind my dad.

'The door was left unlocked?' my father asked.

'Fire regulations,' offered the imam with a shrug of his shoulders.

My father leant a little way over the figure and sniffed, then waved one hand in front of his own face in disgust. 'He's been drinking.'

Voices spoke at once, some puzzled and others panicked:

'If he was my son I would kill him.'

'Allah, Allah.'

'Drunk? Here?'

'Call the police.'

'Come on, brothers, there's a dozen of us, let's have him.' That was Mustafa.

The imam cleared his throat loudly, silencing the assembly. 'Does anyone know who this *gora* is?'

'What does that matter?' my father said.

'Akram knows him,' cried Mustafa.

I glanced angrily at Mustafa. He had grown fat and studious and wore thick glasses. He was rarely seen outdoors, and rumour was that he would go to university. I blurted out without thinking, 'You should keep your mouth shut, white boy!'

My father rapped me, not lightly, across the back of my head.

Taking off my skullcap and pressing it to my nose, I stepped forward and crouched over Adrian. Close up he stank of beer, sweat and the cold rain. Each time he exhaled, red-stained mucus spluttered out of his nostrils, and I felt the iron in his blood coat my tongue.

I stood up, relieved to be away from the smell, and offered the crowd a wry smile. 'Mustafa's right, it's Adrian Hartley who was expelled from school.'

Everybody looked at me and then at Adrian asleep on the carpet.

'There's a bruise on his chin and blood coming from his nose,' I continued.

'Shall we call an ambulance?' someone asked.

'Allah, Allah,' cried the imam, shaking his head.

'It's who?' My father shot me a stern glance.

Adrian coughed and we fell silent, watching as he began to stir. He opened his eyes then slowly eased himself into a sitting position against the wall, drawing his knees to his chest. His eyes swept the room; if there was any fear in him it didn't show. When he saw me he raised his eyebrows, gave a nonchalant half-smile and then winced in pain. He wedged a fist up against his chin, his knuckles raw.

'It's cold outside.' His speech was slurred.

'You can't just come in here!' cried Mustafa.

'Have a heart!' Adrian said with sad eyes. A streaked mixture of blood and saliva dripped from his nose, adding to that already on his T-shirt.

'You been drinking, boy?' asked my father.

'Shouldn't leave your door open,' mumbled Adrian.

'He's probably got nowhere to go,' I offered, hoping Adrian would add to my plea. He studied us with a wry expression but said nothing.

'But. . . here?' said my father.

'He lives on the Old Hill estate,' I said.

'I don't care if he lives in Buckingham Palace, he ought to know better.'

'His dad's an alc, probably hit him,' I added.

'Looks like he needs teaching a stronger lesson,' said my father.

'I'm just saying, it's freezing out.'

'Boy,' my father pushed me to one side and addressed Adrian, 'I'm going to teach—' He stopped, his eyes narrowing. 'Hartley? Son of Chav Hartley?'

'Charlie,' snapped Adrian. 'He doesn't go by Chav no more and he isn't no fire starter, right, and yeah, he'd knock your block off.' He gazed at each of us in turn. He wore a bemused expression, one of helplessness but also resignation.

'He didn't know it was a mosque,' I said.

Gripping the wall behind him, Adrian slowly got to his feet and stammered, 'I'll f-fight anyone.' He left clawed bloodstains on the wall. My father stepped forward.

'No, Dad, he's just not worth it,' I said.

An older Bangladeshi who on Mondays drove the 247 put a hand on my father's shoulder. He shook his head gravely. 'It's his word against ours. If you beat him up you will go to prison.'

'Then my son will do it,' said my father without hesitation.

'Me?' I looked up at my old man.

His teeth were tightly clenched, exposing a thin jawline. He shook off the Bangladeshi's grip. His hand trembled as he pointed at Adrian, and in a staccato exaggerated-Pakistani accent he said, 'That family, Paki-bashers.' The old phrase, one I had not heard for years, and the way it came out of his mouth, made me laugh. I thought others might laugh too, but no one did. His face red, he turned to me. 'You!'

I bit my cheeks to stop the laughter. 'Why me?'

'Why you? You want me to explain? You want me to tell everyone?'

I gritted my teeth and concentrated on not crying or laughing.

'Father of Akram, that's enough,' interjected the Bangladeshi on my behalf.

'This Hartley has been a thorn in your side for how long?' my father said, announcing it to the assembly. I looked at the carpet, tracing its green, roadmap-like grid against a red background.

My father continued. 'After school your mother and I wiped away your blood how many times? Did you not get pneumonia when he pushed you into the canal? Have the police not been called? This Chav Hartley, did I not witness him break Mustafa's windowpane?'

'Yeah, and if he saw you he'd smash you,' Adrian interjected.

'Then Mustafa should fight him,' I suggested, observing that Mustafa had retreated behind my father.

'*You*,' my father pointed squarely at me, 'you sort him out.' He paused to reassuringly squeeze Mustafa's shoulder before returning his attention to me. 'You're not old enough for prison. Take him outside.'

I wondered what Maley would do in my place, but I couldn't supply the answer. Somehow I found myself pushed up next to Adrian against the wall. Unsteady on his feet, Adrian leant against me. From that view the encircling worshippers, primed like an unconvinced lynch mob, made me want to laugh. My father, as head of the posse, looked me up and down slowly.

'I'm gonna be sick,' said Adrian, breaking the impasse and falling unsteadily towards the sacred carpet.

9

Grace stirs and I fall silent, wondering how much of the story she has actually heard. Still seated at the end of the bed, I turn to see her slowly prop herself up against a pillow and reach for the bottle on the bedside table. She drinks from the bottle, takes a pack of cigarettes from her bedside drawer and lights one up. She coughs, then peers over the foot of the bed, observes her towel spread on the floor, smiles and says nothing. Her face seems softer after the sleep and her lower jaw wobbles as though freed of its musculature. Her eyes are glazed and warm and she raises the bottle in salutation as though instructing me to continue.

*

The following morning I went to work for my father. My first task was to make a delivery. When I returned to the shop, my father was sitting behind the counter. He glanced up from his Urdu newspaper and eyed me suspiciously. He was singing along to a *naath*, repeating softly the word *Allahu*. It was playing from a pirate radio on a small transistor hung on a nail behind him.

'I'm going to make up one-kilo bags of rice,' I said, staring nervously at a series of open sacks propped up against the counter.

'What for, coward?'

'And packets of lentils: brown, yellow and black.'

He shook his head. 'Here it is my system!' He continued in a softer but condescending tone. 'When the customer comes in they ask for a pound of this and a pound of that and I make it up in front of them and that way they know I am not cheating them.' He laughed. 'No one here asks for kilos.'

'Then I'll make up pounds,' I offered.

'Sometimes they ask for a pound's worth in money, not weight. What will you do then? You will measure it out for them, won't you? Why don't you do what you cowards are good for and sweep up instead?'

I picked up the broom from behind the counter. The radio crackled, and changed to a long slow lament. I could make out the Arabic word *jannat* (heaven).

My father peered mistrustfully over his glasses. 'You were gone a long time.' I nodded. 'You left the delivery by the door?'

I shook my head. 'Can we tune to the football broadcast?'

'That would be sin,' he said, leaning his ear towards the radio as though guarding it. 'Now that it is playing it is *sawab* to leave it on.'

I rubbed the hard bristles of the broom against a sticky mess of sugar under the counter. 'Mice will get to that.'

My father laughed. 'Scared of racists and scared of mice!'

On the back wall behind the counter and on two other walls were floor-to-ceiling shelves, painted white. Decades earlier, my father had put them up. They were not hung straight and the gaps between each shelf varied slightly, giving them a ragged appearance. Boxes and sacks occupied most of the floor space, some piled high, allowing only a narrow path to the counter. The shop was on a corner and had two windows to the street. Except on Saturdays, when the football crowd marched past to and from the ground, it was quiet outside.

'Where were you?' he asked.

'You sent me to the new mosque, so I went in to take a peek. Why shouldn't I?'

'I sent you on a delivery.'

I reported the events to my father. I had cycled to a large, warehouse-like building. It was unmarked except for a narrow green door on which had been posted a white paper sign bearing handwritten Arabic script. The door was locked and from within came shouting and muffled noises. A guy let me in. Inside were hundreds of men, squeezed together on a makeshift prayer-room floor, and they all looked like wrestlers, only wrestlers with beards and from many countries of the world, including England. I wanted to provoke my father, and so I added, 'I didn't know there were so many *gora* Muslims in this crappy town!'

'Islam is the fastest-growing religion.'

I laughed. 'One day we will all be Muslims.'

My father slapped his palm hard on the counter top and demanded to know what had happened.

'I think I missed it. There must have been some big event but by the time I was shown in they were just chanting, that's all, and then I could swear this guy flew in the air.'

A sea of football supporters drifted past outside the shop window, clad in black and yellow: yellow for the martlet, a mythical bird born without legs to land upon and thus eternally in flight. The supporters wore expectant, hopeful faces.

I returned my gaze to my father. 'Oh, and also I nearly got into a fight.'

My father looked both confused and angry. His face reddened and a bead of sweat dropped off his brow. He wiped it with a small hand towel he kept on a hook behind the counter. He took a long deep breath, shook his head dismissively and ironed out a corner of his newspaper with a fist. I continued with my report in a matter-of-fact tone that I knew would annoy him, my father feigning lack of interest and occasionally pointing to an area my broom had missed.

Stepping nervously in the few gaps between the densely packed worshippers, I had dispensed grapes, walnuts and dates from the box he had sent me to leave by the door. A lad with a long beard and rippling muscles took offence as I strayed in front of his space, and punched my leg. I nearly dropped the box, and smarting from the pain I stood my ground and glared.

The brute force of the blow, and my shock at what he had done, in a mosque of all places, left me bewildered. I noticed a dark circular patch like a third eye in the middle of his forehead. The third eye was acquired by friction between skin and prayer mat. It was a sign of great *sawab*, and was known to take a lifetime of prostration to obtain, and even then, so it was said, only if Allah chose you. I wanted to say to him that it was a fake, his third eye – faking it was not an unknown phenomenon. Instead, and perhaps because I was indeed a coward, I rudely dropped a sprig of grapes into the guy's lap and quickly passed on to the next man.

'You would have liked it,' I told Dad, 'and you could have got *sawab* if you had gone yourself. Don't you always say it is *sawab* to feed the faithful?'

My father said nothing.

'What do you want to hear?' I asked. 'That they preached death to America and death to Britain and death. . . ?'

'Did they?' He seemed genuinely excited.

'Probably.'

'You shouldn't talk about what you don't know, it's dangerous.'

'Truthfully, they were chanting *Allahu* and working themselves up into some sort of hysteria. . .' They were clapping as well, everybody, with necks strained and shoulders rolled forward and broad grins exposing various stages of dental decay. Together, as though in a Mexican wave, they swayed from side to side, and the *gora* spotted within their ranks appeared nervous and comically incongruous. I could tell they didn't understand the words, and their blond or ginger beards clashed with the long white robes and elaborately bound, mullah-like scarves around their heads.

'Hysteria is what your football yobs get up to.' My father gazed thoughtfully out of the window at a passing football fan giving our shop the two fingers and mouthing the word *Paki*. 'Don't be so disrespectful,' he added as an afterthought.

'They must have been well fed.' By the time I got to the front the box was still half full; seeing no easy way back and fearing another confrontation, I placed my box on the floor and, squeezing between two men, lowered myself to the carpet. Facing the assembly and only a few feet from me was the imam, sitting atop a set of triangle steps like a stepladder that had been filled in with wooden tables at the sides. Slim and wearing small round glasses, he was dressed like an English gentleman in a three-piece suit, and a silver pocket watch dangled off his waistcoat. He had thin menacing lips and a loose wiry beard. '*Allahu,*' he led the chant; his voice was slow and controlled and it seemed to linger, almost stop, at the climax of each phrase. '*Allahu.*' He smiled as he chanted. His eyes seemed to glisten and retreat into their sockets and his body swayed, reaching a perfect forty-five-degree angle on each side.

The floor was richly carpeted, but the walls were unadorned painted brick and the lack of windows gave the interior a cold industrial feel. The building must have been newly purchased: people were building mosques all the time, and I knew that soon enough it would acquire the usual pictures of Mecca as well as wall hangings inscribed with words from the Holy Koran. At Christmas-time there would be tinsel too and small colourful lights flashing on and off.

My father raised his newspaper, hiding his face.

'Don't you want to know how the man flew?' I asked.

The telephone rang. There had been many expensive pre-booked three-minute calls to and from my cousins in Pakistan of late, and my father climbed off his stool and shuffled into the back. I watched him go, and the shop suddenly darkened as a cloud moved across the sun. The radio broke into the *azan*, calling the faithful to prayer. My thoughts returned to the mosque.

They continued to clap, the sway of their bodies gathering a determined momentum. Wedged against my left shoulder was a man with long greasy hair. He had no beard, as though he was above ritual, and his bony, craggy face was exposed in sharp relief, suggesting someone who seldom ate. He had full swollen lips and hollow orbits ringed by a thick protuberance of bone as though his eyes should have been much bigger. He sat cross-legged, and around his shoulders was a robe of rich red and gold brocade that draped to the floor. One bent leg that had escaped from under his robe twitched. It didn't jerk up and down; instead the muscles of his leg seemed to contract independently of any visible movement of the limb itself. It was strange and unnatural, as though the muscles were responding to pulses of electricity.

The imam, visibly exhausted, leant back against the step but continued to clap, and the chanting grew louder and its pace faster. There had been an unannounced change in its metre and while the word *Allah* was said in a barely controlled whisper, the syllable that followed, the *hu*, was spat into the room with all the breath the assembly seemed to possess.

Then the greasy-haired guy next to me uttered a long, high-pitched shriek that pierced my eardrums. I turned towards him and watched transfixed as he swayed violently from side to side. His arms were raised high above his head and while he swayed, slowly he seemed to rise. He repeated his shriek several times, the sound of someone in great pain, and then it was replaced by *Allahu* chanted so fast it sounded like another language. Behind us the room had grown silent. The man continued to rise and sway in what looked like a physically impossible movement; although the robe obscured his feet, it was as though he was freed of the laws of physics, as though he was levitating. I saw a flash of movement as the imam leapt off his steps and threw himself onto the levitating man, forcing him to the floor.

The man who had levitated, suddenly I recognized him. He was older now, with teeth that had separated and grown longer and a layer of blood at the crescent line of his gums, but it was his eyes that gave him away, large and wild and rolling in their sockets. It was Bobby. Bobby of the pound note and the bush in Lye Park. Bobby had not aged beyond recognition. I shuddered.

'It's all show,' said my father, returning from the back room. 'These modern imams, they're all fakes.'

'It's true,' I said in a deliberate challenge to his authority.

'The coward has no views worth listening to.'

'Then I quit.'

His coarse laughter issued a challenge. 'Where will you go?'

*

It felt like the right thing to do, leaving the shop. Had I stayed I would have stayed forever. Back home I switched on the TV, leant back on the sofa and kicked off my shoes. My feet hurt from standing and my leg hurt from the punch at the mosque. On the screen, they were racing hamsters through perspex tunnels. It was a straight track about ten feet long and the owners of each of the three hamsters stood at the finish line, screaming encouragement and coaxing the animal with a morsel on a cocktail stick.

'No, I'm not kidding,' said Mum, striding in from the kitchen with a tray in her hands. She was continuing an earlier conversation between us, one that had been going on for weeks and that I had hoped had expired. 'She's a modern girl, she's called Azra and she's from Islamabad.' Mum then repeated what I already knew. 'In Islamabad they even have a Pizza Hut.' She seemed proud of that.

'I prefer curry.'

'Azra is from a good family, clean and she fears Allah.' Mum put my tray gently on the coffee table and took a seat opposite me. She plucked a plastic flower from a vase and examined it closely. 'Lovely, isn't it.' Her eyes glistened. 'How was your first day at the shop? You mustn't argue with your father.'

In the weeks since Mum had started speaking of marriage to Azra, I had gradually formed a picture of my bride. She was a young girl dressed in a pink *kurta-pajama*. In my mind she had huge almond-shaped eyes cast demurely downwards and her smile was sweet and childlike, exposing perfect square-cut ivory teeth that sparkled as though they had never known use. She shared a dusty street with animals and trucks belching black smoke, and it was remarkable how she kept her white headscarf so clean.

'Your father says he can rent you a small unit at the indoor market and you and your new bride can live with us.'

I sighed and took a sip of tea. Taking the fake rose off her, I said, 'Perhaps I could sell pretend flowers?'

'Have a biscuit, it might sweeten your tongue.'

Instead she offered me a glass of water from the tray. I took a sip and felt something strange in my mouth. Rather than spit it out, I swallowed quickly. I peered into the glass, and saw bits of paper floating in the water. 'What's all this stuff?'

Mum smiled nervously. 'You have swallowed a spell.'

I floundered for words. 'A curse?'

'Don't talk about things you don't understand.' Her voice rose in anger. 'It has power and you will marry her in the end.' Satisfied with what she had achieved, she continued in a conciliatory tone. 'You may think you have nothing in common but, my son, once you lay eyes on her you will find something you like.'

'I'd be at the market stall all day. What would she do?'

'We'll get along just fine, Azra and I, in this little house.' She thought for a moment. 'Although we might have to install central heating. They do fear the cold, do new Pakistanis.'

'Wouldn't it be a bit cramped?' I picked at the paper on my tongue with a fingernail, then wiped it on my thigh.

We were seated on two identical sofas placed opposite each other. The armrests were covered with a protective layer of transparent plastic and that, coupled with the fact that they were weighty and almost immovable, still gave them a brand-new and almost official appearance. Between us was a coffee table, in the centre of which was a tall bronze vase out of which sprouted the lurid flowers. To one side was a tiled brown mantelpiece on which stood a green plastic carriage clock that could be set to play the *azan* five times a day. Above that was a picture of Mecca garlanded with tinsel as old and durable as the floral arrangement.

My mother sighed. 'It's our way, but if your generation. . . if you prefer independence, there are always houses coming up in this street. . .' She paused and looked wistfully out of the window to the backyard. 'Or we could build an extension? Azra's very religious, prays five times a day no less. Maybe she can show us all how to live a better life? How to grow closer to our faith?'

I could see her leaving our house clad from head to toe in black, with thin black gloves and a slit to look through, and I saw myself standing on the doorstep behind her.

'No need to pull a face, she doesn't smell.'

Since my mother had first introduced the idea, I had developed a fantasy about the girl Azra. It was a sexual fantasy, and because all I was required to do was to reply in the affirmative to my mother, at times it had felt tangible. However, the sudden insertion of the long black burqa, that precise image, was like a poster from a horror film. I had seen such women in the high street, and despite the Grim Reaper-like invisibility of their cloaks I could tell that, inside them, their bodies were bird-like and tender. Holding each woman's black-gloved hand was some muscle-strapped, bearded teen smiling broadly as though all he did was fuck her all night. Azra. The fantasy had suddenly grown into a name I could hook to my private lust.

'I'll find my own wife.'

The hamster in the left tunnel had won three times in a row. Its owner, a fat bubbly teenage girl, was awarded a pink rosette.

'You'll learn to love her.' It took a lot of effort for my mother to use the word love. It was a word that had never been used, not in our house. It was a *gora* word, a modern word, and articulating it had never been necessary.

'I'll go back to the shop, and I'll ask for a pound of grapes and one clean Pakistani wife.'

'What are you planning? Will you take a *gori*?'

'Only if she cooks a good curry.'

Mum shook her head. 'It is no joke. We will never accept a *gori*.' She leant forward and gripped me tightly by the arm. 'Never.'

'Is that a new gold bangle?'

'I'll show you something else as well.' Mum got up and reached onto the top shelf of the dresser where my father kept his important papers. She selected a brown envelope and returned to her seat. She pulled a passport out of the envelope and smiled broadly. I took it off her and thumbed through it. It was mine, bearing a picture I'd had taken for my recent provisional driving licence. It was strange holding my own passport, and the idea that instead of going to Pakistan with my mother I could use it to run away flashed through my mind.

'So you're all set?' I said. For a brief moment we both stared at the gold on her arm.

'It's just one small bangle.' Mum giggled like a little girl.

I reached for her arm, and as she pulled away her shirtsleeve fell back to her elbow, revealing, I counted, six gold bangles.

'I can't go with empty arms, people would talk.'

For the first time I noticed that my mother had aged, although she didn't show it on her face. She was slimmer now than she had ever been, and the years had crept up on her in other ways and were telling on her hands and arms, crisscrossed with thousands of almost imperceptible wrinkles. Now, as she proudly held up her arm with the bangles, her face lit up. In Pakistan she would have had nephews and nieces and by now perhaps even grand-children. We would have shared a farm and she would be in charge of them all, the grand matriarch. Here she had only my dad and me, and the house, and now that I had replaced her in the shop she would spend endless hours at home waiting for us to close for the night at eleven.

'Next you'll be telling me you've bought the aeroplane tickets?'

'It's for the best, son,' she said softly, pulling her shirtsleeve down over her wrist. 'You were betrothed to Azra the day you were born. You see, we promised our first-born son to Azra's father, my brother, and as Allah, peace be upon him, blessed me with only one child, I'm afraid the obligation falls to you.'

'What obligation?'

'He lent your father the money to come to England. It was his generosity that bought us the shop and kept us all these years.'

'You didn't pay it back?' I was angry.

She shook her head. 'My brother is a wealthy man and demands some-thing more than money.'

The hamsters were now running inside a spinning wheel. The camera zoomed in for a close-up and their moving legs blurred. The wheel was connected to an electrical device measuring revolutions per minute.

'I'm not doing it.'

Mum leant forward and slowly she pulled off the bangles, one at a time, and placed them noisily on the coffee table. She looked at them and then at me and tears welled up in her eyes. She slipped off her sofa and, coming over to my side, sank to her knees. She gripped my legs and, fumbling as though she was blind, worked her way up to my face, then grasped my head in both hands. She pleaded, 'Azra's very beautiful, and the minute you see her you will approve, and if you don't then you will not have to marry her.' Mum pulled back so that I could see the tears streaming down her cheeks. 'She's young enough for you to change her, make her who you want. Son, you've got nothing to lose. For my dignity, for your father, please just consent.'

Unable to look at her, I turned away.

'If she doesn't please you, you can always divorce her.'

I knew she was lying and hated her for it. 'What does Dad say?' I asked, although I had little hope of receiving the answer I wanted.

'He says you can leave this house if you don't accept.' Mum got to her feet and went back to the dresser, walking her fingers along the top shelf until she found another brown envelope. She pulled out a wad of banknotes and threw them at my feet. 'If you want to go, just go.'

'You're bluffing,' I sneered. Slowly I picked up the money. Mum had her back to me, and when I touched her on the shoulder she flinched and turned further away.

I swallowed hard. 'I suppose it was always going to come to this.'

And then, retching against the cursed bits of paper stuck in my throat, I carefully placed the money onto the coffee table next to the plastic flowers and the gold bangles.

10

Grace shuffles towards the end of the bed. 'Did we. . . ?'

I shake my head.

'You sure there's nothing I need to know? I mean, it's fine – if we did I can get a pill.' She swipes her hair behind her ears, exposing a small, star-shaped tattoo on her earlobe where a piercing might have been. Ink in lieu of an earring. 'I don't want another baby.'

'You should know who you've been intimate with.'

'Yeah.' She turns away to face the wall.

'I don't know what I'm doing here.'

'That's nice.'

'I mean I don't know you.'

'It's coming back to me. You're married. Technically. . .' She laughs. 'I blacked out, but. . . still a virgin?'

I shrug my shoulders, one hand propping up my chin.

'This Azra not giving you any?' Grace gets out of bed and straightens, unembarrassed by her naked body. She comes around the end of the bed and bends down; putting a shoulder into my armpit, she helps me off the end of the bed and to the chair on which I have draped my clothes. I see my stick leaning against the back of the chair, and grapple onto it.

I turn to thank her, my arm brushing against her breast.

'On your way,' she says resignedly.

'I've disappointed you.'

'You said you had to crack on.'

I begin to dress. Grace slips into a nightgown, her breasts and a roll of skin at her belly bulging against the satin. Standing inside the bedroom doorway she adopts the posture of sentry, her arms folded. On her face she wears an expression of impatience. 'Your wife, what is it she hates about you?'

'She hates herself. Or hates that she is a woman. If you saw how women are treated like cattle. . . Maybe it's her one and only line of defence, something she can hang on to. Or maybe it's just that she imagined something else. Sunshine. Money. Not these damp houses and. . .' I stop as I try to ease the trouser leg up my left shin. 'I have a trigger point under the skin, about three inches below the knee and a little to the left. If I scrape it pulling on my pants I scream, even when I know it's going to happen and try and hold it in.'

'You sensitive, then?'

'A trigger point is a knot of nerve tissue, but no one really knows why it fires off such awful impulses.'

'We all have one of those,' she says ruefully.

'I know.' I think of the picture by the bed. 'I'm sorry.'

'They can burn yours off,' she says thoughtfully. 'Ask the doctor.'

I look up and offer her a weak smile. 'Perhaps I am in need of it.'

My tunic buttons up like a corset, causing me to stand up straight. She brushes the cap badge with her fingers before handing me my peaked cap and saying softly, 'Don't put it on indoors.'

She helps me down the stairs and to the front door. I turn to look at Grace. Her shoulders sink with an air of resignation. Her lips tremble and for a moment I think she is about to cry.

'They took her to a home. Not good enough, see, me, on account of the pills and whatnot.' She laughs. 'I fought them, yeah, I got knocked out.' With mock pride she points to the gap in her mouth. 'I lost.'

Gripping the cap tightly in my hands, I shake my head very slowly. 'I'm so sorry.'

'I'm not needy,' she snaps. 'You can go now.'

'Didn't you want to trade? Secrets?'

'Myself, I don't tell lies, but you Pakistanis aren't straight. Not one I've ever met.'

'I think. . .' I struggle for words. 'I think you allow them to take advantage.'

Grace takes a step forward, her body almost brushing against mine, and rubs the fabric of my tunic between her fingers. 'You're prickly on the surface.'

'As you say, we Pakis, we're trouble.'

'So come on then,' she looks up imploringly, 'let's trade.'

I pull away and stare at the collection of dogs on the far wall. 'Sometimes you have to do a wrong to address a bigger wrong. You have to do that to make your point.'

'Not worth indulging in those thoughts,' she says.

'Life has to count for something.' I pause to think. 'Wouldn't you trade a year without your daughter for a single day with her?'

'You leave her out of it,' she says.

'Those that took her, don't you want to smash their faces in?'

Grace considers what I have said. 'For months I'm on the pills. I go out but it's not proper work. I come home and crawl under my duvet and hate myself and don't resurface until it's clocking-on time.'

I catch my angular shadow against the wall and stand as tall as I can. 'It's about style – ours is different.'

'Day after day it's the same and then suddenly, as though the sun has come out, I snap out of it and I'm like any other person. I don't mind, not really. I can't change it.'

'If there's a wrong and you can right it – even if it means a huge sacrifice – why wouldn't you?'

'The pills, they stop me thinking the worst, but when I'm on them I never properly laugh, as though my lips can't form the necessary shape.' She sees the direction of my intent gaze and picks up the picture. 'It's just life.'

I feel caught in her grief and suddenly conciliatory. 'She'll come back to you one day.'

Grace laughs mockingly. 'They say it's in her best interests.' She looks up at the ceiling, down at the floor, gazes at the wall. 'They say that, don't they, authority people? But what a kid really wants and what they can't give her is love.' She turns to the window, which is misted with condensation. 'She's out there, proper little princess. She's even getting a horse.'

'But you'll see her today?' I ask.

'Yeah. There comes a point in your young life when an image of your parent is fixed and you as a child are in need of it. You see, she was three and a half when she was taken, and because of that my face is etched like a carving inside her heart. They even let her keep a photo of me next to where she sleeps. That's why they have to let me see her – or her me, as they put it.' She looks up and says hopefully, 'We get to hang out. At least, we do for now. Once a month.'

'Can't you get her back?'

She shakes her head vigorously. 'There's a world beyond soldiering. A world where no one takes orders in black and white.'

'But she's yours,' I say.

'Quit going on about it, will you?'

'A mother. . . her daughter. . . It doesn't make sense.'

'It's just life.' I can see the hurt behind her eyes as they dart about as though she's facing an enemy with a loaded rifle.

'But if you were married, say?'

'Yeah.' She opens the door for me to leave. 'It'd be a suicide mission to take me on.'

11

The door closes softly behind me. There is a powerful chill in the street. I feel a sudden fear, as though I've left something behind or forgotten to tell her something important. I draw breath as though the feeling will disappear into the cold white clouds I exhale. Something about the street, its familiarity, its clean parallel lines and the narrow strip of road between houses, catches me in a momentary wave of melancholy. I try to compose myself and rationalize. I am fond of these dilapidated streets and conscious that this is the last time I will pass through them. As a child, these streets were mine and every time I went out I discovered something novel and amazing: a secluded and sheltered place to build a fire; an abandoned garden with a fruiting apple tree; a square of turf below which someone had hidden a knife with a long, serrated blade. Sometimes I'd make a friend hunting for treasure on some random piece of wasteland, or in the park I'd meet someone who knew someone I knew.

It is half past five and the sky a carbon black. It is too early to proceed, even at a leisurely pace, towards my target, towards the war memorial where the armistice commemoration will take place at eleven.

The wind whistles in the few trees dotted at regular intervals along the main road, and I hear small animals rustle in the hedgerow. The absence of traffic on Sunday mornings gives the scene an eerie, apocalyptic quality, as though I am the sole inhabitant of a land that will never see dawn. It is brief, this time. Soon the sun will rise; dog walkers will be out whistling and shouting commands, shift workers will travel, and before long people will be hurrying into and out of shops for Sunday papers and bread and milk.

By six I reach the Saltwells. To keep warm, I walk as fast as the stick will allow, and I know that this town is simply too small to measure out the remaining five hours on foot. The clouds are low and menacingly cold. I tilt my head to Allah somewhere distant in the night sky. He knows I have been tempted. He hears and sees all, but He is just and His written word tells me that the final transgressions of a martyr are forgiven and that there are many paths to martyrdom, so many that not all are known.

Underfoot, the tarmac gives way to gravel. The canal is so black it is difficult to see where the path ends and its idle waters begin. The birdlife is silent. I carry on into the unlit darkness. A dog barks inside a barge moored by a rope to a hook on the path. It stops abruptly as though muffled by the hands of someone sleeping within. Further ahead is the tunnel where I will pick up my payload. It will be a daysack, to be detonated by mobile phone, and they are watching. Somewhere nearby, the brothers stand guard, unseen. My heart races, and despite the chill I feel a warm trickle of sweat on my brow. '*Bismillah ir-Rahman ir-Rahim*,' I whisper.

It is colder beside the water, as though I am caught on a freezing, expansive moor. This is only a recce; the plan is to pick up the bag later, and I don't want to risk being caught with my load. Turning off the path, I climb a short flight of stone steps, intending to return to the road.

The steps lead to a small wrought-iron bridge before the road proper. From there, I glance back down at the tunnel entrance, and stop. Am I seeing things or did a light flicker inside the tunnel? The light, if it is that, reappears briefly and then disappears. I turn back, return to the path, and approach as silently as my boots will allow. I keep to one side of the path, brushing against the foliage on the verge, my number two dress uniform soon soaked in dew.

Pausing at the entrance, I see a slight glow within the tunnel, and smell smoke. I hear the faint scraping of boots, and a man coughs bronchially. It is only when I get very close that I see, in the faint glimmer of firelight, a circular column of bricks on the path. The great internal wall of the tunnel is composed of many layers of brick, and in one section the first layer has recently been removed and rearranged on the path to make up the waist-high column. Now I see that someone is crouched inside it. My heart starts pounding. That is the location where my ordnance has been hidden. At least, those are my instructions. Where are the brothers? Are they not watching? Where is the daysack?

'Arr war.' A loud, coarse voice is followed by a figure rising slowly out of the circular column. A brick tumbles from the edge and crashes heavily onto the ground. As he stands a brief flurry of flames seem to leap after him, and I make out the outline of a tall man in a greatcoat, his arms at his sides. 'Arr war,' he growls again, 'pull the door and come in.'

There is no door. The man sinks down again, and as I step cautiously closer, I see that he is warming his hands by a small wood fire set within the column.

He eyes my uniform with a broad smile. 'Man of war, welcome. Welcome.' With one hand he sweeps away enough bricks to create an opening for me to pass through. He looks at me, smiling with blackened teeth. His round face is ruddy from the fire, and almost entirely covered in a thick layer of hair that collects at the chin into a long beard. His eyes water, glistening in the firelight.

Hurriedly, he makes a stool out of bricks. 'Come and warm yourself, Sergeant. Cost you nothing.'

Putting down my stick, I ease myself onto the makeshift stool. The bricks are hard but warm. I am conscious that if the ordnance is nearby it could heat up and detonate.

'What are you hiding from?' I say.

'Hiding. Ha. Yes, I get it. Sheltering from the cold.'

'Good place for it,' I say.

'I'm preparing for the future.'

I look around at the walls of the tunnel. The fire illuminates moths circling around us, and the bricks, steaming from the heat, form a pleasant sandy colour as they dry. In the sudden warmth the skin of my face burns, reminding me again of the loss of my beard.

'I lived here when it was a house. Thirteen Golden Hill Road. Postman still delivers.'

'Delivers?'

'Giro. Still get my giro.' He laughs hoarsely. 'But they cut the housing benefit.'

'Well,' I say, 'at least you don't have to pay the bills.'

'Bills?' he says seriously. 'No, lad. No bills. But I have running water.' He points to a service pipe poking out of the tunnel wall, attached to which is a stopcock. 'I know what you're thinking. You're thinking, what's an old fool doing living at number thirteen? I'm right, aren't I? That's what you were thinking.'

I nod.

'Well, I'll tell you, lad. It's because I'm mad. That's right, I'm mad.'

'You're not mad,' I say to befriend him.

'Ah, perceptive. But them civilians out there, they think I'm crazy. Because I see things. Because I won't go into a home. I tell them I'm not deranged. I have a home that keeps me safe and I'm loyal to it. Takes something to be loyal.' Screwing up his face, he considers the motif on my cap badge. 'You and I, we have that in common.'

I shrug my shoulders.

'Wake up, lad, the end is nigh!' he bellows as though I haven't understood him. 'You and I, we will be safe. We are faithful. We believe.' He fumbles about inside his coat, pulls out a half-bottle of spirits. 'Just a nip for the chill.' He hands me the bottle. Inside is a clear liquid. I take a pull and brace myself for the kick. At first it burns slowly, gathering intensity as though boring through the flesh in my throat. I cough.

'You get used to it.' He retrieves the bottle, replaces the lid and puts it back into his pocket.

'You can get used to anything,' I say, massaging my throat. 'We had a saying in the army. It was about having the right kit and food and being prepared for living in the field. Will you excuse my language?'

He nods.

'Any cunt can be uncomfortable.'

He laughs. 'Army, you say?'

'Yeoman's.'

'Say you left something here?'

'I didn't say that.'

'Nah. Got nothing here. Nothing for nobody,' he bellows unconvincingly, his shoes crunching gravel as he stoops towards the fire. 'I thought, there goes a soldier boy. A friendless soldier boy traipsing Golden Hill Road by morning. A kindred spirit in need of a friend and warmth. You've disappointed me.'

'Did you find anything in or about these walls?' I ask nervously.

'The world's coming to an end.'

'Pardon?'

'You'd better believe it. The world is doomed. A great war will engulf the earth.'

'I believe you,' I say. 'Sincerely I do.'

He puts his hands together. 'Hang on. Don't you want to know how the war will begin?'

Deciding to search the area myself, I steel myself with a *Bismillah* and reach for my stick.

He grabs my arm. 'You're jumpy,' he says. His tone is suddenly lucid and inquisitorial and my entire body contracts in an involuntary shiver. 'You speak in tongues. I should report you.'

I shake free of his grip. I am caught in a moment of adrenaline and indecision. I could pick up a brick and strike him with it. I picture an ugly event: his head caved in, body dumped in the canal. But as I said to Grace, it's about style, and that is not mine.

Instead I try to distract him. 'I met a girl. She reached into her mouth and worked loose a tooth. Then she rolled it between her fingers into a silver ball.'

He nods, his face slowly contorting into an expression of confusion. He leans back and thinks for what seems like minutes. Finally he says, 'It's like plucking a rose without getting spiked.'

I lean towards him, my foot scraping against the ground.

He flinches. 'Don't be rough with me, lad. '

'Will you help me find it?' I ask, getting to my feet.

'If you were a friend I might.'

'I've got no money,' I reply, patting my pockets.

He shakes his head. 'It's not money I'm after.'

'What will it take?' I say.

'Come sit. Plenty throw coin at me but no one sits and talks.'

'And afterwards?'

'Tell me about this rose first.'

'As I was telling her my story she fell asleep.'

The old man sinks back against the brickwork, oblivious to the danger that it might topple over. I notice that his shoes are open at the toes, out of which poke lurid shades of infected pink skin, and I look intently at the fire, the light burning my retinas and dulling my night sight.

'A cyclical story of how our beginnings meet our ends,' I add.

'In that tooth,' says the old boy, clasping his knees and leaning forward, 'she stores her sorrows.'

I shrug my shoulders again.

'But you, man of war, you will not understand.'

'I have only the knowledge that God has provided me with.'

The old man coughs violently, his chest jerking inside his coat. As his eyes catch the firelight I see that the cornea of one is ulcerated, its periphery curdled and bloodied. He clears his throat loudly, the sound visceral and urgent, echoing off the brickwork. Finally he spits into the fire and visibly relaxes.

He says, 'You're not one of those Christians, are you, lad?'

I shake my head.

'Savages, Christians. Lure me to a place with hot soup and bedding. I say, baptize me with your force of argument, and they say, beef or minestrone, sir?' His eyes retreat into their sockets and he knocks back a large gulp of spirits, then repeats his refrain, 'Arr war.'

There is a long pause while I look around for my daysack. For a moment, as our eyes lock, his feet scrape hard across the ground. I relax, reading the signal that the ordnance lurks somewhere by his feet.

As though coming to, he says, no longer bellowing, 'Tell me more about this rose with a hag's tooth.'

'Well, not much to say. . .'

'Tell me,' he says loudly.

'Met her only tonight, so I don't—'

'Tell me.' He speaks louder, his voice echoing deep into the tunnel.

'She's authentic. Truthful.'

'You bed her?' Without waiting for an answer, the old man nods approvingly. He reaches behind some bricks and pulls out a green daysack, then places it beside my feet next to the fire.

I stare at it, my heart pounding.

'It's yours, I believe.'

I nod.

'I've taken a sneaky peek inside.' Tilting back his head, he laughs uproariously, exposing blackened stumps in the back of his mouth.

I wait for him to finish. 'I'm just the delivery man.'

'It's crammed full of ordnance,' he says gleefully, his good eye dancing in the firelight.

'Ordnance?' I say. 'You ex-military?'

'You going to cave my head in now?' he says, leaning back on his brick stool.

'No.'

'Everyone thinks I'm mad, but I know what this is.'

'You were right. Armageddon. It's coming.'

'I told them that,' he says. 'I always knew.' He pauses for thought. 'But I didn't see it coming so soon.'

I reach for the sack, but the old boy pulls it away. 'I asked you, did you bed her?'

I stare at him, unsure of what to say.

'And they say I'm mad.' He shakes his head vigorously. 'Go back. Return to her warm bed and think on it.'

12

'You want to finish your story?'

Lying next to Grace once again, my limbs warm and chin tucked into the duvet, it feels as though I never left. She had half expected me to return. No sooner had I knocked on the door than I heard the pad of soft footsteps and it opened. For a second she looked at me but there was nothing to read on her face, blank, soft. I stepped inside and lowered my daysack to the floor. I'm sure she saw it, but she made no remark. Without a word, I followed her upstairs and undressed. Grace is authentic, as I told the old boy, but not truthful, not entirely. She's honest only in the sense that she can't keep a secret. Slipping into bed, I felt her teeth sharply on my shoulder for a moment, and then she turned over and shifted to the far side of the bed.

From outside there is the occasional cry of a cat or a fox, I cannot tell which, the skirmish of animals competing for food scraps and territory.

'You carry on. I'll listen in my sleep.'

'Old Hill tower blocks,' I say. 'Do you know them?'

'Sometimes, if I close my eyes it burns me up.'

'What does?' I reach across and touch her brow, warm and sweaty. She brushes me off.

'I have to clench my teeth and wait,' she says.

I try again, gently stroking the space between her eyebrows. This time, she doesn't resist.

'I have to wait for the lights to put out. It's best then, isn't it? When the lights put out.'

'Your ceiling, do you ever stare at it?' It is a complicated pattern of Artex. Sweeps of plaster folded into each other, in waves and shapes resembling seashells. 'It's trying to imagine the sea.'

'The sea,' she confusedly murmurs. 'Where were we?'

'Old Hill tower blocks.'

'That's right. The lift's always broke.'

'I was naive and full of myself like most teenagers, and after having known only the confines of the family home, I was now free. For a while I stayed with Maley's dad, fixed his garden up, seeing that he was no longer able. Didn't see him often, kept to himself drinking homebrew or he'd be in The Gate Hangs Well. I got day jobs in factories and foundries, lumping timber and casting metal. It was better than shop work, more honest and meagre, and the early rises and hard work toughened me up. Must have been there about six months, had my seventeenth birthday, which we celebrated in the garden with a bottle of wine Mr Male had bought for the occasion. Never had wine before, and he poured it into these dainty little glasses which we sipped slowly all afternoon. He said I could stay as long as I wanted, but also he wished I would leave. For my sake, he said and I admired the honesty of his language. He hadn't heard from his son and I never spoke of him. Some ways, I was his surrogate.

'Coming back from some factory one day, I saw Bobby and followed him to a house where he let himself in. I felt the burden of knowledge, it felt heavy and worrisome. Strange, but that's how it seemed at the time. I had valuable information and I wanted to share.'

'That's kind,' Grace says without thinking.

*

From across the street I had a good view of the three tower blocks opposite. Like a foreboding, my shadow swept before me. When I leant back and squinted, the uppermost floors appeared lost in a mist, giving the impression that up there the rain was thicker. At ground level the grass was deep green as though painted in by a child. The path to the middle tower was bordered with a bed of newly planted yellow daffodils, and sticks and wires protected discrete squares of newly seeded soil. Beyond this the grass was muddy and littered, and small, shaven-headed children, impervious to the damp, pecked about like hens, collecting butt ends into jars.

The entrance to the middle tower was guarded by a large steel door, like that of a prison cell. Fixed to the wall beside it was a heavily studded intercom panel. I pushed button number 142 and waited, watching the children observe a Pakistani on the estate, a rare thing then, with an almost threatening fascination.

The steel door creaked open and slowly a thin old man with a white rabbit in a pushchair eased himself and the buggy out backwards. The rabbit sat upright, its jaws mechanically working on the end of a turnip. Its ears, sensing the sudden change in temperature, twitched and trembled like a leaf. The animal looked up, considered me with round translucent eyes and returned its attention to the vegetable. I caught the door before it could close, and walked into an atrium, its scum-stained tiled walls covered in graffiti, one layer superseding the other. An acrid smell stung my nostrils. Raucous voices issued from somewhere nearby and anonymous footsteps clattered on concrete.

On the fourteenth floor the door to flat 142 hung open an inch or two. Drums, screaming vocals and a crash of cymbals escaped through the gap. I knocked but there was no response. I pushed it open, and flinched as a greyhound leapt out, then skidded dangerously down the deep concrete stairwell.

'Hello?' I called, and stepped inside.

The flat was dark and cold. Faded paisley wallpaper lined the walls, torn and curled in places. The carpet was slippery and had thick concentric stains as though the grime had been trodden in layer by layer. The music stopped.

'What the fuck?' Adrian stood at the far end of the room next to a window. He was dressed in baggy blue jeans and a Sex Pistols T-shirt. He put out a flat palm and I stopped. 'I don't know what the hell you're doing here but if you don't fuck off right now I'll set the dog on you.'

'Dog escaped.' I shrugged.

'What?'

'Went down the stairs.'

Adrian clamped a hand to his forehead. 'Oh fuck, someone will nick him.'

'Won't he know his way back?'

He laughed suddenly. 'Only nicked him myself yesterday.'

'I've seen that lanky, greasy-haired paedo fucking Paki,' I said.

He looked serious again. 'What fucking paedo Paki?'

'Bobby – remember him? The pound note you never got.'

'Okay.' He briefly closed his eyes. 'Don't go on.'

'I spotted him in this new mosque. You wouldn't believe it – the man's a fucking miracle. He levitated! He's going about like he's some kind of fucking prophet.' I paused and raised my eyebrows as though issuing a challenge. 'And I know where he lives.'

We left the flat and walked for a while in the drab drizzly silence without speaking. Raindrops were suspended in Adrian's closely cropped blond hair. His strong broad face was pale and freckled and a thick chin jutted vulnerably. His eyes seemed to scan the horizon and then dart to the side in small movements like those of a rat-catcher in an old movie. He held his shoulders stiffly, and his T-shirt, damp from the rain, outlined the bulge of his pectoral muscles and hung limply over his lean stomach. His hands hung at his sides, clenching into fists and unclenching.

The high street was nearly deserted. 'Normally, if I've got coin I can't go past without going in,' said Adrian, glancing at Ivan's chip shop. Ivan, visible through the glass frontage, wore a chef's cap. When not ladling chips into or out of hot oil, he always stood and smiled at every passer-by. He had left the door ajar, and I took a deep luxurious breath of the smell of vinegar, pickled onion and hot chips.

'I'll just smash that Bobby cunt with whatever.' Adrian stopped and turned to me. 'I'll pretend it was a spur-of-the-moment thing.'

I dug my hands into my pockets. 'You don't have to kill him.'

Adrian exhaled loudly and bit his lower lip, thinking. 'I was going to enlist in the armed forces.'

'You could just scare him?'

'You know, after renting myself to that greasy Paki. . .' Adrian's laughter betrayed his inability to finish the sentence. 'Whatever happens, I want you to know I'm not bashing him just because he's a Paki. I wouldn't do that, I'm not like my dad.'

'Army, navy or air force?' I kicked at a stone, sending it careering into the road.

'I'm not a skinhead. No skinhead amounted to nothing.'

'We're all a little bit like our fathers,' I offered.

'Proper army – infantry,' he said proudly.

'I reckon you'd be good at it.'

He nodded. 'I reckon it's all I'm good for.'

'You get to leave this shithole.'

'Yeah, I got brochures from the job centre: there's winter training in Norway and jungles in Belize, no pain. . .' His chin thrust forward. 'Yeah, I could train myself to feel no pain.'

'I believe that.'

The high street terminated with a newly sprung-up video rental shop on one corner and an old pub on the other. The wind carried a blue plastic shopping bag in circles around a roundabout, and the road ahead sloped downwards, disappearing into a bend, towards the railway station and beyond to the old walled factories bordering the canal.

'You must be making plenty of coin?' he said.

'I've been thrown out.'

He considered me suspiciously. 'I thought you Pakis stuck together.'

'I didn't want to marry no Paki, so I left. My father's last words were *Where will you go?*'

'And you came here! You poor cunt. I could see it coming, though. Your dad's a bit like mine. All mine wanted was a quiet life, earning, spending, his mates and the boozer, but that's all gone and he blames the Pakis.'

'I went to stay with Maley's dad for a bit.'

'Anywhere's better than mine.'

'They'll send you down for murdering that paedo, unless of course you tell them what he did to you.'

Adrian looked back towards the towers, and shrugged helplessly. 'Manslaughter, not murder, still both cowardly things to do.'

'No pain, have that army life instead,' I urged.

'Fucker.' He slowly unclenched a fist at his side and nodded to emphasize each word. '*Something always gets in the fucking way*.'

'Come on, right now. Let's go to the army recruitment office.'

Adrian shook his head.

'It's my fault, I shouldn't have let him.'

'You're the only person that knows. . .' His lower jaw trembled and he pointed a finger inches from my eye.

I took half a step back and gazed up at the grey afternoon sky. It was broiling and darkening, readying for another assault of hard rain. 'I'm sorry.'

Adrian stared at a road sign. 'Did you see that guy with the rabbit, in the pram? That's Paedo John and the rabbit's called Fred. He uses it to lure kids back to his flat. Nothing hardcore like, takes pictures and weirdo-old-man shit, and everyone knows, but he's got coin. If you're short of a fiver, he's good for it.'

I opened my mouth to say sorry again, but nothing came out. I looked at Adrian. He dug his hands into his pockets, his T-shirt flapping around his shoulders. He turned his head to look further into the distance.

*

It seems that for Grace, the lights have been *put out*. The philtrum above her upper lip vibrates loudly and her chest rises and falls in slow exaggerated movements. I don't suppose she has heard anything I have said, and curiously, it doesn't seem to matter.

I picture the ordnance as an X-ray in shades of grey, cylinders of power and a sprig of coiled wire coming from each. The wires connect to a small transparent box, the fuse, which is connected in turn to a cluster of small rectangular nine-volt batteries linked in series to compound the input. The X-ray view shows the inside of the batteries, a dense network of crisscrossing plates.

I continue to stare at Grace. Nagging at me is the irrational thought that it could blow while we sleep. That would 'put the lights out' like she wanted. It's the best way to die, in your sleep. But it won't happen, not without detonation, and the detonator, a mobile phone, sits in the breast pocket of my tunic on the chair. If I squint my eyes I can believe I see its bulging flat surface.

I close my eyes and picture Adrian as merely an outline in pencil; then, picking up my felt-tip pens, I begin to colour him in.

*

Cradley's own army recruitment office was sandwiched between Café Oregano and a clothes shop I couldn't see into because every inch of window space had been covered with the word SALE in tall red letters. Adrian and I stood by the door and smiled nervously at each other.

Adrian took a deep breath. 'Come on, boy, left, right, left.'

As we went in, the sergeant major stood up, leant across his desk and stuck out a hand to introduce himself in a thick Scottish accent. Hurrying across the narrow shop, I was first to it. It was warm and soft. He was a bear of a man, with thick glasses on a large ruddy face guarded by a sergeant major's curly moustache. He wore tight green trousers and polished brown brogues. Over his barrel chest was stretched a thick woollen jumper, and a wide red belt encircled his large girth, a brass buckle shining resplendent at the centre. Sewn onto the left breast of the jumper was a balloon-like para motif, and on the sleeve were three inverted V-shapes with a crown in the indent. On his right breast was a small, discreet enamelled badge bearing the word FALKLANDS.

'H-he's come to join,' I stammered, looking between Adrian and the sergeant major.

Surreptitiously Adrian squeezed my wrist. 'We've both come to join,' he dug a nail into my skin. It hurt and I felt a trickle of something warm, but I decided I'd take it: *no pain.*

The sergeant major ironed a corner of his moustache between two stubby fingers and stared at us. 'What's it gonna be, who's joining?'

'We both are,' said Adrian quickly.

'Comedians, hey? Take a wee look around ye, see if anything catches yer eye.' The sergeant major shook his head and sank back into his chair.

The army recruitment office had once been a video arcade with slot machines lined up against each wall; the owner was a thin fella we called Uncle Stan. I can still picture Stan, counting tall stacks of coins behind a counter where the sergeant major's desk now sat. I peered closely at the pictures that had replaced the slot machines: a green helicopter firing a missile at a Russian tank; the view through a submarine periscope with hairlines dead centre over a ship on the horizon; a troop of soldiers kitted out like green monsters in nuclear-biological-chemical-protective suits, their rifles held before them with fixed bayonets and behind them a lunar landscape.

Adrian and I bent over a leaflet rack next to the door, thumbing through brochures. I picked up one with a picture of a dagger on the front. 'What's happening?' I whispered. 'I thought you were enlisting?'

'I dare you,' he said.

'What would my dad say?'

'Thought you had left him.' For a brief moment his jaw slackened as though he himself was unsure, and then he continued, 'You owe me!'

The sergeant major wrote very slowly as he took down our particulars – names, age and addresses – and afterwards he tapped the nib of his pen on the paper as though he had to think about the details it listed. He squeezed his chin, looked at me, back at the paper and again at me. Adrian and I sat in chairs facing him across the desk.

'What are ye, son? Are ye a Hindoo?'

'He's a Muslim,' said Adrian, his eyes flicking to the name badge on the desk, 'Recruiting Sergeant Major Mackay, a Muslim, no law against that.'

The sergeant major peered over his glasses. 'Are ye sure about this?'

I nodded.

'Have ye talked it over with yer family?' He clicked the pen against his teeth.

'He's old enough, isn't he?' Adrian said.

The sergeant major stared again at the paperwork as though perplexed, then back at us through narrowed eyes. 'Ye're both seventeen, so ye dinnae need parental consent.'

Adrian settled back in his chair and grinned. 'That's what I thought!'

'In the army ye lads could learn a trade. We have cooks, drivers, engineers and medics, even bricklayers. Almost everything ye have on Civvy Street, we have an equivalent in the army.'

I shrugged my shoulders.

'Ah myself first enlisted in the Army Intelligence Corps,' the sergeant major said proudly. 'Ye'll need a trade when ye're back. . .'

'Sir, Sergeant Major Mackay, with respect, we want to be soldiers,' said Adrian.

'Rough and tumble, hey? Ah got caught by that wee bug too.' He pointed to the para badge sewn onto his breast. 'Well, let's have a wee look. . .' He thumbed through a Rolodex next to a large green telephone on his desk. I looked at Adrian excitedly, wondering if he was thinking what I was thinking – that the sergeant major was about to call someone up and send us over there and then.

'So a Muslim, hey?' He seemed defeated by the idea and continued to flick through the cards on his Rolodex, his brow visibly reddening. A solitary bead of sweat trickled down it.

I spoke up. 'Sergeant Major Mackay, my grandfather fought in the Second World War, in the Indian army, but he was fighting for the British.'

'Muslims, Pakis, they're everywhere, and they're as English as we are,' Adrian added.

'Ah, of course.' The sergeant major relaxed back into his chair. 'Fine fighting men. Yer grandfather, was he on the Asian Front or in Europe?'

'He was taken prisoner by the Japanese, sir.'

'Terrible, wicked. . .' He stared at the paperwork on his desk and shook his head. He looked at me again, but now he seemed to inspect me in a kinder manner, as though he was no longer afraid. 'Strong family history. Very good, lad.' He turned to Adrian. 'And ye, chap?'

'BEF, sir. After that POW in France. Escaped, shot and captured, escaped again, then Home Guard on account of shrapnel in one eye.'

I looked at Adrian. There was no sign of pride on his face; it was as though what he was relating was expected, normal. I was struck suddenly by the thought that it *was* normal and expected: during the war, fighting had been the duty of all Englishmen. This was the first time I had ever articulated my grandfather's achievements and suddenly I felt proud that we, the Khans, had been part of the *gora* war.

'We'll let him off for that,' said the sergeant major. Forming a fist with both hands, he put it to his chin and leant forward, speaking slowly. 'War is the terrible reality of killing another man, and the world we live in calls upon men like us to do that job.' We leant forward too, our faces inches from his. This was something serious and we were almost part of it.

The sergeant major took down some further information: the names of our parents, our school, and that of our old headmaster, whom he said he knew and would call for a reference.

Adrian handed him the leaflets we had picked up. The sergeant major shuffled cursorily through them, then placed the pile neatly on his desk and slid it back towards us. 'Army Air Corps?' He shook his head. 'Ya gonna need qualifications for that, and the Paras.' In homage he put his right hand to his left breast. 'They're always recruiting, always looking for the right stuff.' Although he did it very discreetly, I saw him look us up and down. 'And the guards' regiments – well, there's policy and there's policy, if ye know what ah mean.' He put a conspiratorial finger to his nose. 'Not that ah agree with it, a man's a man and that, so the bard said, ach but there's no use sending ye along only to be turned down at the outset now, is there, lads?'

We shook our heads in agreement like small children. Outside there was a sudden downpour.

'Now. . .' he paused for effect, 'the Yeomanry are a fine local regiment. They begin their next round of basic training in a fortnight's time. Ah suppose. . .' He stopped again.

I looked over at Adrian.

Sergeant Major Mackay thought for a moment longer, squeezing his chin. 'The HQ's not far from here and they like to recruit locally. Light infantry and reconnaissance.' He looked us up and down again, more obviously this time. 'Strong lads like ye, suit ye both to a tee.'

Yeomanry. It was a fine word. A word that was as old as England. *Reconnaissance* – I pictured Adrian and me in nuclear uniforms hiding behind a bush then leaping out, guns blazing, the enemy caught entirely by surprise.

The sergeant major tapped his fingers on the telephone. Suddenly he seemed to remember something. 'And of course, the Queen's shilling.' Shuffling his ample weight on the small fragile chair, he pulled on a key attached to his waist and unlocked the top drawer of the desk. We watched mesmerized as he retrieved a small bundle of banknotes. He counted them out into two piles, one before each of us, then ironed them out with his chubby pink hands.

'A fortnight. They conduct basic training in Catterick, Yorkshire. Ah say, ah could just about squeeze ye in.'

There was a pause that seemed to last for minutes. The sergeant major bit his lower lip and peered at us, waiting for an answer. I glanced out of the window, suddenly aware of the silence now that the rain had petered out.

Having shaken hands with the sergeant major, and been told several times *farewell* and *good luck* and *if only there were more like ye – fit, willing young men – then this wee fair isle would be a better place*, I stood by the doorway of the off-licence and felt for the existential weight of the Queen's shilling in my pocket. With a finger I wrote the word YEOMANRY into the condensation on the glass frontage.

Adrian emerged into the street carrying a bottle of blackcurrant cordial and two heavy gold-coloured bottles of cider. 'I've worked it out,' he said, briefly lifting his purchases above his head. 'Done the maths on the alcohol-percentage-over-volume-per-penny ratio.'

I saw that he had also bought a small glass bottle of tomato ketchup. He pushed it into a pocket and offered me an embarrassed grin. 'Can never get enough of that stuff.'

Guiltily I patted my own pocket, where my money remained unspent.

A swan from the canal had lost its way, and at the roundabout traffic was at a standstill. The animal's neck was caught in one handle of a blue carrier bag, and it thrashed furiously, its frantic efforts to escape only tightening the noose. Safely inside the video rental shop, people peered out, their noses pressed against the glass. The swan's elegant body twisted and lurched, and feathers flew off as it flapped its great wings. Nervous drivers watched from their car windows.

'Dare you,' I said.

Adrian put down the shopping bags and strode across the road, slipping off his T-shirt. He threw it over the bird's head, then with one easy flick of his wrist freed it of both plastic bag and T-shirt. He stepped quickly back with a flourish, dangling his T-shirt at the waist like a bullfighter's cape. A car sounded its horn and Adrian took a deep bow. Behind him the bird lurched at Adrian's legs but deflected away, just in time, as another car beeped its horn loudly.

'I'd make a better survivor than you,' Adrian said, returning to the corner and picking up the bags. Behind us, through the video shop window, the civilians looked on, transfixed.

We walked along the towpath of the canal until we found a hole in a high brick wall big enough for a man to squeeze through. On the other side of the wall was an enormous concrete yard. It was like a parade ground except that the concrete was rent with long gashes as though riven by an earthquake. Surrounding it on three sides were cavernous, four-storey rectangular brick buildings neatly appointed with row upon row of smashed latticed windows.

A small steel canopy propped up on stilts projected from part of the wall. Beneath it the ground was dry, and we gathered loose bricks to make seats and settled down, our legs stretched out in front and backs against the oily black wall.

Adrian opened a bottle of the cider, took a long swig and then topped it up with blackcurrant cordial. 'God's own brew, for beginners.' He pushed it towards me.

The cordial spread down through the yellow cider until the contents of the bottle were entirely red. I looked at Adrian, who was drinking from the second, unadulterated bottle.

'Dare you,' he said, raising his eyebrows.

'No pain.' I picked up the bottle in both hands and put it to my lips.

'Tastes of pop,' I said.

Adrian put the ketchup bottle to his mouth and sucked at its turgid contents. 'I've dreamt of this and I'm gonna finish it even if it makes me sick.'

'We don't sell ketchup in our shop.'

'Made chains here,' said Adrian, looking around the yard. 'And the anchor for the *Titanic*.'

'My mate Maley, his dad worked round about here,' I said, taking a large gulp from my bottle.

'Wish I had been around then,' Adrian said, licking the ketchup off his lips.

'Made him go half deaf.' I nodded thoughtfully, remembering to say a silent *Bismillah*.

'Imagine how proud you'd be.' Adrian swept his hand across the view. 'Took twenty shire horses just to pull the anchor across the yard. God only knows how they loaded it onto a barge.'

'Remember Maley?' I asked.

'He disappeared in a lorry, right?'

'He'll never come back.'

'Don't blame him.'

'I would have gone to visit him but don't know where he is.'

'Shire horses,' Adrian said dreamily, 'solid, done up to the nines in brass.'

*

We drank slowly, and as afternoon turned to early evening the sun came out. Behind the wall we could hear birds chirruping out on the canal and ducks as they noisily floated by. A canal barge motored past, and when, a little further ahead, it entered the long tunnel, opera music echoed inside the barrel-vaulted brick walls.

'They do that as they go through Netherton Tunnel. They cut the engine and play grand music from an old gramophone – it's like being in heaven,' Adrian said.

'What do you think it'll be like, the army?' I was shivering from sitting still so long.

'Beef and gravy, mate.'

'Do you think there'll be another war?'

'Bring it on.' He picked up the now half-empty ketchup bottle and flung it across the yard. 'Don't sell ketchup, what the fuck do you sell?' I heard the bottle shatter in the darkening distance. 'No pain!' he shouted, wiping the ketchup from his chin and staggering unsteadily to his feet.

I tried to get up but my legs felt weak, and the slightest tilt of my head brought on nausea. I bent over and vomited.

'Get it all out,' said Adrian, slapping me on the back. 'Tickle your tonsils with your fingers, it'll help.'

It hurt like fury, and after a long and painful bout of gut cramp and vomiting I rose to my feet, wiping the tears from my eyes. My throat burned. I laughed, bending forward as far as I could to test the returning strength in my legs, and screamed into the uninhabited darkness, 'No pain!'

'So,' said Adrian, rubbing his hands together, 'are you going to show me where that paedo lives?'

'I thought we had a deal. Army over paedo.'

Adrian grabbed me by the throat. Caught unaware, I was quickly pinned to the wall. 'I dare you.'

I wriggled free and shoved him in the chest. As he staggered back I saw his eyes, glazed from the drink but cold and determined.

'Do it again and I'll. . .' I said.

'Oh yeah?'

I rubbed my sore neck. Now we were comrades in arms. Army men fought and died for each other like brothers.

I took him to a terraced house not dissimilar to the one I had grown up in. It would have been indistinguishable from the others in the row except for the thick, moth-eaten curtains that hung precariously in his front window. They appeared undisturbed, as though never opened. No light emanated from any of the windows.

Adrian knocked on the door and waited for a minute.

'No one's home,' he said disappointedly. 'Let's go back to mine.'

I could have simply agreed with him and we would have moved on, but we were now in an unshakeable pact. 'He's in, all right.'

'Smash a window then, he's bound to come out.'

'What, like your old man Chav Hartley?'

'What then, what are we going to do?' Adrian hopped from one foot to the other in excitement.

Indicating for him to stand back against the wall where he couldn't be seen, I knocked on the door. There was no movement inside. I pushed open the flap on the letterbox and spoke into it. '*Assalamualaikum*, brother, it's Akram from Khan's shop. My dad sent me round to deliver dates to the brothers ready for Ramadan.' Conscious that my words were slurred, I spoke slowly, trying to focus on only one word at a time.

The hallway light came on and the door was unbolted from within several times.

'You got good security here, bruv,' I shouted to be heard through the door.

The door opened part way and on the other side stood Bobby, his eyes adjusting to the outside light.

I sneered. 'You're not fucking levitating now.'

A flash of panic crossed Bobby's face and he took half a step back. As he did so the swish of his long velvet dressing gown swept up a cloud of dust.

I kicked the door fully open and it struck him in the face, knocking his glasses to the floor. I stepped into the hallway and felt the glasses crush beneath my shoe. Adrian leapt in after me, then bolted the door behind him.

Seeing Adrian, Bobby turned and shuffled away with no apparent urgency, along the hallway and into a darkened living room. We followed. In the background a radio was quietly playing a *naath*. A two-bar electric fire glowed orange, its illumination reaching only the surrounding mustard-coloured tiles on the hearth. Above the mantel was a stack of mouldy sliced white bread about ten deep. A single tatty chair sat in the centre of the room, a packet of cigarettes, a box of matches and a lighter resting on its padded arm.

Adrian and I stood guard by the door. Bobby fumbled about on the chair like a blind man. He found his cigarettes, took one out and rapped it against the thumbnail of his other hand. He put it between his lips and with a shaky fist nursed a head wound caused by the door.

'It's definitely him,' I said to Adrian. I took the matches from the armrest and lit one. I could see the flame's reflective flicker in Adrian's eyes. Turning, I extended the match towards Bobby.

'Let's brand him,' said Adrian, twitching like a greyhound, 'just say you dare me.'

'Brother Bobby.' I placed my index finger on the centre of my forehead. 'Brother Bobby, my friend here says you owe him a pound.'

*

It strikes me as a unique failure that I can climb out of the beds of two women in the course of the same night and remain a virgin. Slowly, and as silently as possible, I reach for my stick, negotiate the door to the landing, and descend the stairs one at a time.

In the kitchen, I shiver in the cold atmosphere. It smells synthetic, of disinfectant and lavender and cold steel. The English don't warm their houses as much as we do. I note they use mugs, none of which appear to match, and have an ample supply of spoons and tea. They leave themselves small Post-it notes as mundane reminders: *pay the milkman*; *cheese in the fridge* (where else would it be?); *call the social worker at 9*; and, more curious for Grace, *see dentist*. Is that new since she met me? It is a self-indulgent idea that somehow, in the short space of time between my leaving and returning, she changed her mind about the missing tooth.

The English are not entirely private about their correspondence. Attached magnetically to the refrigerator are reminder bills for electricity and water, and a magistrate summons for monies owed to the Inland Revenue. A paragraph details her alleged crime and describes her work as *Other Self-Employed*. Do they really expect Grace to itemize expenses and keep receipts? It adds another layer to the complexity of the English: the sparse, neat, freezing kitchen and Her Majesty collecting from places like this earnings such as *Other*. What I find more interesting is her name, *Miss Grace G. Booth*, followed by her address. A discrete square of print in the top right-hand corner of the letter, a dense chunk of type making Grace official. She suddenly seems somehow more substantial, part of a larger world, in a way that elevates her to something greater than what she personally declares.

From the house next door I hear the tinny sound of the dawn *azan*, today's first call to prayer, no doubt played, as it is in my parents' house, from an alarm clock on the mantel. It is barely audible and not something Grace would hear, but at sunrise I am primed for it, often finding myself waking up seconds before it commences, and I hum softly along. Although it is after seven it is still dark outside, the sky heavily clouded.

A pile of papers is wedged between a microwave oven and the tall refrigerator. Guiltily, I flick through them: *Court Summons*, *Family Proceedings*, *Adoption Notice*, *Variation to Contact Order*. The earlier correspondence is addressed to a flat in Old Hill tower blocks, and the most recently dated letter states, if I am correct, that the last time she will see her daughter Britney is today, 11 November.

My eyes are drawn to a newspaper clipping among the stack. It is about six months old, dated in the late spring: *Woman Kidnaps Daughter*. I read quickly, the article describing how *Grace Booth, self-employed, 31*, locked herself and her daughter into a social worker's office and was reported to have said, *I'm going to put the lights out unless you give me back my Britney.* It goes on: *A spokeswoman for the police reported that the child was in grave danger.* The newspaper does not mention any sort of weapon. I stop reading, my heart sinking coldly into my bowels.

Behind me, I hear a shuffle, and there stands Grace with a kitchen knife poised at her throat. Her eyes glare determinedly, the lower eyelids filling with tears, and her mouth is clenched so tightly that it appears as though her jaw will somehow break.

13

'My people have a saying: A woman is born when she gives birth.'

Grace stares at me incredulously, the knife tip making a blanched indent in her skin. Soon it will pierce the surface and she will bleed.

I take slow steps towards her. 'God love you, Grace, but the problem with you is that you were born with a face that could never quite solve the puzzle.'

Her mouth trembles and she glares at me silently as though trying to work out what I have just said.

'I know you've thought about it. Putting the lights out. For good.'

A slow trickle of blood leaves the point of the knife, running down the blade.

'But that sort of thing, it's not for you.'

The trickle reaches her fingers clasping the knife.

'Some escape, some take revenge, and others, well, they just take it. Sooner or later, they lower their expectations and reach some sort of compromise.'

'I can't do that.' As she speaks, the knife slips to within an inch or so below her Adam's apple. 'You don't understand. You can't compensate for what they take away.'

'No, my love. The compromise is with yourself.'

'Whose side are you on?' The knife returns to its earlier position.

'You were asleep, weren't you? I told you all that stuff and you slept right through it.'

The knife presses deeper, the trickle of blood growing, branching into two and then three. The blade is dangerously close to her carotid.

'If you were listening you might have heard something. Something that might make you stop.'

As she shakes her head in confusion, the knife serrates the skin at an angle, drawing tiny pinpricks of blood.

'I knew Britney's dad. I served with him.'

She shakes her head more vigorously, her eyes bulging like those of a trapped animal. The blood runs between her fingers. 'I hardly bloody knew him myself. Said he was serving but they all say that, don't they? Told him I was expecting and he done a runner.'

I say, 'Adrian Hartley. Only Allah knows how I loved that man.'

The knife drops to the floor and her body starts to shake uncontrollably. I grab a tea towel off the sink and wrap it around her neck, applying pressure. I gently guide her back up to the bedroom, where I make her sit up in bed, her back against the headboard. She is wide awake and I pour her a large drink. She wants to know everything, 'for Britney's sake, to tell her when she's older'. She tells me they were never in love and I can say it how it was. Propped next to her, my arm around her, I begin at the beginning.

*

'Nature, what makes it different?' bellowed Training Corporal Longbone.

I looked across at the open fields and then back at the woods from where we had come. The long route march, the last of week three, had worn me out. My feet, in boots that were not yet broken in, hurt with every step, and the sweat was still running into my eyes as I stood in formation as though ready for inspection. Around me, the men of Recruit Company C, to which Adrian and I belonged, eased their weight painfully from one leg to the other.

The corporal dug his thumbs into his webbing and paced up and down the line. He was tall, with big shoulders and a strong, boyish face. 'In nature nothing is straight. Not a blade of grass, not a twig; everything is bent, fucked.'

He stopped at me and extended a hand to finger the collar of my khaki shirt. 'In the field nothing is black,' for a moment his eyes caught mine, 'or white. Remember it well, in the field it could save your life.'

Without warning, the corporal threw himself down and began to wrench clumps of long grass out of the ground, stuffing it into his webbing, around his weapon, pack and helmet. He pulled elastic bands out of his pocket and strapped leaves and twigs around his arms and legs. Then, like a tribesman, he smeared black camo, from a lipstick-like device, across his face.

'On my command, close your eyes, count to ten and open them,' he ordered. 'No peeking or I'll have you on a fucking charge. Go.'

I listened to the light thud of his footsteps as I counted, but after four they were imperceptible. Opening my eyes, I scanned the field, but Longbone was no longer visible. I looked up at the Yorkshire sky, blue and dotted with cotton wool clouds like a child's painting. One of the other recruits reported movement at nine o'clock but no one else could confirm it.

Then I heard a brief war cry, and directly ahead of us the corporal sprang to his feet. A haphazard mixture of man and vegetation, he ran towards us – towards me, I felt – his rifle extended before him: 'Bang. Bang. Bang.' He stopped and caught his breath.

'That was twenty yards. Machine-gun fire is accurate at over five hundred yards. A sniper could be a mile away.' He looked around at us. 'Fall out, buddy up – I want to see you all camo up.'

'I spotted him,' said Adrian, tucking small branches of heather into the rear of my webbing, 'at twelve o'clock.'

'Why didn't you say?'

'He's the corporal,' he said.

'Corporal, sir,' I said, turning to Longbone. He was sitting on his haunches, about five yards away, smoking a cigarette.

'Recruit Khan?'

'Where do we get camo from?'

He reached into a tunic pocket and pulled out the camo stick, squeezing it in his giant fist. I watched his face change; it softened, almost as though he was about to laugh, and then froze into a stern expression. 'You serious, Recruit Khan?'

I shrugged my shoulders.

'Do you think you need it, Recruit Khan?'

The hairs on the back of my neck stood up. Again I shrugged.

'Shrug your shoulders at me once more and I'll carve them off you – you fucking Paki.' He spun the camo stick between his fingers. The entire company had stopped and they stared at me. I looked away, wiping the sweat from my brow.

The corporal jumped up like a gymnast onto his feet. 'Listen up!' he cried in his usual booming voice. 'Let's see who was paying attention in class this morning. Does our quota of Paki,' he coughed, 'Recruit Akram Khan, does he require camo paint?'

There was a long silence, broken finally by Adrian's voice. 'Corporal, sir, camo not only makes our colour less visible but it breaks up the distinct outline of the human face.'

The other recruits laughed. The corporal drew on his cigarette, staring at Adrian through narrowed eyes. 'Recruit Hartley, are you a homo?'

Adrian said nothing.

'Do you love the arse of another man?'

There was silence.

'Answer me, Recruit, or I'll have you on a fucking charge.'

'No, Corporal, sir.'

'I love my wife and I love England. Do you?'

'Yes, Corporal, sir.'

'You love my wife?' The corporal's voice rose into a crescendo.

Adrian opened his mouth. I stared at him, willing him to shut it. 'No fucking way.' He looked at me and then again at the corporal, and crouching to tear at a clump of grass in the ground he half whispered, 'But that Paki, he'd have you.'

There was a hushed silence and I could hear the wind whistling loudly through the trees. Recruit Company C stood perfectly still and looked expectantly at the corporal. Longbone's face flushed pink. He dropped the butt of his cigarette, ground it underfoot and then stared at it. Finally, after what seemed like minutes, he said to Adrian, 'He'd have you, Training Corporal Longbone, sir.'

He turned to the others and clapped his hands. 'Okay, not only do we have to look like the field but to blend in we also have to smell like it. Any ideas?'

As we watched, the corporal's face contorted in concentration. Then a wet patch grew at his groin and urine splashed below the hem of his combat trousers onto his boots. He smiled. 'Pissing in numbers, on my command: one, two, three, piss.'

'Dickhead, you'll get us both killed,' I muttered. The grass at Adrian's feet, now wet, glistened deep green. 'You had no right telling the corporal I'd have him.' I bristled with anger and fear at what the corporal might do next.

Adrian, who fought anyone put in front of him, just didn't get it. 'You ungrateful Paki.'

'You've made it worse.' I turned away.

'You *could* have him,' he said, spinning me around to face him. 'You could fucking smash him.'

'Do you dare?' I glanced towards the corporal.

He shook his head. 'It's your fight.'

'If I had to fight. Well, like you say, no pain. But I'd have to believe it would achieve something,' I said.

Adrian put a fist up before his face and stared at it, slowly nodding.

'You remember that kid Dax?' I said. 'You even beat him up.'

He nodded guiltily, withdrawing his fist to his side.

'Were you there when they all had him?' I asked.

'I had detention,' said Adrian boastfully. 'Besides, I fight alone.'

I gazed into the far distance, at a pattern of white streaks in the sky left behind by an aeroplane. 'I'd fight the corporal if I knew Dax was watching.'

'There was something special about Dax, wasn't there?' he continued.

'He let on that he couldn't cry.'

'I remember now. That was his weak point,' said Adrian softly.

'Something like that.'

'That bastard,' he gestured towards the corporal, who was helping a recruit with his face paint, 'he's got a weak point.'

'You reckon?'

'I know.'

'What is it?'

He shrugged his shoulders.

'Well, that's helpful,' I said.

'Seriously,' said Adrian, 'if you haven't discovered any obvious weak point then try the throat. A finger's width above the bulge of the Adam's apple. He won't get up for a day.'

'Forget about it. Like you said, he's the corporal.'

'Sure, but if you do, think *Dax. . . throat, Dax. . . throat,* and aim for a finger-width above the Adam's apple. Throw a wild punch in the air with your left, and for a split second he'll look up and his throat will be fully extended, and at precisely that moment just fucking smash it – fingers, knuckles, lunge with your teeth if you fucking have to. If you don't put enough feeling into it then you'll just wind him and make him angrier and he'll smash you proper, so get it right first time. You got that?'

'Recruit Khan.' The corporal stood a couple of yards away. I looked at him, wondering if he had heard the exchange between Adrian and me, and my heart sank. He shook his head and raised his eyebrows. 'You Pakis, you really are hung like niggers, put it away at once.'

I put a hand to my wet crotch and looked down. Confused, I looked back up at the corporal. I was about to say that my cock wasn't out but he turned away, laughing. Suddenly I got it. The joke was about me looking for my cock. They all laughed, even Adrian. I stared at the ground and couldn't help but laugh too.

On the corporal's order, we marched in formation to a nearby field and formed a neat queue outside a small wooden building not unlike a garden shed. Three steps led up to a door on one side and three steps led out of a door on the other. Cut into one wall was a long perspex window. Inside, I could see a small desk with a metal chair either side of it.

'Gas masks,' instructed the corporal.

Our gas mask cases hung like a boxy aberration on the outside of our webbing. I reached for mine, slipped it on and tightened the straps. It felt like an imposition, like a great black rubber hand clamping itself across my face. The trick, we had learnt, was to settle into a pattern of slow, controlled breathing. *Breathing at rest.* It was bearable if you were *breathing at rest.*

Briefly opening the hut door, the corporal threw in a grenade-like pellet of CS gas. 'You'll enter when you're commanded to, one at a time. Once inside, you will feel guilty for making the others wait. Understood?'

'Yes, Corporal, sir,' we croaked through the resistance of our gas masks.

The corporal slipped on his own mask and as he opened the door to go in dense white clouds of gas escaped, caught in the wind and billowed upwards into the atmosphere. Despite the mask, the gas stung my eyes. I tightened the straps as much as I could bear, the rubber digging into my flesh. Longbone took in the first recruit, Binnington. With the thick smoke inside the shed, we could see nothing through the window. After about a minute, the exit door opened and Binnington fell out, throwing himself onto the grass, coughing and screaming. His gas mask dangled off his arm.

The corporal stepped out of the hut and closed the door behind him, then took off his gas mask and stood over Binnington. 'Get up, get up now, and stand still with your arms spread out.'

Binnington continued to roll around on the grass, clutching at his face.

The corporal shook his head. 'If you rub it into your eyes you will suffer. Stand up, Recruit Binnington, that's a fucking order.'

The corporal turned to us. Behind him, Binnington, foaming at the mouth, staggered to his feet. His face was bright red, his eyes bloodshot and tears streamed out of them. A neat arc of vomit escaped his mouth and met the grass.

'Man up. Remember to stand still with your arms out. Let the wind do the work. Understood?'

'Yes, Corporal, sir,' we collectively replied.

Longbone took in the next nervous recruit. After about a minute the door opened. Clappison jumped the steps, landing awkwardly on the grass. He got to his feet and ran across the field screaming, his arms held out. The next one went in, and the next. Eventually, as the first recruits in began to recover, sitting on the grass looking thoughtful but relieved, I had the idea that it mightn't be so bad after all.

'No pain,' I heard Adrian say as the corporal stood by the door, gesturing for me to go in. He shut the door behind us. Inside, the white smoke was dense, but close up the visibility was surprisingly good and I could see the corporal clearly as we each took a chair. Looking at his watch, he motioned for me to remove my mask. I took a deep breath and, whispering the words 'Bismillah ir-Rahman ir-Rahim', I prised it off, then put it on the table in front of me.

'Name?'

The effect of the gas wasn't immediate. For a few seconds I felt okay. 'Recruit Akram Khan, Corporal, sir.'

The CS began to sting my eyes and throat.

'Number?'

'Two-four-seven-seven-seven-three-one-one.' The paralysis came in a blunt wave, and suddenly I found it difficult to breathe. My eyes watered and I could feel the white gas forcing its way inside my throat and nose. I coughed, thought about shielding my mouth and eyes with my hands and then thought better of it. 'Cor-por-al, sir.'

The corporal sank back in his chair and looked again at his watch. 'Tell me a joke,' he said.

I was conscious of his eyes staring at me through his gas mask, cold and determined. The gas seemed to have blocked my throat and although I tried, no words would come out. My mind scrambled to think of a joke. I thought I might pass out or collapse; the overwhelming sensation was of burning from the inside out, and suddenly I was afraid I would die. I reached for my mask and tried to get to my feet. I felt the corporal's thick hands clamp over mine.

'Tell me a fucking joke,' he repeated slowly.

I screwed my eyes tightly shut but the gas seemed to be inside, between the lens and the eyelid, burning at my eyeballs, and closing them made it worse. 'Knock, knock,' I said and then coughed, letting more of the gas into my lungs. My chest was on fire and heavy as though weighing me down.

'Tell me a joke.'

I thought, this is where I will die.

Suddenly I felt the corporal's heavy hands grab the straps at the rear of my webbing. Opening the hut door, he flung me out.

*

On Friday evenings and taxicabs queue patiently, far into the distance, along the long broad streets that made up the perimeter of Catterick Garrison.

'It's cheaper by bus,' I said.

'We're earning, aren't we?' said Adrian.

We nodded at the guard at the gatehouse and exited onto the street.

In our first week we had been issued with a bank card, and I had been to a cash machine at the Navy, Army and Air Force Institute and looked up my balance. It was hard to believe that for this, boys messing around, the army was paying money into an account in my name.

'It's a waste,' I said, following Adrian into the back of a waiting car.

Richmond was like no other town I had seen. The houses were made of solid brown stone and the narrow streets, many of which were cobbled, were hilly and steep and swept into a curled distance as though hiding a secret. There were more pubs in one road than I had seen in my entire life, and young men milled about on the ancient narrow pavement, crawling from pub to pub, searching for local girls. The squaddies, who were always in groups and outnumbered the locals, were immediately recognizable: short-cropped hair, moleskin desert boots, tight blue jeans with pockets bulging with money, starch-pressed shirts, and most distinguishing of all, an easy swagger and erect posture.

We found a table in an old neglected pub. A handful of locals crowded around the bar. The landlady, brisk and efficient, lacked charm, but in the absence of music or slot machines, it was quiet, and so for me an easy choice.

'The corporal, he's out to get you,' said Adrian, draining half his pint in one long glug. His glass returned to the table with a click.

I turned my full glass between my fingers on the scratched wooden table. 'It's normal, I bet there's always one he singles out. It's psychological.'

Adrian drank the remainder of his pint and then belched.

'It makes the whole company work harder,' I added.

'I think it's because you're a Paki.'

I shook my head. I put my glass to my lips and tried to drink as much of it as I could in one go. It rose quickly up my throat and behind my nose, stinging where the gas had earlier, and I put it down.

'As far as he's concerned it's his army,' said Adrian. 'He's just like my dad. Why does every fucker think he owns England?' He stood up. 'Another? Or shall we go?'

'Steady, we've got all night.'

'Yeah, but we've got to get in the mood.' Adrian did a little bicycle motion with his arms. As he loomed over me across the table, his number one haircut made him look like his dad.

'If I have to fight him I've got a secret weapon,' I said.

He put down his empty glass and looked at me. 'Dax?'

I shook my head. 'You, you cunt. You'd jump in if he was killing me!'

'Won't need to. Throat. Just remember one word: throat.'

In the next pub there was nowhere left to sit, but we found space by the bar and leant against it. I looked around for black faces but saw none. A troop of squaddies at the far end were raucously singing an army song, and girls dressed in tight, brightly coloured frocks were sitting at a bench against the rear wall, looking on bemused. Sergeants or sergeant majors, distinguishable from the men by their age and handlebar moustaches, drank quietly with their wives.

'We should chat up some girls,' said Adrian, shouting to be heard over the din of conversation and music. I looked around. There were boys with girls, girls with girls, many in groups, some laughing, some leaning into each other in conspiratorial conversation. A clutch of the girls were dancing on the spot, their wine glasses swaying carelessly, while men looked on. It was difficult to tell who was with whom.

Adrian kept his eyes on the entrance. After some time, two girls walked in and stood by the door, scanning the room as though wondering whether to come in further.

'Dare you,' said Adrian, staring at the girls. Before I could answer he was making his way towards them. I could only follow.

'Hey,' he said, 'I'd love to buy you a drink. Let me guess, wine? White wine?'

The girls looked at each other and shrugged their shoulders, but they didn't say no. Not waiting for a refusal, Adrian headed to the bar, leaving me with them.

'Hello.' I extended a hand. 'I'm Akram, we're recruits at—'

'You look like it,' one of the girls said.

'We're not desperate, you know,' said the other.

I offered my best smile. 'I'm harmless,' I looked over one shoulder, 'but my mate, I can't vouch for him.'

They laughed and introduced themselves as Wendy and Dawn. They seemed surprised when I again offered to shake hands. Wendy was blonde and taller than her friend, with a thin face. She wore a short yellow skirt and cropped red top. As though in deliberate contrast, Dawn had short dark hair and wore a plain green dress that covered her arms and buttoned to the neck. She had small eyes and a freckled button nose that made her look the friendlier of the two. Unsure what to say, I shuffled awkwardly on my feet, and put away my unshaken hand. Hoping that Adrian would be back quickly, I glanced over at the bar and spotted him waiting to be served.

Dawn bent towards me to make sure she was heard. 'What's it like?' The soft satin of her sleeve brushed lightly against the back of my hand, and the scent of her perfume lingered around me.

I shrugged my shoulders. Catching myself in a mirror fixed to the wall, I straightened. 'I was gassed at thirteen hundred hours.'

Wendy and Dawn looked at each other and giggled. 'Your friend, him too?' asked Wendy.

I nodded. 'But I was in for a minute longer.'

'Was it a competition?' said Wendy, laughing.

I shook my head. 'I got singled out.'

Dawn leant in and briefly clutched my wrist. 'You be careful, this here is Yorkshire.'

I was startled to be touched by a girl. Although she held my arm for only a second, it had left a faint tingling sensation. I nodded. 'It's beautiful, what I've seen of it, and posh.'

'Posh?' The girls looked at each other again and laughed.

'You haven't seen where we're from,' I said.

Adrian returned from the bar balancing drinks on a tray. 'What was that?' He dispensed the drinks and stowed the tray on the floor against the wall.

'Your friend Akram was telling us where you're from,' said Wendy.

'Least said,' he said.

'Where's Ripon in relation to here?' I asked, changing the subject. 'A friend once told me it was the best place in England.'

'What was your friend doing up here?' said Dawn.

'He was fairground,' I said.

'Cogger's Funfair. Next to the fête it's about the most exciting thing that happens around here,' said Wendy drily. 'Stays for a fortnight.' She turned to her friend. 'Camps on Burnham's fields.' Dawn nodded.

'That's it!' I cried excitedly. 'Dax Cogger.'

'Well, if you want to see Dax I expect Cogger's Funfair will be Yorkshire-based about now,' said Dawn.

Adrian opened his mouth to say something. I silenced him with a glance and said to Dawn, 'How would I get there?'

'She'll take you,' said Wendy, nudging Dawn with her elbow. 'Won't you, love?'

Dawn looked at her friend and blushed. She turned to me and smiled nervously. I felt myself redden too.

'He's free Sunday,' said Adrian.

'Go on,' said Wendy to her friend.

'Just the two of us?' said Dawn, looking put upon. 'This weekend?'

The girls finished their drinks and left soon after, saying they had to meet friends. Dawn gave me her mother's telephone number on a slip of paper, in case I was put on a charge and prevented from going. It seemed quite a precise thing to do and I wondered if she had previously known a recruit, perhaps a former boyfriend. She said she'd borrow her mother's car and agreed to pick me up outside barracks on Sunday at noon.

'You got a date,' said Adrian, breaking the silence that fell upon their departure, 'and she drives a motor.'

'It was when she mentioned the field. Dax was mad about this girl whose dad owned the field. I just want to go, see the field and that. It seems right.'

Adrian shook his head. 'You'd better do that for me when I'm gone.'

'I'll pay homage to Old Hill tower blocks,' I said.

'I hope I'll have staked a claim somewhere better by then.'

'Trick is,' I said, 'never to go backwards.'

After we'd had a few more drinks, each one at a different pub, last orders were rung. Not wanting to join one of the queues outside the many night-clubs, lines of rowdy squaddies with disappointingly few girls breaking up their number, we flagged down a taxi and rode through the dark rural night back to the Navy, Army and Air Force Institute on base. Like prisoners, we had been allowed into the NAAFI only once previously, to purchase sweets, chocolates and, for those who wanted them, telephone cards and cigarettes. There might be army girls at the NAAFI; if not, at least it had a late licence and the beer was cheap.

In contrast to the pubs in Richmond, the NAAFI was a new building with decked pine lining the walls, ceiling and floor. The planks were randomly studded with knots, and standing by the door narrowing my eyes, the room looked as though it had been peppered with gunfire. The bar was largely empty, and at the far end of the cavernous room, soldiers played at pool tables and attended to slot machines. A pair sat in opposition, playing chess. A lone figure, dressed in a green T-shirt and jeans and with a Yorkshire flat cap at a slant on his head, slouched over the bar, his back stooped in a perfect quarter-circle. Above him, behind the counter, hung a large framed portrait of the Queen.

Adrian and I each took a stool at the other end of the bar.

'Let me buy you a drink.' The man swivelled on his stool and touched the brim of his flat cap. 'And your bum boy,' he said to Adrian, 'what's he having?'

It was Corporal Longbone, his voice slurred. Without waiting for an answer, he turned to the barman. 'Two lagers, and the same again for me.' He returned his attention to the small glass before him, turning it between his fingers.

'Th-thank you, Corporal, sir,' I stammered.

He patted a stool next to him. Adrian and I went over and took a stool on either side of him. 'Don't call me sir, not in here.'

We looked at him. He was obviously drunk, his cheeks flushed and nose strawberry red. His eyes were glazed over, and as he focused on me, they seemed to soften and a thin smile spread across his lips. 'I like to know who I've got in my company,' he said.

The barman put our pints on the counter before us. Swiping away the corporal's empty glass, he replaced it with another of whisky neat.

'Something the matter?' Adrian said to the corporal.

The corporal laughed, exposing strong brown teeth. 'Not in here. Here we're all friends. Here you're one of us.' Leaning over, the corporal briefly put an arm around my shoulder. He stank of sweat and whisky. Adrian rolled his eyes at me. 'Out there,' continued Longbone, 'is the British Army. And you, Recruit Akram Khan, you need to prove yourself worthy of the uniform.'

Adrian's eyes slipped down, fixing on the bulge of the corporal's Adam's apple.

Longbone shook his head and for a long minute he stared at his glass. 'But,' he raised a finger, 'you need to get past me first.' Turning to the portrait of the Queen, he picked up his whisky, took a sip.

'I could have killed Her Maj,' he said, addressing the portrait. 'Truth is, I was just clowning around, but I thought about it.' He turned to me again. 'Would you have done it? Recruit Khan, would you, like me, have acted the clown?'

I reached for my pint and drank half in one go. 'That would be murder.'

'England forever England would never be the same again,' said the corporal.

'But for some,' I said, 'it would be martyrdom.'

'Not for an Englishman,' he said.

'For a Paki, for some, I can see it,' I said.

The corporal nodded. 'It would have made me the most famous person to have ever lived.'

'Some would see you as a hero,' I said.

'Everyone would know where they were the day the Queen died.'

'It would be like the enemy within,' I said.

The corporal drained his glass, signalled the barman for a refill. 'We were standing around these tables having tea and dainty cupcakes and she came up and stood right next to me. I put my hand in my pocket, felt my penknife in there.' He laughed. 'Used it to clean the shit out of my boots. Fucking hell, I thought, how the hell did that get in unnoticed by security? And then it occurred to me, I could fucking have her, I could just lunge at this little old woman, one split second.'

The corporal turned to me, his eyes serious and sober. 'So, lad, just so you know, I can spot a clown.'

*

Early the following morning Corporal Longbone stalked up and down the line, his gaze wandering from the polish on someone's boots to the sparkle of a belt buckle or the starched stiffness of a shirt collar. It was dawn, and despite having had his last drink only a few hours earlier, his eyes were alert and his voice loud and fully awake.

'The good news is we will not be going on a run.' The troop cheered. 'The bad news is that instead we will find a quiet field and have a little fun.' We cheered again. He smiled at a large, bulging canvas bag that he had dropped to the ground. 'Do you understand?'

'Yes, Corporal, sir.'

'If any recruit does not want to take part in the fun he may take the run instead, with my assistant, Lance Corporal Bunce. But you should know that Lance Corporal Bunce was out dancing last night and at this very moment he is cleaning his cock and looking forward to an undisturbed breakfast of bacon and eggs. Does anybody require an escort from the Lance Corporal?'

'No, Corporal, sir.'

We followed him to a field with rugby posts at each end. It was an unremarkable morning with a cool breeze and a mildly grey sky that grew lighter by the minute, almost daylight. We were instructed to form a circle about six yards in diameter and stood rubbing our bodies with our hands for warmth.

Longbone opened the bag and retrieved two pairs of sparring gloves, then threw them at two of our number, seemingly at random. 'Fighting men, gentlemen, is what we are teaching you to become, and God help you if you lose your rifle, your bayonet, all your weaponry and don't realize that you still have your God-given weapon. With our bare hands we can thrust, scrape, gouge, claw, squeeze, chop – and today, ladies, you will punch.'

The pair of recruits had already put on the gloves and begun to shadow box, dancing on their toes. Without prompting they seemed to be working their way into the middle of the circle.

'Each pair will have only one three-minute round. You will find the time quite sufficient. On my first whistle, box. On my second whistle, stop. If I blow the whistle at any time before the three minutes are up you are to cease immediately and go to opposing corners.' He signalled to opposite sides of the circle. 'Understood, Recruit Company C?'

'Yes, Corporal, sir.'

'Are you fighting men, Recruit Company C?'

'Yes, Corporal, sir.'

He blew the whistle, and the boxers, who were now eyeballing each other, got to work. Their leg movements seemed clumsy, and as they circled each other, neither threw a punch that made contact. Both snorted and panted, and after about thirty seconds their pace slowed.

'Come on, ladies, we need a fight.'

Momentarily their punch rate quickened, although the efficiency of contact did not, and their blows barely scraped each other's skin. Looking disgusted, the corporal consulted his watch and blew his whistle. 'Get those gloves off and get out of my fucking sight.'

The second pair stood square on to each other and traded punches. They both bled from the mouth and nose, and their faces turned a purple-red I did not think it possible for a *gora* to be.

The corporal blew his whistle. 'Time. Well done, but you could have circled a bit – the idea is to hit without being hit.'

As he looked around the circle, men shrank away from his gaze. 'Khan and Hartley, you bum boys next.'

I stared at Adrian. Suddenly I saw an image of a boy of about eleven with a snub nose and a gentle face. A boy knocked to the ground, getting up, and smiling as though to say, *This will all be over in a second. Won't it?* Briefly and out of necessity, I hated Adrian. I stepped into the circle and slipped on the gloves. Adrian stood a couple of yards away. He put his gloves up to his face and punched them together, shuffling his feet neatly on the spot. The corporal blew his whistle.

I had barely got my hands up when I took a one-two and my head jerked back. Adrian pulled away, circling. He jumped in with another one-two.

The next time I saw his right coming and leant to my left, but he anticipated and his glove glanced across my brow. He was hitting hard but not as hard as I knew he could. I circled, jogging backwards, but Adrian cut me off, one-two-three, the last one to my body, hard enough to make a good sound but not enough to wind me. Adrian was a complete boxer, I thought, as he caught me again and again.

The corporal blew his whistle and we stopped. Panting, I stared at the grass. Longbone addressed me. 'You fucking clown. If you don't hit back, I'm going to put you on a fucking charge.' He blew the whistle again.

I launched myself at Adrian, my arms flailing wildly. He stepped to one side and I stumbled past him into the surrounding circle of men. Half blind with sweat, I felt the hands of a recruit push me back into the middle. I could hear encouragement and obscenities. This, I thought, as I saw again the boy with the gentle face, is a scene from Dax's murder. Rubbing the sweat from my eyes, I refocused on Adrian. He was smiling. His feet were no longer dancing. Instead, he was walking about, circling me with a swagger. It was the swagger of the skinheads outside the Mash Tun pub. He leant in once or twice, as though to throw a punch. He was teasing me. I could see the other men yelling, but the blows had now rendered me deaf, with only a loud, incessant buzzing in my ears. Adrian stepped forward again; this time he punched me neatly, a right cross in the face. Temporarily blinded, I saw a black background with horizontally moving stars, and it was silent, almost pleasing, like falling asleep. He stepped back and with a rolling haymaker, one I could see coming but do nothing to avoid, socked me in the belly. I doubled over, winded.

Longbone blew his whistle and looked at his watch. I panted, my eyes appealing to his wrist. He looked back up at me. 'Khan, you've got one minute to make an impression, otherwise I'm going to fucking have you on a charge.' I knew the minimum charge would be cancelled Sunday leave. 'Hartley, you're holding back – if you don't fucking finish him off you will be offering him your arse in the jailhouse.' He blew his whistle.

I looked at Adrian. He wore a sly grin and his eyes, colder than ever, reminded me of his father's. I could see a chain swinging from his hips and the silhouetted figures of my mother and father in the street, defiant but helpless. With a roar I swung a left at Adrian. He turned on his toes and slipped to one side, raising his hands in the air, gloating to his audience. He wouldn't knock me out. He'd take the charge instead. I knew that. Or did I? I swung again, only to miss and receive two to the head. I circled back around quickly, behind Adrian. He turned to look at me. He smiled, his nostrils flared. I could see his right, about shoulder height, tucked behind his left which guarded his face; the right trembled as it readied for a knockout blow.

I looked upwards, fixing momentarily on a patch of sky. '*Bismillah*.' He raised his eyes, looking for what I had seen. For a split second his neck was extended and I landed my best right, what Adrian would have called a straight right cross. I felt something buckle under my glove. He fell to the ground, clutching at his throat, his legs jerking like an epileptic.

Repeatedly the corporal blew hard on his whistle. I bent over Adrian. 'Cunt, you let me win?'

'I told you,' he wheezed, 'you could have Longbone.'

I turned to face the corporal and glared at him. Putting a glove to my mouth, I licked it, tasting leather, sweat, and the iron in Adrian's blood.

*

Gripping the steering wheel, Dawn stared at the road ahead. With a hand casually placed against my chin, I tried to conceal the worst of the bruising around my mouth. I looked across at her, hypnotized by her silver dangly earrings. She turned briefly and smiled, the freckles on her nose illuminated by a shaft of light through the trees.

'You been beaten up?' she said. 'Told you to be careful.'

I put both hands across my mouth, picking at a scab. 'Funfair arrived?'

She nodded. 'Spoke to Lucy Burnham. She's at college and popped into the chemist's. I'm an assistant there.'

'Lucy Burnham? I assumed Burnham's fields was a place name.'

'It is, sort of,' said Dawn.

'You needn't worry, when you tell me to be careful.'

'How did you meet this Dax? Great name, by the way, fun.'

'I can handle myself.'

'Wendy said you could have made up the whole thing just to get me to—'

'He's dead,' I interrupted.

She was silent for a moment. 'I'm sorry.' I could see her reflection in the windscreen, confused and sort of panicked. It disappeared abruptly as we passed into a shaded part of the road. When we motored back into the sunshine, Dawn seemed somehow different. Her grip on the steering wheel had loosened, and her face in profile was less determined, as though she no longer knew the destination.

'I figured you were going to see him?' Her voice trembled.

'I'm sorry, I've upset you.'

'I just feel a bit put upon. Misled.'

I shook my head. 'Do you think you can truly be happy only once in your life, at one time, in one place?'

She glanced at me uncertainly. It was the same look as she'd worn in the pub when her friend cajoled her to go out with me. 'Was your friend Dax happy here?'

'He was in love with a girl who brought him eggs.'

She laughed. 'That could have been Lucy!'

'I don't expect she will remember him,' I said. 'Strange, how things join up.'

'She might,' she said. 'We could stop by the farmhouse. If she's home we could mention it?'

I said, 'His soul, and I know there is such a thing, it's here.'

Dawn put her hand on my wrist and squeezed gently. Her touch no longer felt exciting the way it had in the pub. 'You've got gentle eyes. You must be kind.' She smiled, an enigmatic smile, the way only a girl could, with plumped, soft cheeks and narrowed, translucent eyes.

'I'm not up to meeting Lucy.' The view outside was of an undulating road blanketed deep inside a lush green. 'This place is as good as anywhere. Why don't we stop here?'

She pulled into a layby and without a word I stepped out and walked along the verge. She followed. 'You're hard work, you,' she called, catching me up.

'Can we just find a spot?' I looked around. We were in a narrow lane bordered by hedges and forest on both sides. Slipping through a gap in the trees, we emerged into a field of long grass.

'And a bit daft for a tough soldier type,' she added.

We sat down on the grass. 'How come this field isn't ploughed?' I said.

'Resting,' said Dawn.

I said nervously, 'I've never had a girlfriend.'

'This could be a Burnham field,' said Dawn. 'They've got land all over.'

'How can you tell?'

'Usually, you can spot the cut of someone's field.' She looked out into the distance. The field sloped steeply downwards, ending abruptly like the edge of a cliff.

'Can we imagine it's the field Dax knew?' I said.

Dawn nodded. We sat, listening to the occasional call of a bird and the rustle of small mammals in the hedge.

Focusing on a patch of white sky, I raised my hands to my face and said a prayer for Dax, followed by the incantation '*Bismillah ir-Rahman ir-Rahim*'. I finished by swiping my hands down from my forehead to my chin.

'Strangest date I've ever been on,' said Dawn. 'You're not right, you soldier types. I've seen it before.'

'It's no use,' I said, wanting to cry, 'being here, knowing he's dead. Murdered. I thought I'd sense him. Stupid, isn't it?'

Dawn got to her feet. Small white stones in her earrings caught the sun. 'You're angry?'

I nodded. 'I still mourn him.'

'Was he a good friend?'

I shook my head.

'An old friend?'

Again, I shook my head.

She looked at me with irritation. 'Come on, I'll drive you back.'

*

'I'll take Khan,' commanded Corporal Longbone.

I snarled at him. It was the live fire exercise, a series of targets divided by obstacles. We were divided into groups of eight, each man accompanied by a company corporal or sergeant, who would keep a close eye on him and, more importantly, his weapon, which was loaded. I would win it. For Dax.

The starter pistol sounded and the exercise commenced. I ran to the first station, my rifle held pointing straight ahead, magazine loaded with precisely ten 7.62mm live rounds. The corporal ran alongside me. 'Fuck it up, Recruit Khan. It's the last big one and you're going to blow it.' He was laughing, his eyes wild. 'You're not English, you're a fucking clown. Do something, you pussy, don't just take it.'

Loudly he collected a bolus of spit in his mouth. I saw it, as though in slow motion, as it shot out of his pursed lips. I watched its trajectory as the wind carried it across my eyes and away. Focusing straight ahead, I stopped at the first station, dropped into the prone position, trained the sights of my rifle and discharged one round at the pop-up target. It fell down. I got back to my feet, slung the SLR over my shoulder, climbed a triangular wooden obstacle, stopped at station number two and fired from the standing position, one round and the target went down. I ran, Longbone's boots clipping my heels, and then dropped down and crawled through a tunnel, my weapon held six inches off the ground in front of me. I hit the other side and made it to station number three. From the kneeling position, I hit the target in one. Beginning to enjoy it, I commenced the long run to station number four.

A punch landed on my shoulder, making me stumble. I turned reflexively to look at the corporal, and just then my right foot sank into a shallow ditch in the rutted ground. I fell. I saw the corporal's mouth open but didn't hear the words. My rifle slipped out of my hands and then I heard a sickening sound, *bum*, as it discharged one round randomly into the landscape. While I watched, my SLR landed nearby with a thud.

A whistle blew. The corporal was screaming at the top of his voice, 'Stop! Stop. Stop. Unload!'

Recruit Company C froze wherever they were and unclipped their magazines. They stood, holding their ammunition in one hand and presenting a clear chamber in the other. I felt their eyes on me, and heard hissing.

The corporal was still screaming, his face inches from mine, his spit showering my face. 'You fucking clown! That stray shot could have killed somebody. You're out. You're out. You're going home!'

He retrieved my now muddy rifle from a shallow stream, unclipped the magazine, which he pocketed, and after turning the SLR sideways to eye its empty chamber, thrust it hard against my chest. 'Get up there and strip your weapon.' He pointed to a small wooden hut about a hundred yards away on a mound overlooking the range. As I limped away, I heard him instruct the others to reload. For a moment I froze with the crazy idea that he was about to command Recruit Company C to shoot me. He blew his whistle, and the troop continued with the live fire exercise.

Against one wall of the hut was a stack of metal ammo boxes. I opened one and ran my hand across a folded belt of sparkling 7.62mms, like neatly lined-up brass pencils. They were cold and smooth. Mounted on a tripod, its barrel pointing at the range, was a general: a general-purpose machine gun.

From my elevated vantage point I scanned the firing range. Recruit Company C ran across it like toy soldiers; reaching a station, they aimed their rifles into the sun and fired at will. *Bam. Bam. Bam.* I placed several heavy ammo cases next to the general and lowered myself behind it. I swung off the cover tray, pulled a heavy ammo belt out of its metal case and laid one end inside a depression in the tray. It fitted nicely. I clicked the cover tray neatly shut and switched the safety to off. The gun felt hard, rigid; it smelt good: of metal, oil and cordite.

Jamming the butt tight into my shoulder and putting my eyes to the flip-up sights, I trained it on the company, the crosshairs searching for the corporal. I adjusted the grouping one click to account for the wind from the right. I was happy.

I heard footsteps behind me. Unusually, the corporal spoke in a sort of low stammer. 'Recruit Khan, you?' Tightening my grip on the general, I turned to look at him. He was panting, his arms pinned to his sides and his eyes wide. 'What the fuck are you doing with the general?'

I offered a nonchalant smile.

'Hang on.' His face became a frozen white mask. 'Is that thing loaded?'

Slowly I swung the general towards him and said, 'First rule of the firing range, guard your ammo. They're going to have you for this.' The sights were now trained on him. 'Dare me?'

His eyes darted between my eyes and the tip of the barrel and his chest rose and fell quickly. His jaw trembled and I laughed. I sprang to my feet, knocking the general. Its barrel swung on its tripod pivot before coming to rest, and the corporal dived for cover.

'Who's the clown?' I said, standing over his prone body. 'Who's the fucking Englishman and who's the fucking clown?'

'Fuck,' said the corporal, slowly getting to his feet and dusting himself off. 'Fuck me, Khan, at this rate you'll make best recruit.'

*

'It gets worse now,' I tell Grace, her head on my shoulder.

There is blood in her hair, seeping through the makeshift tea towel bandages on her neck, on her arms, between her fingers, and I can feel it drying against my ear and down towards my chest. In places it congeals into dots of iron suspended in dark red slurry. At its borders the red is drying black.

'How did he die?'

With a finger, where Grace's scapula meets her shoulder, I trace concentric patterns in the thick blood. 'Our troop was on patrol. He got hit.'

'Could they not save him? Didn't they try?'

I shake my head. I put the finger to my nose and inhale the scent of cold steel. Closing my eyes helps me picture the scene. I can feel the chill off the mountains and smell the flowers and the rot and open drains. I can see our troop pass through a field, and then another, at our backs the moonlit night. Lieutenant Lovell is at the head, speaking softly to his girlfriend, a comms operator back at base. I walk behind him, trying my best to avoid mines, putting my feet exactly where he put his. I remember thinking, it is good of the lieutenant to take point. By rights it is my job, it is the sergeant who takes the mine. I hear the light fall of my boots on the earth and feel a cold sweat on my brow. Beyond the occasional call of an owl, all is quiet.

Lieutenant Lovell gave the halt and the lads settled down to brew tea. They needed no excuse for a brew. Private Hartley padded up to me and, with a twist of his head, indicated for me to follow.

When we were out of earshot of the others, he said, 'You thirsty, Sarge?'

'No, lad.'

'Me neither.'

'Then let's carry on half a k.'

We were rarely alone and I enjoyed his banter, so we scouted, taking a route we knew. After twenty minutes we were about a k and a half from the others.

The day's first *azan* started up from a distant loudspeaker, '*Allahu Akbar.*' I pictured a turbaned mullah standing somewhere nearby reciting into a microphone. It resonated through the languid mountain air of the Hindu Kush, puncturing the silence. It had been merciful, the absence of overnight contact. Terry were out there, smoking opium in dugouts and on rooftops, doing nothing more than quietly taking our measure.

'Can't smoke enough today, boss.' From a pocket Adrian produced a box of cigarettes, a blue packet branded with the English word *sky*. Delicately, with thick, tanned fingers, he pulled one out and rapped the butt end against the box.

The *azan* had for a few seconds been solitary, and now it was joined by another starting up from the beginning, and a few seconds later yet another, until all around was a cacophony of competing calls, from loudspeakers large and small, mounted on poles and in minarets, near and distant, a chaotic and disassociated shrill.

Putting my hands over my ears, I said, 'Noisy bastard mullahs. I'd cut their fucking throats, all but one.'

Adrian stood still, blowing smoke out of his nostrils and rubbing the stubble on his chin. 'You might be the sarge but you're lowering the tone. Sarge, do you know about the Night of Power? It's suspicious, like a birthday for Muslims.'

'Let's not stand around,' I said.

'Sarge,' Adrian acknowledged.

'I think you mean *auspicious*.'

The sun was rising, a thin yellow glow spreading across a snowy summit. Between the peaks and our position several kilometres across the plain was a dry landscape of rock and brown earth, still dark and invisible in the shadow of the mountains, like a void yet to be sketched in. Gradually the fresh light brightened into a syrupy-yellow clarity that you could almost touch, as though Allah was saying, *Here you go, lads, behold the earth*. It brought a new smell too, replacing the pungent night-blooming jasmine: the smell of open fires and baking flatbread mixed with gas from engines – tuk-tuks, buses, taxis, Suzukis – starting up at the chowk in the nearby village. And it seemed that the smell came first, reminding me with a jolt, as I looked around as though for the first time, that in a few minutes it would be daylight. Already the air was warm.

Behind me I heard again the word 'Sarge'. There was only Adrian and me, but it didn't sound like him. The voice was low, summoned with great effort.

I turned. Adrian stood a few feet away, his gaze fixed on me. His cigarette dropped to the ground. Slowly, his face tightened. 'Sarge,' he said again, louder, his voice a sharp cry.

As though doing a calculation in my head, I traced back to the moment before he had dropped the cigarette, before he had called to me. Had there been a click of metal? At his perfectly still left boot a spark flared abruptly and worked its way around the rubber sole, like a small firecracker labouring under a great weight, and then, before either of us had time to avert our eyes, take cover or say another word, it died out. For what seemed like minutes we stood perfectly still. Adrian looked as though he was in great pain, his fists clenched at his sides and eyes now screwed tightly shut. I listened to the sound of his laboured breath.

I slid my rifle and daypack gently to the ground. I took one step forward and then, with one knee bent, my arms circling his waist, I summoned all the strength I possessed and heaved him off. I fell backwards to the ground, the great weight of Adrian landing awkwardly on me, although thankfully my helmet and shoulders took much of the impact.

Wriggling out from under the weight of Private Hartley, I stood up, picked up my rifle and rubbed my chin where Adrian's helmet had struck me. Under the short beard it felt hot and raw but the skin wasn't broken.

'*La ilaha il Allah*': the final *azan* came suddenly to a close. Adrian sat where he had fallen, his head bowed and his hands clamped over his eyes as though trying to block out the world. He rocked back and forth, muttering to himself.

'That's why Terry call it the Night of Power,' I said. I could feel the after-rush of adrenaline pumping through my chest, and my hands trembled. Adrian looked up through a gap in his fingers. For the first time I noticed how closely bitten his fingernails were, reduced to thin arcs. 'I understand it now. After all those years at the mosque I think finally I get it. Why they call it power. Terry say that for one night a year the Angel Gabriel mingles with us on earth, and tonight a Terry angel has saved your legs. Why not? Terry say anything is possible.'

Adrian stood up, wiping the tears from his eyes. He panted, the sweat dripping off him, and stared cautiously at the spot where he had earlier stood. 'Was that an IED?'

'It was just a fuse devoid of charge.' I wiped my clammy brow. 'I had a hunch. . .'

He looked at me, his expression like that of a child, a mixture of confusion and disappointment.

I said, 'It couldn't have been an IED, it didn't sound right.'

'You know it can happen,' he said, 'when they fail to go off.'

'You will find that the earth around it hasn't been dug. It's just a metal plate attached to a fuse. A warning.'

He shook his head. His chest heaved inside his body armour.

'I'll prove it.' Before Adrian could react, I jumped onto the plate. Adrian fell backwards, shielding his eyes, and then peered out from behind his hands, his face fixed in horror.

I stood perfectly still on the plate and laughed. 'Now, cunt, pick up your shit and let's go, and don't forget there's a reason why I'm the fucking sarge.'

'You daft bastard.' He shook his head. 'I didn't have to know.'

I nodded. 'Night of fucking Power. As kids at the mosque we'd stay up all night, rocking back and forth pretending to read the Koran, and every last one of us half expected to see the Angel Gabriel.'

With shaky hands he lit up another cigarette and inhaled deeply. 'That angel must be looking out for me.'

'Anything is possible – on the Night of Power, they kept saying, anything is possible.'

Adrian said slowly, 'I get it.'

'This one year my mother pointed to the window and wailed like a banshee. Her eyes were bloodshot and tears ran down her face. Her head-scarf was all torn and her hair was crazy, wild, and she turned to me and said, "Pray harder, you of all people, you really need to see for yourself."'

'Terry do that, don't they,' said Adrian thoughtfully, 'pray hard.'

'No fucking use,' I said.

He threw his cigarette to the ground, stubbed it out under a boot. 'What would you do if you saw the angel?'

I gave a sinister laugh. 'Well, Gabriel is a man, so no use to me, but as you say, anything is possible.'

Adrian turned to me, in his eyes a mixture of incredulity and relief. 'Really, for a second or two, really I thought I was goners.'

'You're right on one point,' I said. 'I have heard it can happen, when it's not wired properly. There was a lad from Bravo Company who got charred feet. Went on bragging. Bad taste.'

'I felt like crying.' He looked down at the burnt boot. 'I could get myself a new pair from stores.'

Crouching down, I retrieved a map from my daypack. I took a pen from my tunic pocket, one of those that could switch to six different colours. After finding our exact position on the map, I turned to Adrian, my pen poised at the ready. 'What colour? Blue, green, black, red, orange or purple?'

Adrian laughed. 'Red. . . no, black,' he said.

'Black it is. Black-Spot Hartley, I'm going to name it after you. I'll take it to the lieutenant and he'll get it copied back to HQ where they keep an archive and maps. How do you feel about that?'

He shook his head, raising a foot off the ground and staring at it. 'No, I won't change them – these ones are lucky.'

Superstitiously, I wore prayer beads around my neck, lucky beads, or Terry beads as the lads called them, and out of instinct I touched them. 'What you should know is that on an IED the fuse is soldered to the charge, and you would think they're joined, wouldn't you, and that the join is true, as true as life and death, but you'd be wrong. There is a distance between them,' I paused, 'a potential distance through which you could slip an atom, what they call a metaphorical distance.'

'Goners, man!' Adrian still had one hand clamped to his head. He peered over me, his lower eyelids swollen and black with soot. 'That's the truth.'

In black ink I scratched the position of Black-Spot Hartley onto the map. 'Private Hartley, as the senior NCO I want your opinion.'

Adrian got down next to me. Rocking on his haunches, he put on a serious face.

'You always seem to know what's going on down below.'

He appeared confused but nodded just the same.

'In *Friends* do you reckon Ross will forgive Rachel?'

'Rachel had sex with Joey,' he said brightly.

'We only saw them kiss.'

Adrian clutched himself and rocked with laughter. 'Well, if she made Joey use a condom, Ross might forgive her.'

'Do you want to watch a bit before shut-eye?'

'Seen it, Sarge. Next episode moves on to a different story, leaves it open, cliffhanger like.'

I looked at Adrian with a frown. 'You're going to spoil my day, Private Hartley.'

Adrian pointed to the map in my hands and smiled. 'What are the green crosses for?'

'Terry positions,' I said. Six green crosses made over the course of the patrol coincided exactly with those made the previous night.

'Terry's busy looking over his fat hairy belly at the Grim Reaper giving him head.'

I said without looking up, 'Better not take it for granted, Private.'

'Sarge?' He shook his head for what seemed like a long time, as though deep in thought. 'It's spiritual.' He squeezed his palms together and squinted hard at the join between them. 'The true distance between the fuse and the charge is spiritual.'

I pretended to yawn. 'It would have got you that tan you're after.'

'Panic tanning, Sarge.' He stood up and curled a bicep, the tension spreading upwards through his neck and terminating at his clenched chin above which he tried to squeeze out a smile. 'For my going-home body.'

The sun had risen quickly, and at both east and west, as though bearing down upon us, stood the peaks of the Hindu Kush, close enough that during the night patrol we had shivered under their icy weight. Once illuminated they seemed friendlier, as though painted in as a magnificent backdrop to the movie we sometimes felt we were making. If in years to come we forgot everything else, we would always remember the mountains, against which we posed for photographs during the day whenever a new and unexpected vista opened up, and the cold, the white-cold starlit breath through which we viewed each other during the night.

'Come on,' I said. 'Section will be wondering what the fuck kept us.'

We doubled back along a crooked dusty path, a low barbed-wire fence separating it from a wood on one side. On the other was a waist-high poppy crop. The only sign of life was an occasional scorpion darting across our boots.

'When we get back, best not to brag about it,' I said.

Through a gap in the wire we cut into the wood, densely populated by tall upright pines. The foliage had burned to ochre in the summer sun, and under our feet crunched chestnut shells and the bony, desiccated detritus of fallen twigs. We zigzagged cautiously between the trees, checking the weight of each rustling footstep, and with our rifle sights we slowly scoped the perimeter.

'Have you noticed something weird?' said Adrian. I shook my head. 'Trees seem to be getting shorter.'

The sunlight dappled the wood in alternating shafts of light and dark. When I squinted, the tops of the trees seemed to bend into a downward curve in the middle distance and then rise again in a blur at the far end. Save for birds in the trees and the creaking of foliage in the gathering heat, the morning was silent and still.

'You get it too, boss?' Behind me Adrian stood perfectly still, his nose tuned to the air. 'Smells like. . .' he paused as though wondering whether to continue, 'love.'

Something else had replaced the night jasmine, a rounded, perfume-like scent that seemed to be growing stronger.

'Just roses,' I said. 'Big deal here, roses.'

'Boss, Black-Spot Hartley has reminded me, I haven't done my death letter.'

'Just count down the sleepovers,' I said.

'Could you help me write it?'

'Count off seven and you'll be waving out the window at the Hindu Kush and oiling your biceps,' I said.

'I need it all set down, on paper, signed and witnessed. Something for Britney – maybe, as well, something for her mum.'

'Hustling in pubs for an arm wrestle and shagging anything that moves.'

'Gonna go up to Old Hill and see her, make amends.' He lit up another cigarette, blowing the smoke out of his nostrils.

'Thought you said it was a one-nighter – she got one in the oven and you did a runner?'

Adrian threw the empty cigarette packet to the ground, crushed it under a boot. He coughed violently. 'Makes no difference. Girl's mine. Want to be a proper dad.'

I touched my prayer beads and whispered a *Bismillah* for his kid.

'The lads, it gets on their nerves when you pray in Paki, but I don't mind.'

'I bet they don't believe in the Angel Gabriel either,' I said.

'What's it called, when you squash the rose petals inside a book?' said Adrian.

'Get her chocolates instead, from duty free on your way back.'

'I'll take her out. Steak meal and all the trimmings.'

'What makes you think she's waiting for you?'

'I could. . .' He nodded slowly. I waited, but he didn't finish the sentence.

'Your England,' I laughed, 'all that beef and gravy, it's fiction.'

'My Britney is going to get roses,' said Adrian, picking up his pace. 'I'm in need of roses.'

'It's called pressing. You press the flower.'

We followed the rose scent. Shorter, colourful pomegranate trees had replaced the evergreens. Their branches spread low with dense green foliage; from them hung the large round fruit, not in abundance but dotted here and there, like a picture in a child's book. The fruit was blood red with a thick leathery skin, and beautiful against the green leaves – too beautiful, as though unreal, painted in. The pomegranate orchard was well tended, with narrow irrigation channels running parallel to each row of trees.

'You smell love? For me love is an easy walk down to the local where no one calls me a Paki.'

'And out of the window of your local you can see the estate and that shithole you call a mosque?'

'Green fields, mate. Green fields.'

'That's your fiction,' said Adrian, plucking a pomegranate off a tree.

'Steady,' I said, 'this patch has never seen the white man.'

'Then I'll be earning the roses.'

I listened to the sound of his teeth tearing at the leathery pomegranate.

He turned and smiled, blood-coloured seeds dripping from his lips. 'Don't you ever feel,' he continued between noisy mouthfuls, 'like back at base when we do an ammo count, that you did nothing more than just blast the fuck out of anything within a thousand yards of Terry? Don't you ever think you've got to earn something, anything, earn that shitty view from the pub window?'

'Last contact the lieutenant wrote off twenty-two thousand 7.62, twelve RPG and two Javelin. A lot of money for a sandcastle.'

'And the rest,' he said, spitting out the dripping husk. It landed on the ground, quickly staining the dry, yellow earth.

'Last contact I counted two Terry souls as they flew off to heaven.'

'I don't hate them. You got to respect—' he began.

'You have a short memory. If that thing I pulled you off had been an IED you might not be smelling love right now.'

He looked at his boot and shook his head. 'Luck.'

I said, 'Roses, Private Hartley, you can touch and smell, even dry in a book, but luck is another one of your fictions.'

'We know where Terry are and they can set their watches by our movements, yet. . .' he struggled for words, 'yet we prance about on patrol and let each other play on.'

'You live and breathe, Hartley, and that's all there is.'

Adrian shook his head again. 'They'd have just chalked it up, like we do. One of ours for a hundred of theirs.'

'That's reasonable,' I laughed.

'A hundred thousand pounds worth of armoured truck blown up by an IED packed with ten pound of fertilizer,' he said.

'Private Hartley, you are an Englishman. Your shit floats on pork fat content, your skin is pink and burns, your breath is like that of those dogs you love, and if anyone heard you side with Terry it would be most unwelcome.'

'They should have these in England,' said Adrian, rolling a second pomegranate in his hand. 'There must be better mosques than your one in Best Street? Pretty ones that aren't full of Pakis?'

'You forget my mother saw the Angel Gabriel at Best Street,' I said.

'I get it, that's all,' he stammered. 'I get where Terry are coming from.'

'*Haji*, Terry, raghead, Paki,' I said. 'Take it from me, it's black and white, there's nothing to get!'

'Yesterday I saw this Terry give mouth-to-mouth to a newborn goat. Goat got up and was sick all over him. Terry laughed his head off.'

'Random shit. Don't get taken in. Have yourself a deep breath and count off seven sleepovers.'

In the centre of the wood was a clearing, a long strip of closely cropped bright green grass bordered on all four sides by a low wall built of stone and painted white. The larger stones were punctuated with green Arabic script – at a guess the ninety-nine names of Allah. Through the middle of it ran a broad path; over the path, at intervals of about four feet, were tall trellis arches bursting with red, pink and white roses.

A smile spread across Adrian's face. He shook his head and his eyes sparkled. 'Who could hate the Terry?'

I stared in wonder. 'I don't like it.'

'It's a good sign. Britney's mum will take me back,' he said.

'Yeah, and if you concentrate hard enough you might even remember her name.'

'Must have taken Terry years,' he said. 'How the fuck do they water it?'

We stood below the first arch. The early morning sun was already intense and the dense network of intertwining flowers provided the small comfort of a gappy shade. The roses cast a complicated pattern on the grass. Adrian put his nose to one and inhaled deeply. 'It's something, isn't it? Love.'

I shivered involuntarily. 'There are seven rose arches,' I said. 'Like the seven levels of Terry heaven.' I scanned the area through the sights of my rifle. The orchard continued on all four sides from the edge of the lawn and from there, in all directions, and as the tree line grew taller and sloped upwards, the fruit trees were replaced by alpines.

He said excitedly, 'Feel it, man.'

We went and sat on two large stones under the middle arch. He lit up a cigarette.

'Private Hartley, you fall in love too easily.'

'All those nights you stayed up at the mosque, Sarge,' he pulled hard on his cigarette, 'you should have kept your fucking eyes open.'

'Mate, pick yourself a fucking rose, let's go.'

He stared straight ahead. 'It's eerie.'

'What is?'

Adrian dropped the pomegranate, crushing it absent-mindedly under a boot. 'The eyes. You seen them, Sarge?'

He was right. I looked around, suddenly aware of eyes, hundreds of them, staring back at us. The eyes were about six inches long, with blue, green and brown irises, painted at eye level on the trees that surrounded us. The arrangement was obviously designed to be viewed when seated on the stones.

'Evil eye,' I said.

'What?'

'They look creepy but in fact they're supposed to ward off evil,' I said.

'They're fucking queer,' he said.

I laughed. 'My mother swore by them.'

'No, man, it's an ambush.'

'Then it's already too late,' I said.

'Evil eye isn't Muslim, it's fucking superstition,' he said.

Adrian lecturing me about Islam was embarrassing. 'It's not right you going on like that. There's no depth to you. You don't think. You don't care for anything. You're just some random pisscan from the estate.'

'In Old Hill, you Pakis think you've a monopoly on God.'

'Look, man, I should know. I grew up in it. It just never really convinced me. . .' I shook my head, exasperated. 'Thank God for down below, your estate and that, where there are no rules.'

Adrian got up, slung his rifle over his shoulder and strode towards the seventh arch, his arms spread out and palms facing outwards. I followed.

'Nothing worth having on that estate, but your Pakistani mindset, it just doesn't export. You seem to think that God is found in curry houses and corner shops, but here,' he tested the weight of a rose in his hand, 'here, if you Pakis put your mind to it, you can do anything.'

'Allah tells us that in England we should apply ourselves to earning pound notes,' I said.

'Say I'm Terry and hungry and I find a loaf of bread. Do I hide in a dugout and gorge on it all by myself? Do I give it to some poor orphan in return for God's blessing? Do I share it with my Terry mates? Here,' he stared at me and nodded, 'here every day is a test and you have to be true to yourself.'

'Tell you what. . .' I paused, wondering if I should continue. Although it was every Muslim's duty to convert people to the faith, I had never considered it to be within my power. 'If you really want to be like Terry all you have to do is recite the Shahada. It's a one-liner. But you have to do it to the tune of "Twinkle Twinkle fucking Star".'

'Really?' Adrian's voice was childlike, too trusting.

'Do what your heart tells you.'

'But. . .' He stopped as though he didn't know how to finish the sentence.

'But remember, the believers will always lead you astray.'

'Good advice,' said Adrian, nodding.

'Recite the Shahada and I will call you Brother fucking Hartley or Abu fucking Britney and you can find a dugout and fornicate homo-style with the Terry brotherhood.'

'You're fucking with me?'

'No, brother, it's my duty.'

Adrian nodded. 'Abu Britney, man, *inshallah*.'

The word *inshallah* sounded awkward coming from a *gora*, but Adrian's pronunciation was good, as though he had been practising. My loud laughter echoed around us, and Adrian blushed a deep red, wounded. I stopped suddenly, conscious of the noise I was making. 'Okay,' I whispered, 'repeat after me, *La ilaha. . .*'

'Not like this,' said Adrian. 'We probably ought to drop our weapons and kneel.'

From behind I heard the unmistakable cocking of an AK47, the clack of spring-loaded metal against metal, close enough that for a moment, frozen to the spot, I was convinced it had fired. The rose Adrian was holding dropped to the ground. Suddenly I felt sick at the sight of that rose and I waited for a moment to see if he would fall after it. Then I turned carefully and gazed up at an Afghan, the tip of his rifle catching the sun as he trained it on us. It took me a few seconds to take it in, as if my eyes were clearing from a temporary blindness. The Afghan was a mess, as though he lived rough in the garden. He wore baggy trousers and a long grimy shirt, and above that was a densely black beard. His eyes were wild and seemed to creep out from under a poorly tied turban.

His gaze darted from his rifle tip to Adrian, me, and back again. I began to laugh loudly again, at the unreality of the situation. It flashed through my mind that if I was loud enough I might draw the attention of our section, drinking tea no more than three hundred yards away.

He stepped forward and swung the butt of his rifle against my chin. I fell sideways, tasting blood in my mouth. Then, fumbling on the ground for my rifle, I looked up cautiously.

The Afghan stared at Adrian.

Adrian, his voice trembling, said very slowly and clearly, '*Allahu Akbar*.'

The stranger took a step back, his expression changing from one of rage to confusion. He shook his head as though in denial of what he had heard.

Adrian squeezed his hands together, as he had done earlier when picturing the distance between the fuse and the charge. It was an act of submission, seeking mercy, and I wondered if he knew that. The Afghan would know it. Adrian smiled. 'Shahada,' he said brightly. He nodded and with a fingertip he jabbed his sternum, where his bulging chest parted in the middle. 'I Abu Britney – Shahada.' He struggled for the words.

My rifle was lying on the ground just out of reach. I kept my eyes fixed on the Afghan. I was caught in indecision, unsure whether or not to risk making a grab for my weapon.

Adrian bent over and picked up the fallen rose. Holding it out towards the Afghan, he tilted his head up, as though addressing the heavens.

I said slowly, '*La ilaha il Allahu Muhammad Rasul Allah.*'

Adrian repeated the words after me. '*La ilaha il Allah—*' And then, before he could complete the Shahada, he fell backwards as a single gunshot broke through the windless morning calm, a momentary clatter like a heavy door bolt hammered shut, a bullet entering and exiting his neck.

The Afghan laughed coarsely. A thin blue smoke rose from his rifle tip.

I felt sick, with an overwhelming sensation of thirst, as though I was hollow inside, coated with powder and dry like the earth on which I lay.

*

At the village chowk a bus engine started up, the great metal hulk shuddering around it as though only loosely attached. A solitary tuk-tuk driver, wrapped in a thick woollen shawl, slept awkwardly doubled over in his cabin, his feet sticking out. A battered yellow taxicab sat idle, its driver behind it, his recitation just audible as he bent over a prayer mat. A ragged, sore-ridden donkey flinched as I passed.

The road was heavily potholed and fell away in places where a combination of rain and the ISAF convoy of heavy vehicles passing through twice daily had washed and chipped it away. Bordering the road were shops, still closed at this time of day. Outside a clinic that advertised itself as '24-hour family service', a guard, wrapped from head to foot in an orange blanket, dozed lazily on a chair; an old Enfield rifle rested in his lap. The place stank of diesel and open sewers, and on either side of the road was a drainage channel of black slurry.

I stood in the middle of the road and gazed at my watch as though it would tell me something other than the time. The donkey brayed. Forty-three minutes had passed since Adrian had been killed.

The sentry outside the twenty-four-hour clinic woke. He rubbed his eyes and looked at me, and then looked again, as though unsure of what he had seen. He reached for the Enfield. I shook my head. He closed his eyes, pulled the blanket over his head and leant back in his chair. I heard the faint rumble of Apaches chopping the air above the orchard about a mile away; further into the distance but louder, A-10 Warthogs screamed low, sweeping the earth with a sonic boom.

From behind me came the scraping of steel as a roller shutter noisily opened. Inside was a boy, smooth-skinned and wearing a clean, long blue shirt and baggy trousers. His feet slipping inside his sandals, the lad came out carrying tables and chairs, which he placed on the side of the road. Unlit and gloomy inside, the teashop consisted of three brick walls and was no bigger than a garage for a car. At the far end, a bearded man stood behind a counter, wiping his forehead with a flap of his turban and stirring a large copper vessel.

Spotting me, the boy quickened his pace, fleeing into the teashop. I went over, pulled a chair from underneath a table and sat. The furniture was roughly made from planks nailed together, and where a vertical met a horizontal it was supported by poorly fitting triangular wedges of timber. Seeing a rose pattern painted onto the tabletop, I smiled, tracing its outline with a finger. The boy came out and stood next to me. Blended out of mountain tribe genes, he was white, with beautiful pale blue eyes that met mine, and his soft mouth quivered nervously as though he might cry.

'Tea?' I said, putting on my best smile.

He shook his head.

'Chai?'

He nodded and continued to stare. 'American?' he said.

I shook my head.

'British?'

Again I shook my head.

'Gurkha?' he said, confused.

'Pakistani,' I said, leaning my elbows on the table and cupping my chin in my hands.

'Muslim?'

I nodded.

The boy revealed a wide toothy smile. 'Angel Gabriel,' he said in Urdu, shaking his head in bewilderment.

'No angel, just a Pakistani in white man's clothing.'

'Angel!' he screamed excitedly and ran into the teashop.

The boy trembled as he came out with the tea, a tiny steaming cup that he set on the table before me. He stood staring at me again. I patted the seat next to me, but he shook his head and remained standing.

'What's your name?' I asked.

'Usman.'

'Sky,' I said, both hands outstretched towards the heavens. 'In English the word *usman* means sky.'

He watched eagerly as I patted down my pockets. I pulled out my beret and considered the bronze regimental cap badge set into it. The motif was of a double-headed eagle. I turned the beret inside out and rubbed the stitching against the rough tabletop to break the thread.

'Usman, for you.' I tossed the cap badge in the air. He caught it and ran into the shop.

The tea was thick and intensely sweet. In the back of our shop in Cradley was a gas stove. My father would add half milk and half water, throw in a handful of leaves and sugar, and evaporate it off for ten minutes while I, primed and ready with a rusk biscuit, watched impatiently.

I felt the weight of my numb cheek and awoke to find myself slumped on the table. Opening my eyes, for a moment I wondered where I was. Where was Adrian? Had I dreamt there was a boy? I could still taste something dry and sweet – tea.

Lying on the earth, seeing Adrian fall, hearing him fall, seeing the cloud of dust fly up around his limp body, I had had a sudden moment of lucidity. I had thought, This can't possibly be the end. I had felt angry, at Allah more so than the Afghan, as though it was impossible that this was the destiny He had written.

I had got slowly to my feet and picked up my weapon. The Afghan did nothing to stop me. He looked at me and laughed, bent over and laughed, as though submitting to the truth, to death, to the destiny that was written for him. I took a wide swing and the butt of my rifle cracked open his jaw.

His teeth broken and bloodied, his mandible dangling off his face, he swayed for a moment, looking at me, and crumpled to his knees. I stood over him, staring at his wretched, already barely human figure. For what seemed like minutes I said nothing, staring alternately at the Afghan and at Adrian. Adrian lay in a heap to one side, his blood running in rivulets across the dry earth. The Afghan gazed at me, tears springing from his eyes, foaming crimson bubbles at his mouth. He clasped his hands together and croaked, '*Allahu Akbar*.' His voice was irritating. Through my earpiece I heard urgent traffic: *sitrep*, casualty status. I heard the question *medevac*? The word irritated me. It was too late to medevac. I felt for the lever and switched my rifle to automatic. I remembered what my father would say in the back of the shop as he took a blade to the neck of a chicken, and stammering, '*Bismillah ir-Rahman ir-Rahim*,' I discharged a burst of 7.62 into the Afghan's face.

Footsteps approached behind me. My section, all talking at once. It was vexing. The lieutenant touched my arm; turning reflexively, I shoved him as hard as I could. He fell to the ground. He picked himself up, his face like that of a disappointed child. The voices of my section seemed to get louder, more insistent, like a swarm of wasps getting closer. I felt as though I had been stung, as though my body was burning up. I threw off my helmet and Osprey body armour, dropped my weapon. I immediately felt better, lighter and freer, and the flaxen rays of sunshine felt pleasant on my skin. I started to walk slowly away. Although I could no longer see them, like hot breath on my neck I could sense my section watching in disbelief. I could sense the stretcher-bearers hurrying to Adrian stop and stare.

Finally Lieutenant Lovell spoke, his voice like a knife in my ear. 'Halt, Sergeant Khan. That's an order: halt.'

I kept going. No longer encumbered by the weight of my kit, I ran for it, and faster than I thought possible. I pictured the scene of chaos behind me as they threw themselves into the impossible task of saving Adrian. *Medic. Medic. Medic.* As the earth warmed, the rays of morning sun sprang back in fissures and spirals and I had to squint my eyes to get a clear view of the path ahead.

Now my eyes focused on the tabletop. I saw that the teacup had been removed and in its place was my cap badge. I looked behind me. The teashop shutters had been drawn and the chowk was silent, the vehicles had left. Breaking the silence, the donkey stamped at the earth, its neck twisting awkwardly as it pulled at the post it was tethered to.

Across the street a sugarcane vendor sat cross-legged on his cart. On it was a mound of cane sticks, a metal juicing machine with a long handle, and a stack of dirty green tumblers. A string of prayer beads dangled from one hand and with the other he fanned himself with the tail of his turban. A stray dog walked between us and loped off, carrying a limp. Instinctively I touched my neck, and felt for the first time during the tour the absence of my lucky beads. The cane seller's hand moved slowly up and down as though testing their weight.

From the direction I had come, a Suzuki minivan careened towards us, its thin boxy frame bouncing over the potholes as though out of control. Over the sound of its tinny engine labouring under the strain, I could hear a *naath* playing within, one I had heard many times before, a slow lamentation on the phrase '*Allahu*'. Nearing, it slowed right down, almost rolling out of gear. It was white with a red strip running along its side; as it neared almost to a stop, one of its two male occupants turned towards the cane vendor and passed him a weapon. The van accelerated away and I caught sight of myself in the tailgate window, the glass of which had been covered over with a plastic stick-on mirror. My beard, elongated by the curve of the glass, looked like Terry's, and smeared across my forehead was Adrian's blood. The blood ran down my cheeks; there was a gap across my chest where my body armour had been, but it continued downwards from my waist, much of it no longer bright red but a deep crimson colour turning black. The Suzuki sped up, and I traced its rear window far into the distance, twinkling in the sun.

Something else caught the sunlight, and as I turned again to the cane vendor I observed the tip of an AK47 trained on me.

Unhurriedly, the cane seller dismounted from the cart and stood in front of it. Despite his sallow cheeks, Terry-style beard and the turban on his head, he reminded me of myself. We coincided in build and height, but there was something else about him, the way he carried himself, and his smiling, weak, unsure, eyes that betrayed him as carrying out someone else's orders. His hair was closely cropped, his skin yet to be furrowed or pockmarked, and I guessed he was also in his late twenties. I was struck with the idea that he could have been me. I could have been him. The cane vendor, Adrian, myself – it suddenly seemed that each of us amounted to nothing more than where we were fated to be born. I offered him a smile, convinced that he understood what I had just discovered.

He spoke in Urdu. 'Taliban' – with his rifle tip he pointed vaguely towards the granite mountains in the distance – 'will kill you.' Behind him flies buzzed densely around short stumps of sugar cane, and like a chest of jewels the haphazardly stacked glass tumblers sparkled in the sunlight. 'But,' he smiled broadly, revealing the blackened stumps of his teeth, 'you are my brother.'

I nodded. '*Allahu Akbar.*'

His eyes focused on my wrist. Quickly removing my watch, I threw it onto his cart. He glanced at where it landed and shook his head. 'And the Taliban may take mercy on my brother,' the tip of his rifle descended towards my legs, and he spoke slowly, 'if my brother were crippled.'

I turned my head away and upwards, towards the perfectly blue sky. A white vapour trail of A-10 Warthogs skimmed across it. I closed my eyes and waited. '*Inshallah.*'

14

'*Inshallah*,' says Grace. 'I wish I had a word that would make everything bearable.'

'*Inshallah*, you will.'

She wipes away a tear and laughs, clutching her neck to steady herself. For a moment, seeing her head caught at that angle, eyes wide and glazed, blood congealed on tea towels wrapped around her neck, I wish I could draw out the hurt.

I feel a helpless panic in watching her cry and quickly continue with the story. 'After that, I remember waking up in a hospital in England, my parents on either side of me. When I opened my eyes my mother began to wail, slapping her palms against her face. I closed my eyes, wishing I was back in Afghanistan.'

She places a gentle hand on my knee, a silent benediction. 'It will be a consolation for Britney, knowing that Adrian's last thoughts were of her. They wouldn't take her away. Not if he were here.' Then in a louder voice, a sort of plea, she adds, 'He would have fought them. He would, wouldn't he?'

I nod. 'You were saying earlier how your image was fixed in Britney's brain.'

'They'll take that away too. And they'll replace it.'

'Can they?'

'If I passed Britney in the street years from now, I might recognize her,

I might not, but would she me?' Grace thinks for a long time, biting her lip. 'She might turn, take a second glance.'

I sink back against the pillow and close my eyes. My head hurts from the whisky and lack of sleep. 'That newspaper story. It's brave what you did.'

Grace's voice is soft and soporific. 'Britney was born early and needed blood. After three nights we were allowed home, and I was the happiest I've ever been. I lived in Old Hill tower blocks then, and Betts and Alfie from upstairs did my shopping so baby and I never had to go out. We were getting into a groove. Betts had a key to my flat but no one else came. Suddenly, after about two weeks, there's this loud knock at the door.

'"I've been trying to call you for a week." It was the midwife, a black woman with a tidy Afro. With her was another woman, white, older, tall, with a thin face and greying hair.

'"Sorry," I said. "I haven't been out to put credit on my phone."

'The midwife and I sat down, baby on her lap. The other woman took a seat opposite. I looked at her and smiled, expecting a greeting or at least that she would introduce herself. "My colleague's just here as a chaperone," the midwife said, sensing my anxiety. She passed the baby back to me. "What a pretty little thing."

'We talked about how I changed Britney, how I fed her; I pointed out the sterilizer that cleaned her bottles. The chaperone made me nervous. Although Britney slept in a basket, when they asked me to demonstrate how I put her down, I wrapped her up and put her on the bed, next to where I slept. I looked at them and trembled, my eyes darting about.

'"Babies are happier in a smaller space," the midwife said.

'"Being confined simulates the womb." It was the first time the chaperone had spoken.

'I boiled water and put it in Britney's bottle, then put the bottle in cold water to speed up the cooling. I added a level scoop of infant powder to the water in the bottle. The midwife nodded and smiled. The chaperone asked, "Are you not lactating?"

'About then, Britney woke up. She had a powerful cry. Luckily, I had just done a bottle, so I fed her.

'"Funny, isn't it," I said as I finished the feed, "you put it in one end and it comes straight out the other."

'I undressed the baby – it's no easy thing pulling those vests off her head, especially when you're being watched. I took off the nappy and cleaned her. The midwife stopped me there to examine the baby's bottom. The chaperone narrowed her eyes and peered closely at the baby. "Ecchymosis, discrete patch, one centimetre, lateral right thigh."

'"It's nothing to worry about," the midwife reassured me. "I'll book you in at the doctor's this afternoon."

'You might wonder how I remember all this? It was written up later, like a play, every detail and word spoken. I've read the documents a hundred times.

'At the doctor's, there were two other people in the consulting room. They sat against a wall. The doctor described one as a student and another as a chaperone.

'I put Britney on his couch and undressed her. He looked at the baby's thigh for about one second, turned her over, ran his eyes over her and shook his head. "Nothing to worry about, Miss Booth, just keep an eye on her."

'On the way home, I put credit on my phone.'

Grace nudges up to me for comfort. There is a bottle of water on the bedside table; I use it to wet the dried tea towels around her neck. She screeches at the cold water but keeps still. Slowly I peel away each layer, exposing a small clotted triangular wound bordered by multiple grazes. Like a child she gazes at me, grateful.

I settle back so that we're now lying side by side. Taking a lock of her hair, I twist it between my fingers until it pulls her scalp. She grits her teeth, unwilling to vocalize her pain.

She kicks away the duvet, her legs rubbing against one another like scissor blades. She pulls her nightdress up to her waist, exposing the dark hairy triangle of her cunt. It might be an invitation but it amplifies her vulnerability. It cheapens her in some way. At the same time, I am grateful. It is an offer to my ego. She knows I won't act on it, and so do I.

Closing my eyes, I remember the moment when the cane vendor pulled the trigger. A slow-motion spark at the tip of his rifle. My knee buckles underneath me and I fall, and before I hit the dusty ground, I see a shower of glass tumblers ping into the air, and the flimsy wooden cart fall to pieces, and the cane vendor himself pinned to the spot with fire, peppered by Lieutenant Lovell and what remained of his troop. Trigger-happy ISAF and thousands of rounds of 7.62. ISAF hated to lose.

Lieutenant Lovell was in love with Second Lieutenant Coates. She was a Black Country lass and had a soft spot for me, for Adrian too. Lovell, engrossed in his wireless conversation with his lover, had let Adrian and me detach ourselves from the troop and felt bad. You look after your own in Terry country, and that, combined with his soppy state of mind, meant that the worst he would say was that after the shock of Adrian's death I'd had a moment of *temporary insanity*. I had *paid for it* too, with my knee, or so read his report. *Recommend honourable discharge.* With that, a wodge of compensation was credited to my bank account.

I was in rehab for months. They depressed me, the cheerful amputees and flirty nursing staff. I mourned Adrian and blamed myself. I was the sergeant, and although Lovell's report was kind, I knew I had been reckless and led him into danger. I lived mostly in a daze, lost day to day in my own self-recriminations, and so, when finally I came to leave rehab, naturally I went home with my parents.

They had fixed me a bed in the guest room downstairs, but I wasn't having that. I managed to hobble up and down the stairs. It was really only then, through the enforced exercise, that I learnt, albeit with my own peculiar gait, to walk again. I was tricked, but I was complicit, if not as a participant then at least as a silent observer. I had returned for want of a warm and familiar bed, and even that, my sole comfort, was soon to be shared with a stranger from the mother country.

Of the ceremony I don't remember much, except that it was conducted in our house, and that it was short, with only my parents and an imam present. We ate, the men in the living room and the women separately upstairs. I had hardly finished my meal when my mother came down. 'Now you go.' She pointed to the stairs. I looked over at the imam, who had just shovelled in a mouthful of biryani. He raised his eyes, the rice spilling from his lips.

My new wife, Azra, still in her wedding dress, lay flat on her back on my bed. A veil covered her face, behind which her eyes were screwed tightly shut. For a minute I stood over her, watching the rise and fall of her small chest, barely perceptible, like a precious thing wrapped inside a blood-red shroud.

Mum and I had been mesmerized at first sight by the dress Azra now wore. We had seen it on a mannequin in a shop window. Azra was still in Pakistan at the time. The dress was red with gold brocade around the neckline, cuffs and ankle-length hemline. It was studded with dazzling glass beads arranged to form roses. The owner of the shop wouldn't haggle on the price, and in protest my mother had walked out, leaving me alone, surrounded on all sides by beautiful, alluring mannequin brides, their toenails painted red. I was alone with the shop owner, her foot tapping impatiently on the floor. I dug my hands into my money belt and reluctantly counted out the price she demanded.

Now I slid into bed, nudging against my bride. The glass roses of Azra's dress dug roughly into my chest. I pressed harder, defying the tiny pinpricks of pain, strangely hoping I might draw blood.

Earlier she had sat resplendent beside me on our sofa as the imam had conducted the short ceremony. Before that I had seen her once only, covered from head to toe in her black burqa. Trembling beside her on our wedding day, I dared not look at her, staring instead at the row of gold bangles on her arm. As she leant forward to sign the documents, a dot of gold glinted on her nose but the rest of her face was obscured by a long silken veil. Her long slim hands were clad in thin white gloves, and her feet in narrow sandals protruded from beneath the dress, the nails painted red.

But in bed with Azra now, the dress took on a new meaning. It represented a cold scratchy barrier between my new bride and me. Through the barrier I reached for the soft bulge of her breasts, and felt her chest arch with a long intake of breath. I felt myself harden, every muscle in my body contracting towards my groin, and from the tip of my penis I felt an escape of something wet. Was I supposed to help her out of the dress? It must hurt, I thought, the beaded fabric pressed between her body and the mattress. My hand ran down her flat belly, pulled up the skirt and reached for a drawstring that tied under-trousers at her waist.

Azra turned towards me, pushing her knee up against my groin. Her nose stud glittered like a distant star. Then she shrank away towards the far side of the mattress, pulling the bed sheet tight against her body.

'It's normal,' I stuttered in Urdu. 'Don't be frightened.'

I reached for the light switch on the wall and clicked it off. In the darkness I fumbled again for the drawstring, my fingers slipping underneath the waist of her trousers. I could feel the rapid rise and fall of her diaphragm and between her legs she felt hot. She seemed to tremble and I could hear her laboured breath. She jerked awkwardly away from my touch once more. I no longer felt in control; afraid I would come in my trousers, I pulled away. I switched on a bedside lamp, a softer light that cast an elliptical illumination against the wall.

'It's okay, Azra. I won't force you.'

'I don't believe you,' she replied.

'We've got the rest of our lives,' I said.

'You swear on Allah?'

'I swear on Allah.'

Slowly she sat up, the bangles falling to rest at her wrist. Her face, in profile, was shielded by the veil.

'Won't you look at me?' I stared ahead at the window, the curtains drawn against the night. They were new and pink. Mum had said that all brides liked pink. Azra shook her head, her headscarf rustling loudly against the headboard.

'Why not?' I asked softly.

'I can't.'

'You're my wife, you can.'

Azra laughed drily. 'Is that what English wives do?'

'I wouldn't know,' I replied quietly. 'I've never had an English wife.'

'Ten years ago,' she said, 'I was given a picture of you. It was when I was in my final year at school.'

'I wasn't ready for love,' I said.

'You looked kind. I praised Allah.'

'I was too young. We both were.'

'I stared at it every day, wondering what you would be like. And then one day I came home from school to find my father had torn up the picture.'

'I'm sorry.'

'No, you're not. Saying sorry is feeble and too easy. It's like *love*, a word you've borrowed from the English. My father,' she continued, 'sent me to a madrasa. There I would be useful. I could repent my shame, the shame of having my betrothed fall into the arms of the infidel army.' She shook her head ruefully. 'In Pakistan such rejection falls like sin on a woman's honour. I became a teacher at the madrasa. I had eighty students and I was happy. Now, so many years later, in Pakistan I am considered an old woman; only now you pay the dowry, and my father, he comes for me. For once he is happy. He comes to the madrasa bearing papers from England. He says when I am settled I should send for him.'

'All I know is what my mother told me. She said you were patient and would wait.'

'So you could do what you liked and I would just pray and wait?' She shook her head again.

'You're a beautiful woman – you should have married someone else.'

Azra put her hands to her face as though she was about to cry. Floral-patterned henna tattoos wove around the backs of her hands. They twisted and turned, branching threadlike down each finger.

Suddenly I understood. 'My mother didn't tell you, did she? Nor your father. No one told you I was crippled.'

She shook her head but said nothing.

My left knee instantly throbbed. The lower leg, mutilated by entry and exit holes, had healed like a withered branch on a tree. When I stood, it hung like a dead appendage. Now, in bed, I straightened it, approximating its true position. I kneaded at the joint between titanium and flesh, my face screwed into a knot of pain, feeling for the ridges of cold metal beneath the skin.

She shrank away a little. 'I saw it at the airport.'

'When I'm lying in bed,' I said, 'and there's no weight on my knee I feel like any other man. Sometimes I dream that I'm walking like I used to. It can't be fixed, and as my wife you should know that. At the hospital they wanted to cut it off and give me a prosthetic leg. They said I'd be able to run with a metal leg. I don't want it cut off.'

'Maybe you want it this way,' she said.

'When it hurts really badly I'm happy because I think the life is coming back to it.'

'You have two arms and one good leg. I've seen worse.'

'Yeah, but you didn't marry them, did you.'

'I wouldn't have minded. If he was kind.' Her lips, thick with red gloss, were just visible at the edge of her veil.

'All these years they had you wait for a cripple.' I felt like a grotesque medical specimen.

'My father had even purchased my wedding gold, and to everyone in our sector he had boasted that he would send me out clad in a *lakh*'s worth of gold. The day we learnt of your defection, my father swore, he beat me, he cried.'

'Your father's anger should have been at me.'

'He has forgiven you. And your knee, to me it is of no consequence.'

'Azra,' I said loudly, 'you lie.'

'I throw myself on Allah's mercy, but I do not lie,' Azra sobbed. I listened to the noise from downstairs. The TV was on loud, the familiar opening tune of the nine o'clock news. From the kitchen I could hear the clatter of pans as my mother tidied up after the wedding feast.

'Allah?' I said. 'Which Allah? Every Muslim I ever met had a different Allah. They fight over Allah. They die over Allah. But here's the funny thing, no two of them could ever agree on what or who Allah is.'

She clamped her hands over her ears.

'Mercy?' I continued undeterred. 'In the name of Allah they make war that has no end. The Taliban killed and we killed but there were no martyrs. There was only maiming and death.'

Azra moved towards me and took my chin tightly in her fingers. Through an opening in her veil I saw her face for the first time, slim, angular and beautiful. Her irises were brown, her gaze penetrating, and the whites of her eyes were as opaque as paper. Her thick lashes had been painted with mascara and a faint pink blush dusted her cheeks. She had a thin, pointy nose and a gently curved chin, and I knew, I knew she was out of my league.

Azra spoke forcefully. 'I married you and I will accept your body as it is.' She took a deep breath and went on. 'But an infidel who has fought for the enemy? Allah, no! Not an infidel. I cannot have married an infidel.'

'I may not know much about women but it is not right that a thing of beauty like you should speak such hard words. I am not what you say, but you cannot measure me against the imams and students of your madrasa.'

Azra slumped back against the headboard, breathing heavily. I stretched out a hand and touched her shoulder. She shrugged it off.

'Why aren't you married?' I said. 'Are the men in Pakistan so stupid?'

'My father dictated it had to be a cousin and it had to be England. Is that a precise enough answer for you?'

'Well, now that you are here, what is your decision?'

'You have not denied that you are an infidel. Only through Allah do we understand our lives.'

'You need not worry. I am a believer. But I do not believe blindly.'

'You either believe or you don't. Which is it?' she asked.

'From what I've seen, the believers are intoxicated with belief. They seem to have no responsibility beyond prayer and sacrifice. For them that is enough, but it is not enough for me.'

'A true believer is not living for this life. Rather, the next.'

'Maybe,' I said, 'but for some believers the circumstances of this life are not so great, and while they're preoccupied with the hereafter they're not prepared to change the present. There is no honour in poverty.'

'Things are so much better for you, are they?'

'I used to believe that you create your own luck, but now I'm not so sure.' I pulled my bad knee to my chest, kneading the knotty scar, and added gently, 'Let's not argue,' my voice almost a whisper, 'not on our wedding night.'

'I believed that together with my husband we would each grow closer to our faith.'

'If it's my leg, I don't blame you.'

'No, really not your leg.'

'Prove it.'

Turning away, she said, 'I am sorry.'

I shrank back against the headboard, unable to think what to say next. There was a long silence. I reached across with one hand, feeling her firm thigh and upwards to where it joined her belly. I slid my hand past the drawstring, inside her trousers. She had shaved, it seemed, the tips of my fingers reaching deep into territory that was moist. Azra shuddered, her breathing heavy. Once, twice, she swayed, as though her body in its entirety was in rhythm with the movement of my fingers. I turned, clutching the back of her neck in my free hand, and pulled her towards me. She relented, her body going soft, and allowed herself to face me. Briefly, Azra's eyes met mine, but then her hollow gaze dropped to her lap. She wriggled free of me and retreated until her body hung partly over the far edge of the bed.

'It's normal. It's what we're expected to do. We're husband and wife,' I pleaded.

'You don't understand.' She clutched a pillow to her chest.

'Didn't anyone tell you what you're supposed to do?'

'Your mother, she said just close your eyes and let him do what he wants.'

'I mean, it's natural. It's what we're expected to do, and once we've got it over with it will all be okay.'

With her chin cupped in her fists, Azra stared at me. Gently, she began to cry. The tears ran like grey raindrops across both cheeks. Her mascara spread around her eyes like a blot of black ink. Finally, still sobbing, she spoke. 'Together we will shame the sanctity of marriage as it has been written. Release me and marry an English woman.'

'You love someone else?' I had not thought of this before and suddenly I was gripped by certainty of its truth.

'A real man must lead a family. A man of strength, and none is stronger than he who fears Allah.'

'You do, don't you? You love someone else?'

'My father, he didn't believe in free will.' She turned to face the wall and sobbed. 'All he could ever think of was England, but your England is cold and its heart is dark. What use is this land of infidels?'

I stretched across and touched her shoulder. 'It's okay.'

'Okay?' cried Azra, swinging abruptly around, tearing off her veil and throwing it to the floor behind her. 'You are my husband but you're ignorant.' She lay down and shuffled on her back into the middle of the mattress. She undid the drawstring, pulled down her trousers and opened her legs, her foot grazing mine. A shudder of adrenaline passed through me, but I was unable even to look at her. She continued. 'Okay, now do what your mother told you to do. My faith is strong and it's only my body you despoil. Have your pleasure.'

My hand extended a little way towards her, shaking uncontrollably. I withdrew it, brushing against a glass bead that had fallen off her dress onto the mattress. I picked it up, turning it over in my fingers. Pulling the sheet over me, I turned around to face the wall and switched off the lamp. In the darkness I rolled the bead between a thumb and forefinger. It was poorly cut with sharp edges. I thought about my mother and what she would be expecting. It was silent now downstairs, but I had not heard my parents come up to bed. Perhaps they were listening out for us? The cry of a virgin's pain mixed with the grunt of their son's pleasure. I rubbed a sharp edge of the bead against the soft pad of my thumb. I dug it in deeper, my pain somehow amplified in the silence of the house, *Allahu*, and then again, *Allahu*, and again, *Allahu*, and again and again until it bled. It took all my effort not to cry out my prayer. I reached my hand back into the centre of the bed and smeared the blood across the sheets.

15

Grace drains the last of the whisky, contorting her face like a child fed medicine. Gradually her body relaxes, her eyes half close, but a scowl remains on her lips.

'It went on for over a year. A health visitor replaced the midwife, and later I got assigned a social worker. It wasn't wise to ask a lot of questions; plenty on the estate were having to deal with the same, and besides, they had a job to do. The last thing you wanted to do was rub them up the wrong way.

'And then I got a letter inviting me to something called a child protection conference. The letter explained that we would be discussing *Britney's best interests*, and that *there was no need of a solicitor*. I had never been to a conference before, and I expected there would be lots of people, all listening and learning. I bought a new folder and pens and paper.

'I left Britney with Betts and Alfie and put on my Sunday best. I was told to wait in a waiting room. I was the only person there. It was obviously important, but where were the others? There was a sign on the wall – CCTV IN OPERATION – and leaflets advertising firms of solicitors.

'I was shown into this room with a long polished table. There was a bottle of water and an empty glass in front of each seat, and a pad and pen branded with the council logo. The wooden chairs were proper old-fashioned and heavy, and the same logo was also on the padded backrests. The room was almost full. My social worker pulled out a chair and beckoned for me to sit next to her. The rest of them sat opposite us: the health visitor; the chief social worker; my GP, Dr Moxham; the chaperone woman I had met once. There was also another doctor with a long title and a short name, Dr Ali.

'I began by writing down the names of all the people. I hadn't finished when the chaperone, seeing what I was doing, started up. "For the benefit of everyone, I remind those here that this meeting is recorded." She then thanked me for coming, saying it was a good sign that I was *engaging*.

'The chaperone started reading from a report: "Miss Britney Booth has been taken to see her GP Dr Moxham twelve times in as many months, and has had the benefit of the opinion of the community paediatrician, Dr Ali." I could see they each wanted to smile as their names were read out. "I have visited her on one occasion – sadly, professional time constraints limited me to that – and the combined visits made by other health professionals here present," she looked around the room with a grave expression, "amount to thirteen."

'The chief social worker took a single piece of paper from the pad in front of her and began to fold it. I watched her fingers work.

'Dr Ali was invited to speak next. "I'll cut to the chase and try to use language that we can all understand," he said. "I have reviewed Britney's notes, kindly supplied by my colleague Dr Moxham and others. Britney is otherwise fit and well, but I have recorded bruising to her extremities consistent with NAI."

'"Non-accidental injury," my social worker whispered in my ear.

'The chaperone spoke. "We are not so much concerned with Britney's current injuries but, as covered in the Children Act 1989 and fully consistent with more recent safeguarding directives, those injuries that the child might be expected to sustain in the future."

'I slid down in my chair, my ears ringing. The chief's piece of paper was now one-sixteenth of its original size.

'The social worker nudged me. "Miss Booth, would you like to say something?"

'I stood up. "There's nothing wrong with Britney. Them bruises, maybe they're something to do with the blood she got when she was born. These things happen, don't they? On account of my condition, I don't get out as much as some mothers might, but I sit Britney by the window so she can look out and get her vitamin D." My cheeks felt hot, and as I talked I was choking on my own spit. "I don't know what you're all on about. Can I get a solicitor? Am I entitled?"

"'Miss Booth." It was the chaperone. "We are here looking for a compromise. All these professional people around the table want only what is best for Britney, as I know you do. You may hire a solicitor – although as I am sure you have been told you don't need one – but such an instruction would have to be entirely at your own expense. You are on benefits, are you not? There is no point in me adjourning this meeting – and therefore delaying what would be deemed to be in the best interests of Britney – if the instruction of legal counsel is unlikely."

'Defeated, I shook my head and sat down. I noticed that the piece of paper wouldn't bend into a sixty-fourth.

"'We will take a short break. I am sure you would welcome that, Miss Booth. It might allow you the opportunity to get some fresh air, and perhaps we can reconvene" – she looked at her watch – "in twenty minutes' time and proceed on a more conciliatory basis."

'I took a seat in the waiting room. After a few minutes the social worker came and sat next to me. She whispered, "Grace, I'm on your side, but they want something out of you today. They want you to give something up. They want your agreement. If they don't get it they'll apply to the court."

'I didn't know what she was talking about. "They want me to take her out more?"

"'They would settle for an agreement on a care order. You'd still get to see Britney, I'd make sure of that. Britney would live with someone else and you would visit. Supervised, of course. If you agree today," she paused and looked at me sympathetically, "I could try and convince them to give you two hours a week."'

Grace pants, her breath hot on my face, and her eyes search mine for an answer I cannot provide. I draw warmth from her, skin on skin, brown and white. Without warning, my knee jerks, and agony shoots through me. Automatically, but with no real hope of relief, my fingertips search for the pain. Wordlessly, Grace pulls my hands away. Her fingers lightly knead and press the knotted joint; to my surprise, the pain subsides. As it goes, I relax back against the pillow. Then her fingers begin to walk up my thigh under the duvet, and I stiffen, raising myself off the bed a little. Her hand reaches the elasticated waist of my underpants and she pulls them down. Slipping her head under the duvet, she applies her mouth to me. I tense, every muscle centring to a knot in my gut. I climax quickly, and she comes up for breath, resting her head on my chest. I caress her prickly hair. Small, scrambled bubbles of oxygen burst in my brain as though bringing life to previously dormant nerve tissue.

As I stare down at our bodies pressed together, a picture swims up in my mind. A brown man in a dusty village, clad in rags with a dirty turban on his head. A memsahib walks past and he bows before her, careful not to look at her directly, his hands pressed to his chest in supplication. She is dressed in an unblemished white frock and behind her walks a servant holding a large bleached cotton umbrella. Following the memsahib, of course, were men. Always chaperoned by men, and in this particular case, an ample, moustached English fellow, a recruitment sergeant no less.

It is the only image I have ever been offered, from where I don't know, perhaps a relative, that might represent my father's father. This, what Grace and I are doing now, they would have called it *mixing*. The white man's greatest treasure was his memsahib, and yet I feel no desire to exert power over Grace. In a fantasy, I would have grasped her hair tightly and held her down, hard, in vengeance for my grandfather.

It shames me that this is all I can think of, and I am thankful that her eyes are closed, as though now, after what has occurred between us, she could read my thoughts from my face. Inside my head something drains away, like the fluid from a lanced abscess, and as the euphoria fades, it is replaced by something tighter, more whole, as though the two hemispheres of my brain are more closely integrated, have reached some sort of understanding.

And for reasons of food and foolish bravery, the allure of the memsahib still clouding his thinking, hearing the recruitment sergeant call out his name, my grandfather would have taken one step forward and stood to attention: 'Yes, Sergeant Major, sahib.' My grandfather, one Sepoy Khan, would all his life, even during the torturous years as a prisoner of the Japanese, before he succumbed to typhoid, remember the day of the passing by of the memsahib. The English brought law and the drought abated and the crops grew from grains purchased by Sepoy's salary; the family thrived, and the generations flourished until food was no longer an issue, and it was only once we were fed that we Pakistanis remembered that old grandpa was buried in an unmarked grave in Burma near an embankment where a railway line was once dug. As my mother always said, hunger is the worst thing. And we were angry. But we are a patient culture that bides its time.

From what Grace has related, it seems that the *gora* have turned in on themselves, and as though the fate of the *gora* and that of the Pakistani are diametrically opposed, right now I feel happy, strangely content. The sum of everything that has occurred before is somehow distilled, and more than that, balanced, as though all negatives and positives have been cancelled by each other, and in this moment, my head comfortable against the pillow and the weight of Grace's head on my chest, I feel a peace I had not thought possible.

Still now, six months later, I do not know why I agreed to marry Azra. Waking up the morning after our wedding night, I turned over in bed and spread out and for a moment I forgot that Azra was there. Then I felt my thumb throb as though the skin might burst. A bright shaft of light through the open curtains caught my eyes. Startled by the sound of someone rapping on the front door downstairs, I sat up against the headboard. I heard the door open and the voice of my mother and that of a man. She showed him in, seating him in the front room, and called up the stairs, 'Akram, your brother for you.'

I dressed and with a sense of foreboding made my way downstairs.

As I walked into the room and our eyes met, the visitor put down his tea and sprang up from the sofa. He smiled a broad, pink, gummy smile that contrasted with his paper-white albino skin. He was a large man, rotund, the skin stretched smoothly over his cheeks, giving him a boyish appearance. His upper eyelids were crisscrossed with fragile veins enlarged through the thick lenses of his spectacles, and he blinked frequently as though even the soft indoor light was too harsh for his milky eyes. A white turban covered his forehead, the odd pink tendril slipping from underneath. He had a sparse straggly beard with a pointed tip.

'You remember me, brother?' he bellowed. His eyes seemed to veer back and forth as though struggling to focus. In one hand he carried a large bunch of mixed flowers wrapped in gold cellophane. He thrust them at me and congratulated me, telling me that the big news all over town was that *dear Brother Akram has taken a wife.*

Smiling, I produced the expected response: '*Mash Allah*, it's you, Mustafa – Mustafa, my old friend!' I hadn't seen him since I had left at the age of sixteen, but underneath the extra weight he was immediately recognizable. I put the flowers on the coffee table next to the bronze vase containing the plastic roses, then leant on my stick.

'I am sorry.' He glanced at my left leg, suspended an inch off the ground. 'I heard about your injury. But you,' his gaze lifted, catching mine, 'you look strong.'

'If I squint my eyes I don't see my bad leg,' I laughed.

'I see you have finally given in, family and wife. Fine thing. No life without wife.' He laughed and elbowed me in the side. 'No life without wife!'

'Sit down, brother,' I said, gesturing towards the sofa.

Ignoring my offer, he nodded deliberately and said, '*Inshallah*, I will pray that your wife will soon bear you a son.'

I nodded, feeling myself blush. '*Inshallah.*'

'It's good you have returned, brother. I have also. . .' He paused. 'I have, so to speak, also returned.' He looked around the room as though sweeping for unseen listeners. Then he clasped both of my hands in his, warm and chubby. 'It's time we were reacquainted, you and I.'

I extricated my hands and dug one into a pocket, seeking my cigarettes. Mustafa's eyes followed my hand, and for some reason I took it out, leaving the cigarettes undisturbed.

'Come, Brother Akram,' he said, 'spare me a few hours of your time. I beg forgiveness from your good wife' – he pointed towards the stairs – 'but I will not detain you for long, and you can get back to business.' He winked, and added confidently, 'You and I, brother, we will now go out.' He turned towards the door. Over a long white shirt he wore a British army-issue combat jacket. His baggy white trousers were pulled up to his ankles, above green Adidas trainers.

Once outside he walked slowly, and I was able to keep up. Like me, he too seemed to have difficulty walking. Mustafa spoke all the time, hardly pausing for breath. We soon reached the high street, where the traffic crawled bumper to bumper. I had to laugh as we passed a small orange car clad in a sporty body kit. From it emanated loud Punjabi music, its solitary male occupant nodding vigorously to the drumbeat. He turned towards me and snarled self-consciously through the open window, a gold front tooth and his mirrored sunglasses both reflected in the car windscreen.

Amid the noise of the street, I intermittently lost the precise words but kept the thread of Mustafa's conversation, which focused on his children, three boys attending a madrasa in Birmingham and two daughters sent to be educated in Pakistan. Mustafa and his wife now lived in a council house next door to his mother, who had also been rehoused, and had knocked out the dividing walls to create, as he put it, a four-bedroom mansion. Burqa-clad women pushed toddlers in buggies. Following Mustafa's lead, I sidestepped onto the road to create a respectful distance between us as they passed. Mustafa had another wife – or were there several others? – and further children, in another mansion, in Pakistan. The boys were fed on the milk of cows in the yard: it would make them strong, he said. He talked about bringing them over to the UK, and I pointed out that polygamy was illegal here. Mustafa, with a glint in his eye, said it was perfectly possible, indeed the British authorities respected it. On the footpath, little boys rushed boisterously between their mothers, while their little sisters clutched each other as they trailed behind, heads covered by a simple scarf pinned below the chin. The aroma of frying *jalebi* and curry spice filled the air. Young women with short fashionable hairstyles appeared quite natural and at ease in colourful *kurta-pajama* as they sauntered past, their hips swaying and painted lips moving fast as they talked with each other or into their mobile phones.

'Smell that,' I said brightly as we passed Ivan's chip shop. 'Smells of old England!'

'Rendered pig fat,' said Mustafa sharply, 'what they call lard.'

'Ivan might deny that.'

'You have been away longer than I. There is more.' He pointed to a Malik's Halal Poultry. 'The chickens they slaughter are bought from an English farm. They share a field with pigs and feed on their excrement.'

I shook my head and tutted.

'Brother, it is very difficult to keep clean in this country.'

'You know that for sure?' I replied.

'All I know is that over there' – he indicated across the road – 'is a budget beer shop belonging to the treasurer of Best Street mosque.' He looked up at a swirling orange bulb outside a taxi office, Royal Cars. 'And that our minicab driver brothers hose down the drunken vomit of their passengers every Friday and Saturday night.'

The warm rays of the sun bathed my face and arms, and tilting my head up I saw a cloudless blue sky. I took a big breath in and exhaled long and hard as though the warmth of the air would cleanse me of Mustafa's cynicism.

Mustafa squinted hard at the sky, putting his hands together. His lips barely moved, the hum of a rapid-fire prayer alternating with the sound of his tongue pressing it against the roof of his mouth.

'What is the prayer for?' I asked.

Mustafa swiped his hands vertically down his face and nodded, sucking air through his teeth. 'My brother,' he replied. Did he mean me?

As though suddenly drained of energy, Mustafa shuffled on, taking short steps. When confronted with a kerb or a protruding paving stone he seemed to take great care in how and where he placed each foot. He reminded me of a child learning to walk.

Men and women stopped to smile at Mustafa, then did a suspicious double take when they saw me. My parents would never have openly admitted to my career but, just the same, everybody would know what I had done. An Afghan perched cross-legged on a mobile phone kiosk gave Mustafa a knowing nod, a gesture Mustafa reciprocated by placing his right fist over his heart and making a deep respectful bow.

'You say you've been away?' I asked.

'Same place as you, brother.' Mustafa put out his right hand, inches from my eyes. 'Three is a sacred number.'

I drew back to focus on his hand. The three digits between his thumb and little finger were missing, the stubs gnarled, some longer than others but none progressing beyond the middle joint. The nails on his thumb and little finger were paper-thin and brittle, the faintest pink blush showing through them. I shivered involuntarily.

Mustafa smiled, exposing perfect white teeth. 'As long as it takes, brother, we will bide our time. We will have justice.'

'You were a jihadi?'

'Sunshine out there played havoc with my eyes,' he joked.

I laughed nervously. 'You didn't get a tan.'

'Worked mostly at night.'

'You were the enemy?'

'I was good with my hands.' He smiled and wriggled his stubs. 'And can you believe it? I had to blacken my face; just like your British soldier friends I painted streaks of camo across my face.' Carefully he mounted the steps of the Kashmiri Karahi House and Sweet Shop.

A brother, not looking where he was going, brushed between us on his way out of the store, a carrier bag swinging at his hips. A few feet on he stopped, swivelled on his toes and exclaimed, 'Brother Mustafa, it is you! *Mash Allah. Mash Allah.*'

The stranger rushed back, clasped both of Mustafa's hands in his own and said, '*Allahu Akbar*, brother, you are safe, *Allahu Akbar*.' The speaker glanced at me with penetrating eyes before returning his attention to Mustafa. 'Anything you need, Brother Mustafa, please call upon me. My brothers and I, we await your call, don't forget us.' The man had a long black beard. In the centre of his forehead was a thick circular patch of skin, dark and slightly raised – a third eye, a marker of a true believer.

Mustafa made a deep bow. 'I will, brother, I will, but right now,' he pointed to the stranger's carrier bag, 'your wife will be cross if you let those sweetmeats melt in this heat!'

Ali, the owner of Kashmiri's, stood behind a refrigerated glass counter. The curved glass at the front reflected a distorted image of Mustafa and me, our faces long and curved and Mustafa's beard spiralling to a thin point. In the chilled compartment were brightly coloured sweetmeats shaped into cubes and spheres and crusted with chopped nuts. One type of milky *barfi* was covered in gold leaf.

Ali put his right fist over his heart. 'Salaam to you, Dr Mustafa *bhai*. I saw you from the window and could not believe my eyes. Had you not come in, I would have come out to greet you. Welcome most humbly to my shop.'

'Brother,' said Mustafa, 'I need to trouble you for fifty boxes of assorted sweetmeats.'

Ali nodded. After fumbling in his pockets, Mustafa pulled out a long thin piece of paper like a till receipt. He handed it to Ali and asked him to deliver the sweetmeats to the addresses written on the chit.

The shopkeeper considered the list and nodded. 'Yes, *bhai*, of course, *bhai*, I will close up shop and do it personally.'

'May Allah bless you,' said Mustafa, pulling out a large wad of brand-new banknotes.

Ali shrank back towards the wall behind him, shaking his head. 'No, *bhai*, here you will not pay. I will not accept a penny. Please, *bhai*, give it to the poor.'

'Brother, you are kind. The poor have never needed it more.' And as Mustafa smiled, I understood 'the poor' to mean a fund for jihad.

Outside the shop we leant against a column of brickwork at the centre of the glass frontage, eating samosas out of a paper bag Ali had insisted we take. Mustafa spoke, flakes of pastry caught on his lower lip. 'Brother Akram, in our own ways we were both jihadi.'

'Ali in the shop called you doctor?' I said.

His milky eyes stared into mine. 'Ali, *mash Allah*, is one of the faithful, and although I prefer the honorific mister over the title doctor, people really respect the doctor.' A smile spread across his lips and he returned his attention to the bag of samosas.

'Mister?' I enquired, further confused.

'I was awarded the honorific by no less an institution than the Dental Faculty at the University of London.'

'You were placing fillings in Talibs' teeth?'

Mustafa put a hand on my wrist. 'My dear brother. If you understood the anatomy of how a tooth is suspended by ligaments into the bones of the skull, you would then understand how the dental complex is possibly the weakest part of the body. Allah, in his graciousness it seems, has designed the system to limit our time on this earth. When the dento-alveolar complex fails – and inevitably sooner or later it does – its sequelae is a potent infection spreading like a sponge soaking up water into the eyes and the brain. I, with nothing more complicated than a pair of forceps,' he beamed proudly, 'gave renewed life to our brothers and sheikhs.'

'You met the sheikhs?' I asked.

'I was often taken blindfolded—' He broke off, clearly deciding he had said enough.

'So a sheikh bit off your fingers?' I tried not to laugh.

'I don't talk about the sheikhs.' His eyes stared wistfully into the distance and he nodded before continuing. 'As part of my training I was taught ethics. Patient confidentiality. But I will tell you this. Even the great sheikh trembled at the sight of my needle.'

'You met—'

Mustafa interrupted. 'It was a cause of concern to me that I was unable to sterilize my instruments, and a strange irony that only through the pursuit of a solution to that problem was I introduced to acids and nitrates and chlorides, and there too my medicinal knowledge of chemistry was useful.'

'You laid IED?'

'There was always a shortage of mobile phones.'

'Mobile phones?'

Mustafa laughed before continuing. 'My preferred detonation method was by text message. A short text message sent to a mobile phone wired to the fuse.'

'What did the text say?'

'For luck I used the numbers seven-eight-six.'

'We in the army, we didn't do jihad,' I stated, but no sooner had I spoken than I realized he would make capital out of my alliance with the *gora*.

'No. Really? Not jihad? Then what for?'

I shrugged my shoulders, conscious that I now had to support my statement. 'I was there for my mates and the army, for Queen and country, for England, forever England, green hills and that. It's the thing they drum into you.'

Mustafa didn't reply immediately. With a loose tail of turban he wiped the sweat off his brow, and as he pushed up his turban it revealed his third eye, a callused circle of brown skin that stood out against his white forehead. Proof, if it were needed, that his real Pakistani colour could be beaten to the surface.

I was afraid of what he might say and looked away when he finally spoke. 'Are you really stupid enough to believe all that? Have you looked at yourself in the mirror? When you were drinking with your mates in the NAAFI did you not look down at your brown arms and little black hairs poking out of your skin and think *what the fuck am I doing here?*' He inspected me closely, running his eyes over every contour of my face. 'You're a cripple, and where are your mates now, and where is this green Eng-a-land?'

'I got compo. I have a pension. You're in England now too, so where are your jihadi?'

A pink blush spread rapidly across Mustafa's face, and he spoke angrily. 'Have you not seen them? Are you blind? That man who stopped me outside Ali's, the one with the shopping bag, he might look like a nobody to you but he works as a specialist surgeon. The fellow at the phone card kiosk is an Afghan veteran. And, and. . .' In his fury, Mustafa struggled for words. 'Did you not witness how Ali would not take my money? If I stood here and called, a hundred men would come to my aid. Here, my foolish brother, my dear brother Akram,' he spread out his arms as though he spoke for all of Cradley, 'here, everywhere are my jihadi.' He spoke loudly, almost shouting, panting for breath between words. 'We cannot all fight, but we each do our bit.'

Suddenly, Mustafa stooped over and struggled for air. Letting my stick take my weight, I nudged a shoulder into his to offer support. A thick red tracked up from his neck and quickly engulfed his cheeks. He put his maimed hand to his face, clearly in pain. I could feel heat coming off him. A number of brothers who were out shopping, some a few feet away and others across the street, stopped and stared. Some pointed Mustafa out to their wives or companions, but each stood at a reverent, almost fearful distance, as though primed to help and waiting for a signal.

'What's wrong?' I asked.

'When the fuse blew off my fingers,' he gasped, 'I had a minor heart attack. They could seal the ends of my fingers with a branding iron but my heart they could only monitor. I have not been the same since. At first I thought my confidence had gone, but doctors say it is worse. They say we albinos have weak hearts.'

'Serves you right for messing around with fuses.'

Mustafa's laughter seemed valiant amid his short, panicked intakes of breath. He grappled for my shoulder and straightened. Like a bottle slowly drained, the redness gradually disappeared below the collar of his combat tunic. Seeing the brothers staring at him, Mustafa simultaneously bowed and put his right fist to his heart. The brothers across the road, and others surrounding us from a distance of only a few feet, slunk off.

'I should have been martyred like our kid.'

'Our kid?' My mouth was suddenly dry. 'Faisal was martyred?'

'You don't know? Didn't you see Ali offer his respects by not taking my money? Or the surgeon brother say he awaits my call? What did you think that was about? Our Faisal even made the TV news.'

I shook my head, feeling the hair on the nape of my neck stand on end. 'I remember him best as a kid – as a baby smiling out of a broken window.'

'He was strong, like you, Brother Akram. And proud. He is with Allah.'

'What exactly happened?'

'Exactly, I cannot tell you, for security reasons you will understand.' He stared at me but I offered nothing in return. 'I took our kid out laying ordnance. What your people fear the most. An IED.'

I shook my head.

'He wasn't a natural,' continued Mustafa. 'Mine went off and blew a hole in a Mastiff. Our kid, his didn't go, did it? We were watching from a dugout, and despite what I had taught him, like a brave fool he rushed out to reset it. Just as he got there this ISAF sniper spots him. One round to the head.'

I said without thinking, 'Those snipers are shit hot.'

'He was a British citizen. I took his body by Land Cruiser back to Peshawar. The police affidavit cost five English pounds and the official report read that Faisal was shot by a dacoit. I flew him home to our mother. It was her wish.'

'Allah's will,' I said. 'I'm sorry.'

'Allah's will,' repeated Mustafa. He shook his head but in his voice there was no sense of mourning. 'Only British soldiers talk about sorry. Faisal's martyrdom was the happiest day of his life. It is an occasion to celebrate and to distribute sweetmeats. Our kid is in Paradise.'

'How will you ever know that for sure?'

'Faith, my dear brother Akram. Faith. Justice.' He stared into the middle distance. 'My only regret is that I will not join him. I am cursed with a gene that gives me the skin and heart of a *gora*. I am not long for this world. I don't let on, but I know it.'

The morning sun lent the air a crisp, yellow quality. The colour of shop signs, of the clothes people wore and passing cars, seemed subdued but at the same time more intense, as though colour alone could spring to life.

'Brother Mustafa, the doctors, they don't know everything. They can't always estimate lifespan.'

'You're right,' he replied in a tone of resignation. 'But I sense it. Day by day I feel the strength drain from my arms and legs. I will accept my end.' He looked up at the sky. 'But in the meantime I will continue to do what I can to please the guardians of the hereafter.'

'We are from different countries, you and I. I say statistic and you say martyr. I look at death in war as a screw-up and you regard it as noble. I hope you are right and I am wrong. I really hope so.'

Mustafa laughed. 'You and I, we would have made a good team. You are the left hand and I am the right. Together we are neither one way nor the other but somewhere in the middle. They say middle is the best, no?'

'I've never believed in the middle. In the middle there are lies.'

Mustafa considered me for a long time before replying. '*Inshallah*, in you, brother, I see something special.' He looked at his watch and added, 'But right now I have to attend to Faisal, and I cannot attend to him on my own. I need a brother. As you have witnessed, even on this street I could have asked a hundred brothers, but no.' He shook his head ruefully. 'They are ordinary men, stupid thoughtless men, men whose sole function is to shuffle after their wives and carry the sweetmeats. Let them eat and sweeten their tongues, but you and I, brother, we have seen and understood. We have no fear of death. We have been warriors.'

He swept his hands through the air as though to show the way, then held my gaze. 'Will you, Brother Akram, will you honour me in doing the *ghusl* for my brother Faisal?' It wasn't really a question.

I followed Mustafa in silence, observing his unsteady gait. His walk made mine look almost normal. He ambled from side to side and his feet slapped hard against the pavement, as though at any moment he would lose his footing. I felt sorry for him. The blast, it seemed, had affected his balance too.

Twenty minutes later we arrived at a newly built mosque, in red brick with a large green dome. Diggers were already excavating an adjacent plot for what I assumed was an extension to the building.

An older Pakistani man, tall and thin with a long beard, and wearing gloves, a surgeon's cap and a face mask, met us in an anteroom at the back of the building. His eyes looked familiar but I couldn't place him. '*Assalamualaikum*, I am the duty attendant.' He took us each by the hand, shaking mine overlong. His gloves were wet.

He showed Mustafa and me into a larger room, tiled from floor to ceiling. It had an industrial feel, with galvanized pipes and vents overhead and the sound of working fans that seemed to suck the air out of the room, leaving it cold and clinical.

'Only two of you?' asked the man, taking in my walking stick.

'We'll manage,' said Mustafa cheerfully, his eyes drifting to a large steel door at the end of the room.

'I would be happy to assist,' the man replied, his tone mournful.

There followed a silence broken only by the air-conditioning. Without speaking, the man issued both of us with vinyl gloves and a blue plastic apron. He opened the steel door with a flourish like a concierge at a grand hotel and strode with soundless footsteps into the cold smoky white air. He fumbled for a light cord and a ceiling light flickered. An overwhelming dry smell of formaldehyde escaped from the room. It burned the rims of my eyes and deep inside my nostrils, and for a moment I tried to stop myself inhaling. As the light sucked to a constant state of illumination it revealed a stainless-steel trolley beneath which a macabre galvanized pipe led into a drain in the tiled floor. On the trolley lay a white body bag stamped ISAF. I shuddered.

'You'll find everything you need.' The man pointed to a deep square sink and a shelf above it crowded with bottles and vials. 'There is soap for the body. For our brother, I have prepared a splendid *oud* mixed with frankincense and myrrh.'

Mustafa began to chant, '*La ilaha il Allahu la ilaha il Allah.*'

The duty attendant pressed a small green bottle into my hand and whispered, 'I am atoning for my sins.'

Confused, I turned to look at him. Pulling off the face mask and lifting up his surgeon's cap, he offered a toothy grin. In the centre of his forehead was a deep gnarled burn that had healed badly into a dark keloid brown. I had held him down and Adrian had burned him with a cigarette until we could see the white of his skull bone, until he passed out. 'Bobby? You?' I mouthed silently.

He shook his head. 'Fakir Ahmed Fazal Alam,' he said. Bowing deeply, he left the room.

Mustafa's chanting was soft and deeply melodic, and his body swayed.

When I was a small boy my mother would climb into my bed in the evening. Lying next to me, she would sing me to sleep, '*La ilaha il Allahu*'. Although then I could have scarcely known what it meant, it was and still is the most beautiful thing I have ever heard. She would often pause for minutes at a time to speak to me about hell, tell me ancient stories passed down through the generations, or sometimes she would read from a pamphlet: about eternal fire that burned you up only for Allah to give you immediate life so that you could be burned up all over again. There were also hammers that beat you into the earth like a wooden peg. In hell, everything was hot, black, spiked, and water for the thirsty inhabitants was molten steel mixed with hair from the pig.

Standing on opposite sides of the trolley, Mustafa and I draped a black sheet over the body bag. During the preparation of the body, Mustafa explained, the sheet would remain over Faisal, as a mark of respect: it was important that Faisal's naked body remain concealed from the gaze. Mustafa added that he had done the *ghusl* many times for martyred brothers – brothers white, black and brown.

By wedging a hip against the side of the trolley I was able to free up both of my hands. Glancing frequently at each other and communicating only with our eyes, Mustafa and I worked carefully to release Faisal from the rubber bag that had carried him from Afghanistan. His skin might tear if he was dragged. When Mustafa grew tired and out of breath from chanting, I picked up where he had left off. We chanted and otherwise communed silently with Allah. We each seemed to know what was required, whether to lift or to pull, and at what moment.

As the body slid out of its bag, a foul-smelling gas escaped. Faisal's head was heavy, cold and rubbery. His waxy eyelids were closed and his mouth fixed into place by a circular bandage. He had a short beard and a full head of densely black hair. As he cradled Faisal's head in both hands, I examined Mustafa for emotion but did not see any. Using wet cotton wool, he slowly cleansed the body, beginning with the face. Like the ritual ablution before prayer, Mustafa's hands swept across every inch of his brother three times, his missing fingers seemingly no impediment to the task.

In the middle of Faisal's forehead was a yellow plaster. I carefully removed it to reveal an entry hole. At the back of his head would have been a dirty jagged exit hole, but I did not look. Mustafa put his gloved hand on mine. Catching my eye, he shook his head as though we both knew that this death was a crime that would require vengeance. There was something special in Mustafa's eyes, a softness, a glazed-over vacancy; magnified by the lenses of his spectacles, they looked pleadingly into mine.

Putting his hands underneath the black sheet, Mustafa soaped, dried and then rubbed scent into his brother's skin, and as required we lifted Faisal onto one side and then the other so that Mustafa could reach. The body felt waterlogged and heavy but it did not feel like a human being. No one seemed to exist inside of what lay before us. His soul, that thing that had given life to his body, had long since flown. His soul, the very essence and the only thing that mattered, had left his body for Paradise. I caressed him tenderly as though expecting to feel something, but the overwhelming sense I had was that no one was there – not in that body. It wasn't a great revelation – it was simply that what lay before us, the sheer mass of putrefying muscle and tendon and organs, barely contained by a sac of waxy, semipermeable skin, could no longer be termed human. Faisal wasn't with us, and at that moment I was convinced that there was a heaven, and that the earthly body we were cleansing was a mere husk of the man who had once occupied it. For his twenty-two years on earth Faisal had merely lived in it, like a coat, and I was certain that he had no more need of it. I was sure that the body before us was a vessel in which Faisal had been carried and that he wasn't sorry to leave it. I wasn't sorry he had left it. I wasn't afraid for him. Faisal was in a better place.

Bobby, his face sombre, wheeled in a plain wooden coffin on a trolley. He stood and watched, humming a *naath*.

Mustafa and I lined the casket with three sheets of white linen that draped generously over each edge. After bringing the trolley up parallel to Faisal, with a great heave we carefully lifted his body into the coffin. We wrapped the sheets over his body, tucking them into the sides and tightly over his forehead to conceal the entry hole, leaving an opening so that his face could be viewed. Finally, we placed the cover on the casket and from the green bottle scattered incense over the lid.

As Bobby wheeled the casket away I felt suddenly tired. We had worked in a period of suspended grace and under a veil of hypnotic chant, but now I realized that I was drenched in sweat and that a sort of coffee-grind treacle had rubbed off Faisal onto my hands and arms. I had worked hunched awkwardly over the trolley, my weight borne on one leg, my stick discarded on the floor by my feet.

As though reading my mind, Mustafa reached down for my stick. A single tear tracked down his cheek as he said, 'I hope you are cleansed of the British, of England's green and pleasant land. Here lay no savage beast.' His tears flowed more heavily, and he added, 'I chose you because I knew you would have respect for a fighting man, and I now know that you see what I see, the sacrifice, the nobility of our kid's martyrdom.'

In the anteroom, Bobby helped me out of my gloves and apron. Taking a wet soapy sponge, he slowly wiped my arms and then dried them with a towel. I said nothing, shivering at his touch.

16

Grace pours tea as we sit facing each other across a small kitchen table. She pushes a mug towards me and raises another to her lips. She blows on the hot surface, takes the tiniest of sips and puts it down.

'After the child protection conference, I got a surprise letter from the council offering me an old brick house in a proper street. This house! I jumped at the chance to get off the estate. No place to bring up a kid. Nothing happened for ages, no one visited, and although I dreaded the postman, no more children's department demands arrived. Britney was doing well, and after all the fuss I avoided the doctor's. My mind was good and we got out once a day to the park and to the shops.

'One day we were walking along Cradley high street, window shopping – I was skint – and a policeman literally bumped into me. He helped me up and then stared at me. "Grace Booth?"

'"Yes, sir." I saluted him, all jokey.

'"We've got a picture of you on our wall. We've been looking for you."

'"How strange to be famous," I joked. "I've been home."

'Turns out I was in contempt of court. They had been writing to me at the old address. I went to see a solicitor, Mr Ingram, who told me not to worry and that I was entitled to legal aid. The worst part was the waiting. Mr Ingram was waiting for the other side to photocopy the paperwork, which he'd then photocopy and send to me. It took a month. A van turned up. A man got out, loaded three heavy boxes of papers onto a trolley and wheeled them into the house. Surely some mistake. I telephoned Mr Ingram in alarm.

'"There'll be much more paperwork yet," he said. "You'll also receive several letters advising you of appointments, with Cafcass and a psychiatrist. You must keep all of them." He was about to put the phone down when he added, almost as an afterthought, "I'm afraid there is bad news. Although I've fixed it so that you're no longer in contempt, there have been court appearances in your absence." I asked him what that meant. There was a long silence over the phone. Then: "All is not lost, Miss Booth."

'Over several appointments, the psychiatrist asked me about my childhood. It wasn't a good one and I cried once or twice. Cafcass were more interested in what went on around me: Who were my mates? Boyfriends? Did I know so-and-so from the estate? Was my house tidy? How much did I spend on cleaning products, milk, fags? Britney had her own appointments, and sometimes I'd take her and be told to wait outside. She told me that one time she was asked to *draw a picture of Mummy* and at another they *played dollies*. At the back of my mind were Mr Ingram's words: *All is not lost.* I tried to push them to one side but sometimes they got the better of me.

'The court hearing kept getting put back. Twice, reports weren't ready. Once the social worker didn't turn up, and another time Mr Ingram said we weren't ready. I suppose he had a job to do and wanted to get everything perfectly right. All this time I had Britney. Sometimes I'd look at her and burst into tears. I treated her special, as though every day was Christmas Day.

'Finally Mr Ingram called me to say there was a court hearing. It was listed for five days. Britney was almost three by now.

'I had two lawyers, Mr Ingram and his barrister friend, and we sat on the right. The Social had two lawyers that sat on the left, and even Britney had her own official solicitor, a serious-looking bearded man who sat between our side and their side. Behind us sat the social workers, Cafcass officer, and doctors. Two young men, dressed in tight suits with short trousers like something straight out of *Oliver Twist*, wheeled in two trolleys full of papers. The judge had a plait wound on top of her head like a blond crown. She carried a bronze leather holdall, and before she said a word she pulled a lipstick out of her bag and smeared it on.

'The other side's barrister stood up and listed all the people he would be calling to give evidence, their jobs and qualifications. He finished with, "Ma'am, our position is fully stated in the paperwork."

'The judge briefly took off her glasses. "You really expect me to read all that, Mr Ellis? This court is concerned with expediency and outcomes. I have read the pertinent documents, but really, Mr Ellis, any more paper and I fear the floor beneath us will collapse!"

'My side stood up and spoke for ages about how the system *sought to sever the link between a daughter and her mother*. After another five minutes of non-stop talking, he said, "Therefore, ma'am, we seek not to rely on the Cafcass reports, those of the psychiatrist, and the medical reports prepared on behalf of the child."

'The judge frowned. "Mr Duncan, what are you saying? In a nutshell?"

'My side went very red, mumbled something about taking further instructions, and sat down.

'Britney's barrister said only a few words. He described her as a *bright, mostly happy child*, but then he said, "There is, however, an overwhelming body of evidence that the child repeatedly presents with injuries not con-sistent with unexplained spontaneous bruising, if indeed such a condition does exist."

'I had to stand up. "Your Honour, my daughter had blood given to her..."

'The judge took off her glasses and smiled at me. I stopped talking and smiled back. "Miss Booth," she said in a soothing voice, "you will get your chance to tell the court your side of the story. I know this is hard, but please be patient." Abruptly she seemed to change her mind. "Why don't we start with our first witness." She turned to the usher. "Escort Miss Booth to the witness box, please."

'The usher took me to a small wooden enclosure and with the Bible in one hand, I read an oath written down on a card in front of me.

'"You may sit," the judge told me.

'My side stood up. He called me Grace and asked me my name, address, and if I had an occupation, and I said no. He then asked me about the birth and I was allowed to talk about the blood transfusion that Britney got in her first hour of life. I told them that had started all the trouble. I described our house, what we did each day, what I ate, what I fed Britney. Her room, toys and books. It was like having a pleasant chat with a friendly uncle.

'The other side was next. Even though the barrister was asking me personal questions his eyes were cold. "Miss Booth, what impact does your mental illness have on your relationship with your daughter?"

'Britney and I were okay so I really didn't know what to say to him. Don't they tell you not to say anything in court? Keep silent? Deny?

'"I do apologize. Perhaps if I word it differently? Do you sometimes lose control?"

'I shook my head vigorously.

'"Is it possible that sometimes you lose it, and you're in some sort of daze, and afterwards, even though you were never asleep, you seem to wake up? Is it possible that you don't even remember losing your rag?"

'I was trying desperately not to cry. I stammered, "I-it's something to do with the blood she got."

'"I'm sorry. I didn't mean to upset you, Miss Booth. I'll change my line of questioning."

'I breathed a huge sigh of relief.

'"Miss Booth, is it true that between the ages of seventeen and twenty, you sought clients for sexual services?"

'I shook my head. What else could I do?

'"I refer the court to page six hundred and thirty-one of bundle four." He had a really good memory of his files. "It was recorded on the police database as a non-crime." He bit his lip and waited for an excruciating amount of time. "No further questions, ma'am."

'I slumped back in the chair.

'Britney's barrister was last. "Miss Booth, if I was Britney, your precious, beautiful little girl, and I could talk honestly and like a grown-up, what would I say to you? Would I say, 'Mummy, please stop hitting me'?"

'I was crying my eyes out.

'The judge spoke. "Miss Booth, I am sorry for you but you will see that there is a compound of evidence against you. No one here is thinking anything bad about you. We are simply here to decide what is best for Britney." She turned to the others in the room. "I think that's enough for now. Adjourn for one hour."

'In the waiting room outside, Mr Ingram put an arm around me. "You shouldn't have to sit through that all week. They're offering two hours a month supervised. It's better than losing her altogether."'

*

I have never known a comfort such as this and never will again. It has come late, and even now, as I squeeze her hand, I wonder if her warmth is a comfort I can own. Does not this scene, Grace's hurt and pain, which I can do nothing to alleviate, and she with it, belong to Adrian Hartley? Could Adrian, Britney's father, have helped her? Adrian, where all seemed to begin, my earliest memory, and all will end.

It is not a picture of Adrian that comes to me but that of another fighter wrapped in an ISAF-branded body bag, cold and waxy, scrubbed clean and smelling of rosewater. After finishing Faisal's *ghusl*, I was near to collapsing from exhaustion. Somehow, by mid-afternoon, I had limped home. I scrubbed myself for half an hour, then without a word to my new wife I fell fast asleep. I didn't wake for eighteen hours; when finally I did, I was in pain far worse than the previous morning. My thumb throbbed sharply. I shrank back from the sight of it as though it offended me. The pad of my thumb was hot and swollen around the laceration by the glass bead, and yellow-green pus oozed from the wound. I recoiled at the thought that it had become infected from contact with Faisal's body.

As my eyes adjusted to the morning light, I saw Azra standing beside the bed and leaning over me. She buttoned up the face part of her burqa, her eyes staring at me through black mesh. That small act seemed to stir the air around her, and I caught a waft of her scent, containing *oud* and something else, a reminder of Afghanistan, something I couldn't place.

'Come on,' she said. 'We have a duty.'

I dressed quickly and followed her outside. She walked fast and I struggled to keep up. I felt light-headed and thought I might also have caught a fever. The exertion brought the throbbing in my thumb to an awful, sickening intensity.

Azra shivered inside the burqa. Turning to me, she said, 'I can't breathe in that house of yours, it's so small and cramped.'

'Are you cold?' I asked. It was warm out.

'My father told me it was better here,' she said, gazing along the terraced street.

'These houses were built for workers.'

'My father said that in England the government gives you a house and money.'

'Here you can earn more in a day than you can in a month in Pakistan.'

'You earn nothing!' She spat out the words with contempt. After a moment, she gave a loud, exaggerated sigh.

As she scanned the rooftops one foot absently slipped out from beneath the hem of her burqa. Dark and slender with toenails painted red, it was gracefully encased in a gold strappy sandal, and the malleoli at her ankle jutted out sharply. I watched her foot move about as though it was testing the tarmac. It accidentally struck the base of my stick and quickly retreated back under the black robe.

'If you earned,' she added, 'you wouldn't live in a house like yours.'

'This is a civilized country,' I argued. 'Everyone who needs it is looked after.'

She didn't reply.

'It must be hard for you,' I continued, changing the subject.

'Nothing is hard after what I have seen in Pakistan.'

Azra and I arrived at Mustafa's, a semi-detached new build. There were many like it in the street, and save for a white-plastic imitation Greek porch guarding the door it didn't stand out. His mother answered our knock. A diminutive woman, she was as wide as she was tall, not fat but square. She had a dark moustache that I couldn't help but stare at.

'*Assalamualaikum*, Aunty,' I said.

Aunty returned our salaam, kissed us both on the hand and led us into the front room. Two sofas were placed either side of a coffee table. The sofas were covered in transparent plastic and the coffee table had a glass top. Above the mantelpiece was a picture of the Great Mosque in Mecca and below that was a familiar-looking clock, green plastic in the shape of a mosque with a painted golden dome. Like an alarm it could be set to ring the *azan* five times per day.

'Allah's will,' I said to Aunty.

The women, as though speaking as one, repeated my words. 'Allah's will.'

Relieved of formalities, we all sat down. I put my hands before my chest to pray and the women followed. Azra wore slim black gloves with a gold ring on her left middle finger. I whispered a short prayer for the deceased, and finished by swiping my hands down my face from forehead to chin. The women did the same.

'I'll fetch tea.' Her feet found her slippers, and Aunty left the room.

'This house is better than yours,' said Azra, looking around at the freshly painted interior.

I whispered, 'Because we all contribute to jihad they're loaded.'

I noticed a framed picture on the wall, of Mustafa on the day of his university graduation. He must have blinked as the camera flashed and in his hands he gripped a paper scroll. There were other pictures dotted around, of Mustafa and Faisal, of countless small children side by side on a string *charpoi*, their little legs dangling off the sides.

'I wouldn't want a son,' Azra said. 'The war will go on.'

'Chance would be—'

She interrupted. 'I couldn't let him go. Naturally he would want to martyr himself. It's selfish of me, but that's how I feel.'

'What *do* you want, Azra?'

'Daughters. Eighty daughters to replace my girls at the madrasa. And I want back the years you took from me.'

My thumb throbbed and I tried to laugh off her words. 'Who could afford the dowry of eighty daughters?'

'It would take a rich man.' She stared straight ahead.

'Could you really replace your students?'

'Girls are like mules, owned and transportable,' she said angrily. 'You of all people should know that.'

In the silence that then pervaded I could hear Mustafa's mother in the kitchen. A kettle boiled and porcelain clattered against porcelain. Crinkle wrapping was torn apart. I pictured biscuits tumbling onto a plate.

'Why are you here, Azra?' I said finally.

'Because you sent for me.'

'I thought that for a wife her husband comes first?'

'Allah comes first.'

'Then the husband is next?'

'The infidel is last,' she replied sharply.

A waft of brewing tea caught my nostrils. All four walls of the front room were wallpapered with a dark paisley design and as I traced its complicated outlines it hurt my eyes.

There was a knock at the front door, and slowly I raised myself onto the stick and answered. Ali seemed surprised to see me, but quickly recovered, handing me several boxes of sweetmeats. Without a word he returned to his van, the engine still running. I put them on the coffee table and slumped back onto the sofa next to Azra.

'Take off your burqa so Aunty can see you,' I said.

'Why?'

'I have known her all my life and she would want to see my wife. And try to smile.'

Aunty returned to the room with a tray that she placed on the coffee table. On the tray was a plate of assorted biscuits and three steaming mugs of English tea. She saw the boxes of sweetmeats on the coffee table and opened one. Gazing kindly on the newlywed couple, she smiled and implored us to eat. As she settled her ample weight on the sofa opposite, she blamed her cholesterol for her not joining us. 'My son Mustafa,' she added, 'has forbidden me from making *desi* tea, even for guests – he says I will not be able to resist a cup!' For a moment she tried to laugh. 'He is such a thoughtful boy.' She paused, deep in thought, and then gave a short sharp wail. Tears ran down her face and she blew her nose violently into a handkerchief.

I reached over the coffee table and placed a hand gently on her head. 'Faisal is with Allah, you must believe that.'

The tears stopped abruptly and she looked up. 'I am destined to lose both sons.'

'You don't know that, Aunty,' I said.

'It is *sawab*,' said Azra. 'Your boys are blessed and you are selfish to cry; even a mother must give way to Allah.'

I shot Azra a stern glance. Again I wished she wasn't wearing a burqa. I wished I could have seen the impression my anger had made on her hypocrisy.

Aunty nodded, holding her hands together in her lap. Her shoulders rolled forward and she stared at her hands, picking at the edge of a fingernail.

Azra spoke again. 'The boys at the madrasa, upon reaching maturity and with their hearts overflowing with the desire to perform Allah's work, they would cross the mountains. Not one ever returned. With unseen tears, as we watched them leave, we whispered their funeral prayer.'

'Thank you,' said Aunty to me, 'and thank you for doing Faisal's *ghusl*.' She reached out and took both of my hands in hers. Her hands were warm, the skin yellow. 'You and Mustafa have been friends since you were infants and to him you are like a brother. Your assisting him with the *ghusl* is an honour to our family.'

I hadn't told Azra about the *ghusl*. She gripped her chin in one hand and cocked her head, staring at me. Even through her burqa I could sense that she now regarded me with at least a little respect.

Still, she continued on her theme. 'Our job was to fill their hearts with the Holy Book. It would take about seven years to learn it by rote, occasionally a little quicker, though often, for those who resisted their fate, it would take a year or two longer for the imam to beat it into them. We took them in as infants, mostly abandoned on our doorstep, and sent them out as men. As warriors fit and strong and ready for the short walk across the pass and the long war thereafter.'

I ignored her. 'About Faisal's *ghusl* – it was indeed my honour to be asked, Aunty.' I picked up a mug and put it to my lips. I blew on the hot surface and added, 'Your son Mustafa, he is fearless.'

'Mustafa was a dentist, you know.'

I nodded.

'But he followed Faisal abroad. It was Faisal who had the calling, Faisal who first studied the Holy Koran. But Faisal was easily led and hot-headed, and his brother Mustafa felt he had to follow, to look after him.'

'A dentist. A good job,' said Azra to me, as though in rebuke.

'As a young man, Mustafa was always hunched over a table, his head in a book. He was a good dentist but they took away his licence on account of his poor eyes.' Aunty paused for breath. 'Mind you, he still pulled teeth. Mustafa would joke that to make up for his eyesight he would feel his way around his patient's mouth. It was in London he first practised dentistry, and in the evenings he would devote himself to the Holy Koran. In London he met brothers who taught him to read the Holy Book as a direct instruction to a way of life. Well, when the authorities found out he was operating without a licence they stopped him from practising dentistry, and do you know what they said to him?' For a brief moment Aunty forgot herself and laughed. 'They said to my educated son, why don't you retrain as a butcher? So what does Mustafa do? Ever resourceful, he gathers up his tools and follows his brother Faisal to jihad. "My tools," my son once said. "In the service of jihad my forceps are of greater value than the gun."'

She nodded slowly. 'He always thinks of others. The Taliban were more in need of a dentist than they knew. They took him to far-off places deep inside the mountains and led him blindfolded to work on their leaders.'

The *azan* sounded out of the alarm clock on the mantel: '*Allahu Akbar...*'

'He didn't just pull teeth. He was the nearest they had to a surgeon. Mustafa carried out their justice.'

This part Mustafa had failed to tell me. I wanted to hear more.

'We should go.' Azra got up to leave. I gestured to her to sit down, but she remained standing.

'Mustafa said it was more humane to do it with anaesthetic, cleanly and surgically, than with a scythe. The hands of a thief – the arms of a traitor – primitive justice.' Aunty was clearly irritated by Azra, still standing, her thin black frame looming large in the small room. 'Stay,' she continued. 'Pray with me. It would honour my family if my dear son Akram led the prayer.'

I could sense Azra seething inside her burqa. It felt like a small victory. 'Very well, Aunty,' I said. 'As you wish.' I picked up three prayer mats folded on a side table and spread out the first one on the floor.

'You can't touch the mat with that,' said Azra, her voice a low shriek.

I looked down to see the blackened rubber stump at the end of my walking stick pressing into the prayer mat.

'Your cane,' she said, 'it is dirty.'

'You will follow me,' I said, emboldened by Aunty's presence.

'You have soiled the sacred surface.'

I appealed to Aunty with a smile.

'Ladies behind men – come on, girl,' said Aunty brusquely.

The women fell into position behind me. I couldn't bend or prostrate, so Aunty brought up a chair. Comfortably seated, I led the proceedings, listening for the gentle sound of Azra's gold bangles clicking against each other as they rose and fell on her arm. I conducted the prayer as slowly as I could. I was no longer aware of my painful thumb, and my voice was clear, without a hint of fever. I sang, not recited, the Arabic words, stressing each syllable precisely as I had heard them in Afghanistan. It felt good, like being an imam, and I felt a cheap satisfaction to know that Azra had to follow, as though finally, however reluctantly, she had to bend to my will.

17

'It was the one thing I looked forward to, my monthly visit to the contact centre. I'd wait in a room with plastic chairs, bright pictures on the walls and toys on a mat on the floor. They'd bring in Britney, and for two short hours, under the watchful eye of the social worker, we would play. There were conditions: I wasn't allowed to encourage her to call me Mum, although she still did. I wasn't to be too affectionate or over-kissy. Taking photographs was not allowed. *Imagine you're her big sister*, the social worker had advised.

'They promised that over time they'd look to increase our contact, and one day, out of the blue, a kind secretary from the social worker's office calls me up and invites me in for a meeting. I hope that they're calling me in to increase our hours, and I put on my Sunday best. It takes ages to find the office and it doesn't help that I don't even know who I'm meeting. Eventually I'm shown into a shabby room with flaky, painted brick walls and tall metal windows onto the street. It reminds me of an old classroom.

'"We're here to discuss what's best for Britney."

'I'm sitting opposite the chaperone lady, just the two of us, and I nod earnestly.

'"What do you think that is, Miss Booth?"

'"To hang out more with her mum?"

'"That's disappointing. I was hoping. . ." She shook her head. "Never mind. I wanted to tell you about a family, miles from here. They live in the country with land and animals and are particularly fond of their horses. They have two older children, teenagers, a boy and a girl. My colleagues from their borough sent me their file and I've had a very good look through it."

'"What part of the country?"

'She shook her head again.

'"What's it got to do with me?" I felt suddenly sick and wanted to leave.

'"Miss Booth, you're still young. You can start again. Maybe, in time, have other children."

'There was a square window cut into the door of her office and a colleague of hers was waving through it. "Wait here." She stood up, her chair scraping loudly. "I've got a treat for you."

'The door opened and in walked Britney, nervous at first. She saw me and beamed. In her hands was a card she had crafted.

'"I'll leave you two for a few minutes. Think on it, Miss Booth. It's best for the child."

'I settled Britney on my lap on the floor. We looked at her card, two stick figures in crayon under a yellow sun. I stared at her small pudgy hands and wobbly red cheeks. She looked back at me with huge round eyes. I couldn't cry, not with Britney in the room, and maybe I did, for a moment, lose my mind, just like the barrister in court had said I did.

'Leaving Britney on the floor, I got to my feet and locked the door to the corridor. The chaperone came back after a short while, her face through the window surprised to find the door locked. She knocked lightly at first, trying not to frighten Britney, then a bit harder, her eyes wide and fixed. She called her colleagues, who crowded into the corridor outside, different faces silently taking turns to pull worried expressions through the window. Britney and I played on the mat with wooden farmyard animals, ignoring them all.

'Finally, the police were at the door. At first a woman officer tried to talk to me, but I ignored her and we continued to play, our backs to them. Then a male police officer, saying he would have to bust open the door. It was only then that I picked up a paperknife that lay among the papers on the chaperone's desk, went up to the window and put it to my neck.

'I guess they figured that as long as I stood by the door, Britney, at the far end of the room, was safe. That's why, why I think anyway, the door bust open in my face. I was knocked out cold. Later the nurse in the hospital told me I was choking on a loose tooth in my throat. They must have bundled Britney out of the room.'

There is a glazed expression on Grace's face, but no tears. I stand up, reach across the table and rest her shoulder against mine, cheek to cheek. I tell her that, just like her illness, everything is cyclical, nothing ever really ends. I tell her that when I close my eyes to pray, I see a rainbow of colours streaking across a sky and carved within the blue of it are the words prescribed for the close of each recital. I tell her that I too dread the end, that I feel lost, empty, as though suddenly abandoned by Allah.

Grace slumps back in her chair and nods. 'Don't mind me.'

I kiss her on the forehead.

She seems to compose herself quickly. 'It's all make-believe, you know.'

'What is?'

'A condition of mind.'

Confused, I wait for her to continue.

'We allow ourselves to believe in stuff we shouldn't. Sometimes it's automatic, like when Britney was born and I held her and I said to her, "Me and you, girl, we're in this together, forever." It's the same for you with your Allah.'

'Maybe you're right,' I say. 'Adrian had a phrase for it.'

She leans in and listens intently.

'No pain. If something was too awful to think about, he'd tense his jaw and tell himself, no pain.'

*

It was the first prayer I had ever led, and sadly, it was soon over. Behind me, Azra and Aunty were getting to their feet. I was still dreamy, winding down, when I heard a loud slow clap and then Azra's voice, 'Now you must feel like a real man.'

Burning with fury, I respectfully took leave of Aunty and quickly left the house, stepping into the fresh warm air of the day. I heard the door close behind me, and a second later Azra's full weight charged into my side. My stick collapsed from underneath me and I nearly fell. Extending her painted toes from beneath her burqa, Azra kicked the stick away, out of my reach. I balanced on one leg.

'Be a man and walk,' she said.

The stick lay on the pavement about ten feet away. I stared at her, sweat dripping from my brow, unable to comprehend what she had done.

'And after that take a hand to your wife for her insolence,' she went on. 'But before you beat her, recall that she is not yet your wife. You have not yet made her your wife. A marriage must be consummated, and if your wife won't bend to it then you must make her. Allah made man and woman and to each their respective strengths.'

I longed to see her face, masked by the black drop of the burqa. 'Azra, pick up the stick.' Bearing all my weight, my right leg had begun to hurt. 'I demand you pass me my stick.'

'Crawl for it.'

For balance, I lowered my bad leg. The slightest touch of my foot to the ground was immediately followed by a searing pain from the knee up to my spine. My leg jerked reflexively, the movement threatening to topple me over. The sole of my good foot began to burn on the hard tarmac. I looked around; a curtain in a nearby house twitched but other than that there was no one in sight.

I clenched my teeth. 'I will not crawl.'

'Crawl for redemption.'

'What?'

'We sent them out only to be murdered by the infidel. By you.'

'I bet you were in love with a Taliban.'

Azra laughed drily. 'Love. What would you know about that?' She threw a glance back at the house we had just left. 'You might fool that old woman, but I know your fate is to burn like the infidels.' She took in a wide view of the street. 'The British infidels are born to their lot, but you? You went against your own.'

My face was clammy with perspiration. As the burqa prevented me from seeing the expression on Azra's face, I decided I wouldn't give her the satisfaction of seeing the anger on mine. With great effort, I relaxed my jaw and put on a nonchalant expression, focusing my thoughts on stiffening the muscles in my supporting leg.

'What did they offer you to turn against your own?'

I remembered to wriggle my toes the way we would when standing for long periods on parade. Immediately, I felt a slight relief.

'You murdered the brothers you were born to.'

I closed my eyes, listening to the gentle breeze, the sound of cars in a distant street, the familiar *bong* of a hammer. I thought of an old soldier's trick and tuned my nose to the smell of my surroundings. Too often soldiers forgot that the enemy lay under their noses: the aroma of baking flour as chapattis cooked in nearby houses, a faint whiff of spiced oil, tobacco and a wisp of hashish. I smiled inwardly, remembering that out in the field this, mixed often with paraffin fumes, would alert us to a Taliban camp.

No longer able to hold me, my leg buckled and I collapsed painfully to the pavement. Azra shook her head and proceeded slowly down the street, her hips swaying inside the burqa.

I crawled to my stick, then dragged myself up and limped fast and recklessly in the opposite direction, threatening to stumble at any moment. In no time at all I was descending a steep set of steps that led down, as though a new subsurface level had opened up, onto a path alongside the canal. It was quiet down there, almost brighter, as if, unencumbered by buildings, the sun penetrated deeper. Swans and ducks, dappled in sunlight, meandered casually along on the water, occasionally flopping up onto the ground as a brightly painted barge motored lazily in the direction of Netherton Tunnel. The vessel's engine was a low rumble, background noise, like the sound of wildlife.

I rested on a wooden bench near the abandoned mill. It now had a steel door and a glass window, partly open and protected by a screen of chicken wire. From within I could hear a rhythmic beat, *clack, clack, clack*, and a voice not unlike a training sergeant's, issuing admonishments and instructions. I got up and went closer. Through the open door I saw a brother in a Lonsdale vest working a punching bag. Another couple of brothers, their black beards spilling out of protective headgear, sparred viciously.

I turned away from the door and carried on, and where the path ended I scrambled up, at times painfully on my hands and knees. On top of Turner's Hill the grass was dense and battered constantly by the wind, growing in tall wild clumps. It was darker at the summit, even on a clear day. An electricity pylon marked the highest point and I sat down on a small grassy ridge nearby. It was exposed, and every few seconds the wind changed direction, gusting around me. Before me birds swooped obliquely in and out of view as though carried on the currents. On all sides I was surrounded by hills, hills that were invisible from the town below. There was Clent, Malvern, and further out, the Welsh black mountains. Between the hills were strung factories, tall industrial chimneys, and neat rows of terraces, the older ones with grey slate roofs squeezed tightly together. A knot of spidery orange metal I identified as the playground in Lye Park. The castle sat on a hill at one end of the panorama and at the other, as though diametrically opposed, stood three tower blocks. In the far distance, where Rowley Works once sprawled for miles, was a flash of neon, signalling the entrance to Merry Hill shopping centre. I squinted my eyes against the obvious, the century and a half of labour and industrialization, and obligingly they disappeared into a blurry grey. The scene now before me wasn't natural – nature had been blunted – but suddenly it seemed ancient and unchanging.

Turning, I was surprised to see Bobby, and I felt bitter at the sight of him, as though Turner's Hill was a place only I visited. That day he too carried a limp. Down below on the water, Mustafa would be waiting for me as arranged, and probably he had sent up Bobby to keep a sly watch. The fakir Bobby held a long staff in his hand, and he wore long flowing robes in green.

'What you doing up here?' He had to shout to be heard over the wind. In the absence of a turban his long hair blew across his face and obscured the third eye Adrian and I had branded him with, each grey tendril picked up by the currents, soft and feathery.

'I've come to see the edge of the rain.' I looked out across to a distant range, counting the peaks to myself.

Bobby turned to command the scene in a full sweep, then sat down next to me. 'But the sun's out.'

'I can wait.'

'If you don't mind me saying,' he leant in closely and raised his eyebrows, 'only pervs come up here.'

'You would know.' I stared straight ahead at the view.

Pushing aside his hair to reveal the scar on his forehead, he said, 'Thank you, brother, for this. It was Allah's will and it woke me up to what I had become. I did not seek medical attention; I suffered it, I consumed the pain, hoping for more.'

His scar reminded me of Adrian, and I felt overwhelmed with my love for my dead buddy. 'If I was superstitious,' I said, 'I would think you were there in the pomegranate orchard the day Adrian Hartley died, you were the eye marked on the trees.'

'You saw for yourself, at the mosque, I am gifted with something. The mark on the trees, it was a warning.' The wind almost swallowed up his next words. 'I, brother, I have learnt much through suffering.'

I looked down at the drab landscape and said bitterly, 'I have learnt nothing through suffering.'

He grinned, his strong teeth like tombstones. 'You will, Brother Akram – you have only have to look up.' His hands pointed towards the heavens.

'You think you can be forgiven?' I shook my head. 'Just like that?'

'You think you can live among us yet fight us,' he replied.

'I thought I was done with fighting.'

'Touch me,' he said.

I turned away.

He reached for my hand and put it to his chest. I could feel his heart beat fast. 'Touch me to signal that I am forgiven.' Caught by the wind, his long hair winnowed behind him, and on his face spread a broad smile.

I shook my head, pulled my hand away and went to grasp my walking stick, fallen just slightly out of reach. Surprisingly strong, Bobby heaved me to my feet and carefully put the stick in my hand. As I found my balance, he dropped to the ground and sat with his legs crossed and hands in the prayer position.

Making my way back down towards canal level, I fell several times, grazing my hands on the gravel and incurring scratches from the thicket that lined the path. When I reached the base of the hill, struggling to catch my breath, the brothers who had been training in the mill passed me without a glance. Now wearing high-visibility orange vests and swinging an iron weight in each hand, they ran short sprints up the hill while their instructor counted down from ten. They ran in formation as though they were military.

I returned to the towpath. A barge, painted bright green and with small round windows cut into its side, motored past. A name was stencilled onto the paintwork: *MusicMan*. Just after it passed me, the noise of its engine changed into something more laboured, and I watched nervously as it slowly reversed and sidled up to the towpath where I was standing.

Mustafa, wearing broad, mirrored sunglasses and a sailor's cap with an anchor stitched at its centre, was manning the steering column. '*Mash Allah. Mash Allah*,' he said, putting his hands together in supplication.

He pushed a plank onto the towpath and helped me aboard. 'What happened to you?' he asked.

'Fell,' I said, flinching from his touch. He nodded knowingly at my scratched and muddied face.

We motored towards Netherton Tunnel. Mustafa disappeared into the cabin to switch on a CD player. I lowered myself to the wooden deck, rolled up my trousers and took off my shoes and socks. Averting my eyes from the sight of my left leg, I slid to the edge of the barge and lowered both feet into the ice-cold water. Here, like this, I was no longer aware of my defect.

The vessel crept into the tunnel. Mustafa cut the engine and the music rang out clearly, a deep rousing tenor echoing off the arched brickwork. Then a woman's voice, soft and fluttery like birdsong, straining to be heard over the violins, trumpets and crashing cymbals. I pictured an orchestra playing in a lush garden.

Mustafa's heavy feet shook the deck as he made his way over to me. His hot breath was startling as he bent over and whispered in my ear, 'I prayed all night that you'd come.'

The voices alternated, the man's and the woman's, singing a *naath* in Arabic, '*La ilaha il Allahu la ilaha ila Allah*'. The weightlessness of my feet in the water felt, for a moment, like a miracle. Then both voices sang at once, perfectly in sync, the sum of them greater than their individual parts. They sounded like angels calling out to Allah. The boat drifted further into nothingness and the volume of the song slowly rose.

Mustafa lowered himself down onto the deck and placed a bottle of whisky and a pack of cigarettes between us. He put two cigarettes into his mouth and lit them, then offered me one. 'Drink and smoke,' he said, unscrewing the bottle top and pushing it towards me. 'We who have not long must enjoy ourselves.'

He began to chant, '*Allahu, Allahu*,' his head nodding to the beat. I was enjoying the echo against the walls. 'They won't find us here, Brother Akram. *Allahu*. No wives here. *Allahu*.'

Leaving me with the bottle, he switched on a flashlight and stepped off the barge onto the towpath. The barge drifted on, as thought its direction were divinely set. The beam of the torch elongated along the tunnel walls. It lit up Mustafa in silhouette as he searched for something among the brickwork. Moments later he jumped back onto the barge, the force of his landing vibrating through the wooden planks. He now carried what looked like a military daysack. Still holding the bag, he clambered onto the low roof.

Mustafa extinguished the flashlight, and deep in the tunnel the darkness was complete. I saw a small spark as if two live electrical wires had been touched together. It was momentary, but as it glowed blue it lit up Mustafa's face, bent towards the source, a cigarette dangling carelessly from his lips. He appeared ghost-like, whiter than I had ever seen him. The smell of tobacco, cordite and worked steel clouded the air above, familiar like the smell of a live bullet issuing from a chamber; the spark flickered a second time, and I saw Mustafa's broad pink smile and his fragile blue eyelids bordering un-wavering eyes.

Leaving the daysack on the roof, he returned to sit beside me. 'You like this tunnel? British engineering. Only fifty yards short of two miles.'

'I've always wanted to go through it playing opera music, but this is better.'

'In here,' he said, 'it's the hereafter.'

'It's certainly something,' I said, my eyes beginning to adjust to the dark-ness. 'It's somewhere between worlds.'

'This atmosphere is good for my eyes,' he said. He put an arm around my shoulders. As I picked up the bottle he leant his mouth into it, knocking back a large gulp.

'Brother, it really burns.' Violently he shook his head and screwed up his face. 'How can the *gora* like whisky?'

'You start with something weaker, something like cider and blackcurrant.'

'You have lived with the *gora*. You know their ways.'

'Whisky is fine neat but improves with a mixer.'

'I was never part of their society, therefore I am ignorant of their habits.'

'It must be a cheap blend,' I added, unable to inspect the bottle in the darkness. 'What you want is a pure single malt; that, with a drop of water, is tolerable.'

'You, Brother Akram, have an advantage over me.'

'I would have preferred a pint of Banks's – tastes like dishwater but I got used to it.'

'Society,' Mustafa repeated, tasting the word. 'It is time you knew your own. You, Brother Akram, your fate was sealed before you were even born. Up to this day, it has been child's play, but from now on you must step up and become your own man.'

I took a swig from the bottle and drew on the cigarette. Like a tender lover, Mustafa rubbed my back. 'Take your time, brother. Take six months, even a year. Learn about who you are. Let Allah take over your body, let Him put whiskers on your chin and ease your pain.'

I laughed. 'Can you fashion me a third eye?'

'With a gentle rub of gunpowder I can, or maybe a match,' he laughed knowingly, 'but I warn you it will burn.'

'Through the pain I might learn something,' I carelessly challenged him.

He shook his head. 'No, brother. You must also span the other society. When you are needed you must also blend.'

'What do you want me to do?'

'Become a brother to the brothers. Grow the sign of a believer's beard and know one thing above all else, that only through Allah's grace do we understand the term *justice*.'

'Allah is a strange thing. One that has followed me all my life.'

'When you wake up and see the impotence of our people in the face of the white man's crusade then you will come to me and say, "Brother Mustafa, tell me what I can do. Equip me with the power of what I must do."'

'Are you certain I will do that?'

'When you say "Allah", think *justice*. Just substitute those words.'

'All my life, as a kid and at school, it wasn't so much about being brown and not white; even then, really it was a religious war.'

'It's not just religion. It's a supremacy of morals, ideas; it is the future of mankind. That duty as it has been written, that of killing for vengeance, that noble act is not for the cowardly sweetmeat carriers or the men who trudge blindly around shopping centres behind their wives. It is for men who follow their faith to its natural end.'

A loud drumbeat accompanied the chant. Feeling giddy, I sang along with it, '*La ilaha il Allahu la ilaha il Allah*,' my voice and the bass echoing loudly into the distance, bouncing off the mossy brickwork like a clap of thunder.

18

Grace helps me upstairs and I dress clumsily, using the edge of the bed and the bedroom wall for balance. Her arms folded at her waist, Grace watches quietly but does not help. She wants to slow it down, my inevitable departure, as do I.

She follows me to the door, my cap in her hand. I flip the daysack over a shoulder. Her eyes dart to it.

'We soldiers do love to hump.' I try to laugh.

She opens the door and I step out into the street. She stands on the step, half a foot taller than she actually is. 'It's not soldiers I fear. It's those that come not in uniform.'

I nod gently in understanding. 'Don't put your lights out, Grace. Promise?'

'I'll see Britney once more, in a few hours.' She holds back her tears. 'After that—'

'You will see her again after that.'

'You can't help me?' Her voice breaking.

'Remember what Adrian would have said. No pain.'

Briefly, she laughs and cries at the same time.

'Hold on.'

She nods, wiping her eyes with a fist.

'One day you'll be walking along the street minding your own business and this beautiful young woman will walk right past; then a few feet on she'll stop and glance back, and she'll be like, "Fuck, Mum?"'

Grace smiles, considering the scene I have painted, but says nothing.

'And when she does turn, be yourself, she will love you for it, and tell her all about her dad.'

'I've decided to stop,' she says earnestly. 'You know, the job.' She shrugs her shoulders. 'Wasn't much good at it anyway.' She reaches up on her tiptoes and places the cap on my head. There is a long pause as we try not to look at each other.

'Got to crack on.' I offer a quick smile and half turn to go.

She half closes the door. 'Was it a coincidence? Us?'

'Allah has a plan for each of us.'

'Don't be such a cryptic bastard. You came to get it off your chest?'

I nod. 'I came because Adrian would have wanted you to know.'

'Will I see you again?'

'*Inshallah.*'

A thought lingers on her lips and floats out of view as I turn, my boot scrapes against the pavement, she closes the door and the latch clicks shut.

Grace's voice, '*Inshallah*,' rings in my ears. It was the second time she had said it; it sounded curiously different on her lips, as though it was more important when spoken by the *gora*. *Inshallah* – God willing. A cruel God meting out a brand of justice none of us, least of all Grace, can comprehend.

I walk, pounding the pavements of my hometown, lost in a daze, my face battered by the wind, my thoughts returning to the One from whom I came, Allah. I am conscious of the daysack weighing me down but it feels good, exhilarating, it reminds me of recruit training, of endless route marches. And then of daysacks humped on patrol, weighted with teabags, sugar, powdered milk, stove kit and ammo. Although I attempt to tread quietly, each boot step clips against the pavement, sharp and loud. A weapon slung across my bent arms would counterbalance the daysack, would make me feel whole. The wind blows intermittently and the sun has not completely broken through the cover of purple-grey clouds: the best conditions for a route march. I recall cooling wind on a perspiring brow and false peaks in the distance and training sergeants and corporals lining the route at mile intervals drinking tea from large green canteens, bellowing encouragement mixed with insults with a wit peculiar to the army.

I reach a roundabout at the base of a hill and proceed upwards. Time is closing in, counting down. The occasional minicab races past, well above the speed limit, and I, a crippled former soldier heading towards the monument, occupy an infinitesimal and fleeting space in the thoughts of its driver.

An unmarked white coach trundles past, belching black smoke. In low gear its engine creates a vicious racket, as though its hulk is squeezed onwards through a thin slip of air. In its rear window, now receding slowly from view, hangs a drum sergeant's dress tunic and the top end of a black case with comforting curves that evoke the brass instrument within. Perhaps one of the coach's occupants sees me, *one of their own*, and considers a wave, and the vehicle moves on faster than he can raise his hand. The cap rubs against my damp brow and I take it off, allowing the wind to my hair. Grace, fingering the double-headed eagle pinned to the cap, had called it two-faced. I had never thought of it that way, but now it seems apt. She described the two personalities of her disorder, a dark phase that could last for months and then, as though the sun had broken through the clouds, give way to lightness. She had lost her child in her helplessness – a state I cannot imagine. Grace, almost without thought, revealed the dark gap in her mouth and smiled, a trusting smile. She did that so that I could see her for what she was. I could stay or go: to her I could easily have been just another man passing through, and in some ways I have been just that.

To the east a small shaft of light penetrates the clouds, opening a gap, and instinctively I say a *Bismillah*. Out of the bend the road slopes steeply up towards the town centre, where a stone cross stands on a flat piece of ground, and behind that is a dip where once was a moat. Beyond that, in jagged spurs like those of a looming mountain, are the remains of a castle casting a broken shadow as old as old England. England was then for the

English, and as the great castle sprang up, how grand it must have seemed to the peasants in their dwellings at the base of the hill – imperious like a structure of the Lord. And within the castle must have resided a lord who, having read his barometer (looted during his most recent foray into France), might have stood looking down from the highest wall, clapped his hands, and proclaimed that by virtue of his God-given powers, he knew that a storm was coming. And when the storm did come how the peasants, who knew nothing of barometers, must have bowed to the words of the lord, who, they whispered, was a reincarnation of the Almighty.

Now, in our time, the only illusionist that remains is Allah. Even as children we are taught the simple secrets of the physical world, but Allah remains our Lord, unidentifiable and unseen.

As though I have been unconscious for these last few minutes, the traffic seems to have suddenly built up. A string of vehicles wait at a traffic signal where a broken arch signifies a gate to a once medieval castle. A child waves from the side window of a car. I smile and return the gesture. She reveals a plastic poppy and shakes it at me. The girl presses her nose against the glass. The car moves away.

Towards the crest of the hill the white coach has stopped at a car park and its occupants are climbing out. Men and women in military dress uniform. On the concrete, some are putting the finishing touches to their attire: doing up brass buttons, squeezing peaked caps onto their heads and patting down berets. A man with a large belly – a band sergeant major, I judge from the stripes and crown emblem on his arm – is going from person to person, dusting down their shoulders with a clothes brush. Instruments are unpacked from their cases and tuned, a noise that slowly builds into a cacophony of broken squeals. The car park's rough concrete and dilapidated signage appear as an inappropriate, ugly backdrop to the splendour of the military scene. The military would, with their bellies and their instruments, their gleaming brass buttons and sashes of red against black and green, defend every inch of England, for ever England – once, I too would have defended every inch of its green pastures, but not the car parks or the dreary urban uniformity under a grey sky. Out there that's not how any of us remembered it.

The body of the long coach bisects the scene. On one side are the memorial and the assembling band, and on the other is a volunteer tea stand. Folding tables and chairs are set out, and after ordering a tea, I take a seat shielded by the cover of the bus and place the daysack beneath the table, hoping no one will notice it. The daysack is a field patrol item, not something a soldier would carry while in ceremonial dress.

I rest my head in my hands and picture the most beautiful scene I ever saw. It was in Afghanistan. We were finishing up a night patrol and dawn had just broken. The sky was streaked with reds and pinks, and the pink was so thin where it met the snow-capped peaks of the Hindu Kush that it seemed to melt into the white snow. It was impossible to determine where the earth ended and the heavens began, and at the sight of its magnificence my eyes watered. Then from a distant loudspeaker I heard the call to prayer, the still cold air carrying it to my ears as though it was sung right beside me. I stood on a plain between mountains on each side, and the plain was still dark, still to be illumined by the sun. I shivered and looked around as though for the first time in my life I was properly seeing. The scene had no borders, no left or right; on each side it melted into the dewy air. Everything I needed – rations, a stove to boil water, ammunition – I carried in a daysack, and in that moment I felt like picking up my pack and just walking straight ahead to get as high as I could, to lose myself in the Hindu Kush.

I remember thinking that there would be only one thing better than the view from down on the plain. If I were up on that peak where the air was so thin and the wind chill so cold that I could endure it for only minutes, there I would be closer to Allah. Imagine the light-headedness, the exhilaration, the peril. I could almost touch it. For those freezing minutes I would be truly free and experience something beyond beauty. I would be in some vital place man does not inhabit, more alone than can be imagined. My appreciation of Allah would be equal to my fear of death, but despite that fear I would feel no pain. At any moment the winds would sweep me off and my sublimation would be complete. That would hit it. That's what I want. That is Allah.

A volunteer replenishes my tea, now gone cold. From the other side of the coach I can hear the drum sergeant bellowing instructions as he orders his band into place. I hear the scraping of chairs and the noise of civilians taking their places mixed with the excited shrieks of children. The brass band plays a few notes of a military marching song, a final practice, and as it falls silent I can picture the audience on the other side of the coach as they cheer and clap.

I stand up, pull my daysack out from underneath the table and swing it casually onto my back. My watch reads five minutes to eleven. I march slowly but earnestly, my limbs straight, thumbs perpendicular to my body, my chin tilted up, my stick leading me on.

Up top it flattens out into a square of tarmac, and in the centre is the war memorial, a simple stone cross about ten feet high with steps at the base. The cross is engraved with the names of men, and the steps below it are covered with a wreath and a blanket of poppies. Around it on all sides stand men and women, civilians and military – army, navy and air force in their best dress uniform. I note the band, about twenty members, and pick out the clack of the sergeant's boots as he walks down the line and makes his final inspection. Beyond the band are the ruins of the castle, thick crumbling stone walls rising like spurs of ice. The wind has got up again and I steady my cap, feeling a warm trickle of sweat pass obliquely across my forehead. My heart speeds up but not excessively, a faint repeating thud in my chest.

Unchallenged, I move among servicemen and women. I wear a fixed smile and an air of thoughtful detachment.

Allah. Allah. It is time to think of Allah. Now is the time for exhilaration. I am on a steep cliff surrounded on all sides by the heavens and I feel light-headed. I sense the excruciating pain of wind chill like needles on the skin of my face. I unbutton the breast pocket of my tunic and pull out a mobile phone. An old Nokia. I smile at the familiar keys, my eyes moving to the number seven, then eight and finally six.

I pass through the crowd. They face towards the memorial and no one turns to look at me. Here there are children, here old boys in resplendent uniforms and twinkling medals. Here are civilians, men and women. I make for where the military uniforms are most dense. I hold the Nokia in my right hand and lean on my stick with my left.

A solitary bugle sounds the 'Last Post'. Everyone removes their hats.

I move again, fast. My distance to the memorial: twelve feet. Ten feet. Six. I flit deeper into the crowd. I whisper verse, any verse; the first thing that comes into my head.

The bugle's last note echoes as a two-minute silence commences. I wait. Let them have their silence.

Finally, a padre begins to read a prayer. *Ever-living God, we remember. . .*

The face of the phone reads three minutes past eleven. I should have keyed in the detonation code by now. My instructions. . . The text message. . .

. . . gathered from the storm of war into the peace of your presence. . .

I take a deep breath.

May that same peace calm our fears. . .

I have the power to end their prayer.

. . . bring justice to all peoples and establish harmony. . .

I let the padre finish. I even join in at the end. 'Amen.'

The band starts up a familiar theme from army days. The people open hymn sheets ready to sing. All eyes are downcast.

I am ready now, and I fumble for the keypad of the Nokia. Then someone tugs on the tail of my tunic. I turn to see Grace; next to her is a small child of about six. Vaguely I recall the girl waving a poppy from the window of the car climbing the hill.

The Nokia begins to vibrate. Fuck. Why is it vibrating? Surely only I can detonate the ordnance? Is it because I am late? Are the brothers set to detonate it without me doing anything? If so, they must be watching. Do I answer it?

As I look around, the end of a scarf billows into view, wrapped tightly like a noose, disguising a wound now clotted and healing. Grace smiles broadly. 'Surprise!' She nudges the child, Britney, towards me. In a dimpled fist Britney clasps a poppy. I recall a scene bordered by the elevated Hindu Kush where a man called Adrian set out to fetch roses for a daughter called Britney. A daughter he had never met.

I feel an intense pain in the depths of my gut.

Grace looks beautiful. Her face nicely made up, smart clothes, not a trace of her lack of sleep visible in her bright eyes. They make a fitting pair, mother and daughter. They look alike. Who would guess their hardships? Who would believe they are about to be separated?

I stare at the Nokia. Still vibrating. On the screen the time reads seven minutes past eleven. I need to do something. Seven is a good number. Seven levels of heaven.

Grace is smiling at me. She is saying something to Britney.

I have to think quickly.

Something about me. About Britney's dad.

My feet are frozen to the spot. Soon the call will time out. What then? Will that create the first charge? The charge that creates the spark that fires up the batteries that. . .

For Adrian I finish the Shahada – '*La ilaha il Allahu Muhammad Rasul Allah*' – and instinctively I reach for Britney's poppy. Twisting it between my fingers. I glance at the child, see the silver light in her eyes. And then at her mother, smiling at me out of a silver tooth. Their pale faces buffeted by the wind seem to demand something akin to salvation. And they offer love. Simplistic and naive but love just the same. An image of Adrian flits across the view – the face of a man stepping on a false trigger plate that he thought would ignite a charge that. . . I smile out of fear. Adrian diminishes from view to be replaced by Grace and Britney, both of their faces cold but hopeful, within their eyes something less than a plea.

I want love. I only ever wanted love. I grip the poppy tighter, and my eyes widen as the Nokia, still vibrating, slips out of my clammy grip.

I am Akram Khan, formerly Sergeant Khan of the Yeomanry, and I was once admired. Once a man called Adrian told me: *If you Pakis put your mind to it, you can do anything*. I now know what he meant. There is love. Love enough for us all.

NADIM SAFDAR was born to Pakistani parents and grew up in the Black Country. He is married with three children and lives in London.